Praise for
Sheila O'Connor

"**Moving** and **thought-provoking**."
—*Kirkus Reviews* on *Until Tomorrow, Mr. Marsworth*

★ "[A] timeless piece of middle-grade fiction.... **A special book**." —*Booklist*, starred review of *Sparrow Road*

"The small town setting hits just the right note and perfectly illustrates the tension and division of the era. **This is a most satisfying read**."
—*VOYA* on *Until Tomorrow, Mr. Marsworth*

★ "Readers finding themselves in this quiet world will find **plenty of space to imagine and dream** for themselves."
—*Kirkus Reviews*, starred review of *Sparrow Road*

"O'Connor's characters are **intriguing and easy to love**."
—*School Library Journal* on
Until Tomorrow, Mr. Marsworth

★ "[A] story filled with adventure, suspense, and family drama... **A thought-provoking page-turner**."
—*Publishers Weekly*, starred review of
Keeping Safe the Stars

"**The remarkable relationship between Reenie and Mr. Marsworth shines**, as do the larger historical insights and the book's resonant themes of pacifism and patriotism."
—*Publishers Weekly* on *Until Tomorrow, Mr. Marsworth*

"*Sparrow Road* is a book that strikes—and gentles—with Truth. Here is a world of Sorrow and Comfort, crafted by an artist who dares to suggest, without sentimentality but with a hard-nosed realism, that a broken world can be renewed through love and daring and community and art. What **a sweet and hopeful and engaging story**."

—Gary D. Schmidt, Newbery Honor-winning author of *Lizzie Bright and the Buckminster Boy* and *The Wednesday Wars*

★ "Family loyalty, stubbornness and love in a . . . **totally satisfying blend**." —*Kirkus Reviews*, starred review of *Keeping Safe the Stars*

"Keep a Kleenex box handy as you read it . . . **an excellent choice for a class read-aloud**."

—*School Library Connection* on *Until Tomorrow, Mr. Marsworth*

★ "The **characters are well-developed and authentic**, and their resourcefulness and fierce family loyalty are admirable. Set during the last few days of Nixon's administration, *Keeping Safe the Stars* brings up questions of morality and explores the notion of trying to do what is best for one's family."

—*VOYA*, starred review of *Keeping Safe the Stars*

"In this heartwarming piece of historical fiction, critically acclaimed author Sheila O'Connor delivers **a tale of devotion, sacrifice, and family**."

—*The Children's Book Review* on *Until Tomorrow, Mr. Marsworth*

Also by Sheila O'Connor

Sparrow Road

Keeping Safe the Stars

Until

tomorrow,

Mr. Marsworth

Until tomorrow, Mr. Marsworth

Sheila O'Connor

PUFFIN BOOKS

PUFFIN BOOKS

an imprint of Penguin Random House LLC, New York

First published in the United States of America by G. P. Putnam's Sons, 2018
Published by Puffin Books, an imprint of Penguin Random House LLC, 2019

Visit us online at penguinrandomhouse.com

THE LIBRARY OF CONGRESS HAS CATALOGED THE G. P. PUTNAM'S SONS EDITION AS FOLLOWS:
Names: O'Connor, Sheila, author.
Title: Until tomorrow, Mr. Marsworth / Sheila O'Connor.
Description: New York, NY : G. P. Putnam's Sons,
an imprint of Penguin Random House LLC, [2018]
Summary: "Desperate to keep her older brother from being drafted in the Vietnam War,
eleven-year-old Reenie strikes up an unlikely friendship with Mr. Marsworth,
an elderly shut-in, who helps her in her mission"—Provided by publisher.
Identifiers: LCCN 2017030531 | ISBN 9780399161933 (hardback) |
ISBN 9780698173712 (ebook)
Subjects: | CYAC: Brothers and sisters—Fiction. | Draft—Fiction. | Vietnam War, 1961–
1975—Fiction. | Recluses—Fiction. | Pacifism—Fiction. | Grandmothers—Fiction. | BISAC:
JUVENILE FICTION / Social Issues / Friendship. | JUVENILE FICTION / Historical /
United States / 20th Century. | JUVENILE FICTION / Family / Siblings.
Classification: LCC PZ7.O22264 Unt 2018 | DDC [Fic]—dc23
LC record available at https://lccn.loc.gov/2017030531

Puffin Books ISBN 9780142425541

Printed in the United States of America

Design by Jaclyn Reyes
Text set in Sentinel.

1 3 5 7 9 10 8 6 4 2

For Amellia, Anna, and Connor

who asked me to read more

and

for Mikaela, Dylan, and Tim

who made this story possible

Dear Mr. Marsworth,

Hello from Reenie Kelly from Missouri, your brand-new
summer paperboy. You can count on me to deliver your
Tribune. I'm staying with my gram at the top of Gardner
Hill. Temporarily. Any problems with your paper, you can
find me at Blanche Kelly's. We'll be stuck at Gram's on
Gardner until our family has a home.

No one thinks a girl should have a route except for me, but
Gram said that I could split the route with Dare. I'm eleven,
twelve in August. Dare's thirteen. I'm not too young to have my
own route, Mr. Marsworth. I helped Dare deliver papers back in
Denton, and I helped my oldest brother, Billy, before Dare. It's
high time I have at least six blocks of houses to myself.

This week I've gone door-to-door to say hey to all my
customers, and so far I've met all of them but you.

I can't knock on your door because I can't unlock your gate,
or climb that pointy iron fence around your yard. I've rung
your rusted bell, but no one comes.

I saw a shadow in your window so someone must be home.
Gram says that you're a loner, but a loner can say hey. And I'm
a loner too now, Mr. Marsworth. I'm a new girl in Lake Liberty
without a single friend. Two loners could say hey through
that tall fence. Mom always said some friendly never hurt.

When we meet up face-to-face, you'll see for yourself a

girl can do this job. (If customers don't want a girl, Gram says I have to give my half to Dare.)

Give a man a handshake, that's how Dad taught Dare and Billy to do business, and since this is my first business, I want to do it right.

Is there a time that you could meet me, Mr. Marsworth?

Yours Truly,
Reenie Kelly

P.S. Could you tell me if you own a mean dog, Mr. Marsworth? That iron fence looks like it's meant for a mad dog. It's best if I'm prepared before I start my route next week. In Denton, the Palmers' vicious shepherd bit me twice.

P.P.S. I know folks wish Glen Taylor wasn't moving to Mankato, but I promise I'll do twice the job Glen Taylor ever did. You won't be disappointed in my service, Mr. Marsworth. A week from Friday when his route is mine, I'll prove to you I'm right!

P.P.P.S. Do you want your paper rolled or folded? AND how will I collect if I can't get past your gate?

Thursday, June 13, 1968

Dear Miss Kelly,

How fine to learn the <u>Tribune</u> hired well. For a long time,
loyal customer, a conscientious papergirl is worth her
weight in gold.

I have no doubt a girl can do the job.

In terms of my delivery: I prefer my folded paper in
the milk box by 6:15 a.m., and in return I shall pay you
promptly, every other Friday. Please just leave the bill
inside my box. My customary tip is fifty cents for first-
rate service.

I anticipate wonderful service.

I do not own a dog, but I can say with great conviction
my cat, Clyde, will not attack. His prey of preference would
be houseflies, now and then a mouse. If you are neither fly
nor rodent, you'll fare well.

Perhaps your grandmother is right, I am a "loner."
Although it's not a term I would have used, I will wear the
shoe that fits. On the other hand, I doubt you are a loner.
It's never easy to be new, but you won't be new for long.
I've never known a Kelly short on friends. Your father was a
magnet: most popular, most daring, and your mother, Betsy
Kelly, was a brilliant, bright-eyed girl. Brilliant.

Have we made a proper introduction now, Miss Kelly?

I have no need for handshakes; I won't complain to the Tribune. Any child of Betsy Kelly's will be a perfect papergirl, I'm sure.

However, I must close with one request: Might you refrain from clanging? I assume you are the freckled redhead ringing my old bell. A man of my late years naps at odd hours.

Sincerely,

H. W. Marsworth

H. W. Marsworth

P.S. My apologies, Miss Kelly. Some words are difficult to write, and worse, woefully inadequate, and thus I shy away. Such would be "my sympathy," which rarely sounds sincere, and doubly sad when writing to a child. Yet I extend my sympathy to you. I am sincerely sorry for your loss. I know it's been some time since your mother passed away, but she was among the best this world has known. Such a strong young heart. How terrible that she left this earth too soon.

Friday, June 14, 1968

Dear Mr. Marsworth,

Thank you for your sympathy. Everyone says sorry, and most people are sincere, but I just wish those sorries could bring Mom back. It's sixteen months and twenty-seven days since Mom's been gone, and we all miss her still, even though the Kellys keep our sadness to ourselves. Dare and Dad especially. We're not a family to keep crying, because crying doesn't help.

If you liked Mom then you'll like me, because deep inside I have a piece of Betsy Kelly's heart. (Mom gave a piece to each of us the day before she died.) And I have her gift with old folks, I really truly do. Back before Mom was sick with cancer, the two of us delivered lemon bars or fresh-baked cookies to shut-ins twice a week. Mrs. Jamison. Miss Pearl. Even crabby Mr. Anderson on Grant Street. Mom couldn't bear to see old folks forgotten.

Even after Mom was gone, I made my Girl Scouts Good Deed Project a shut-in back in Denton. (Dad FORCED me to join Girl Scouts, I know Mom never would.) My shut-in, Asa Carver, liked to smoke Pall Malls and talk. He told stories about bootlegging, and how he'd smuggled whiskey from Windsor to Detroit, and how once he'd jumped a train to California just to see that big Pacific for himself. The happiest he'd been was as a hobo.

An old man who told good stories was my best friend in fifth grade. Asa Carver liked that I was tough, and he understood my sadness because he'd lost his sweetheart Lu. He didn't even care I was a kid. I fit right in with Asa, and he fit right in with me. If he were still in Denton, I'd write to him this morning, but he's gone off to Kansas City with his son.

I'd sure like a Good Deed Project in Lake Liberty right now. A Good Deed Project in a new town might make me less alone. How would you like some friendly visits from a kid? Maybe once or twice a week? I won't clang your bell. You don't have to shake my hand. Mom would want to see me be your friend.

Do you know how slow the time goes when you're bored? (Tick . . . tock . . . tick.) I can't play another game of solitaire, I can't. And Gram's little black-and-white TV is mostly static, so instead of As the World Turns I'm staring at the snow.

And it's not like I have my family for my friends. Dare's living out in Gram's woods with his pup tent and Sanka coffee. Even Float, our family spaniel-beagle mutt, sleeps outside with Dare. Most-popular Dare Kelly doesn't want to make friends in this town. He's so mad that we left Denton, he hardly even talks.

Gram's full-time at Brindle Drug, and Billy's full-time at Casey's Conoco, and Dad's gone to North Dakota to build roads with Uncle Will.

So why are all the Kellys working, you might wonder? Why can't anybody play?

1. We lost all our money with Mom sick.
2. Then we lost our house.
3. Then Billy turned eighteen, which means we need $$$$
   for his college. If a boy's enrolled in college, he isn't forced
   to fight in Vietnam. Mizzou is the one way to save Billy
   from this war. (Mizzou = University of Missouri just in
   case a man in Minnesota doesn't know that college.)

So you can see that it's pretty lonely at the Kellys'. Some
nights, I still play chess with Billy, but he usually falls asleep.
He's grease-stained and exhausted from his long days down at
Casey's, but he can't say no to chess. Or he can't say no to me,
he never could.

Maybe I should be your Good Deed Project, since I'm a
shut-in now myself. Ha-ha-ha.

Sugar cookies or lemon bars? I'll make either one.

Yours Truly,
Reenie Kelly

Monday, June 17, 1968

Dear Miss Kelly,

Rest assured a friend will come your way, one always does.

I'm afraid I cannot be your Good Deed Project, and you cannot be mine. Unlike your shut-in, Asa Carver, I'm not the type of man who can entertain a child with wild tales of my youth. I have no taste for whiskey; I've never smoked Pall Malls.

This summer I am solitary by necessity and nature.

Are there not other Good Deed Projects to be found? Might you inquire with Blanche Kelly? She would have a better sense of local "shut-ins."

It is noble work you're after, dear Miss Kelly. I have no doubt you are good company with your lemon bars and spunk. You'll make some shut-in very happy in this town.

Sincerely,

H. W. Marsworth

H. W. Marsworth

P.S. If you're at a loss for friends, you can always grow a garden. Something beautiful and blooming might be solace for your soul. Please take these marigold seeds I didn't get in the ground. Perhaps they'll find a home on Gardner. Temporarily.

P.P.S. As to Billy and the draft: I wholeheartedly concur with you, Miss Kelly. Your beloved brother Billy must not go to that war.

Monday, June 17, 1968

Dear Mr. Marsworth,

You're the best part of Lake Liberty, you are! A second letter in your milk box! A little gift of seeds! It was almost like my birthday, opening your box to see the things you'd left inside.

I'll find a place to plant those marigold seeds. I promise that I will.

I'm grateful for your gift, so please don't think I can't take no for an answer. I hate it when Gram says I can't take no. I can take no for an answer, but it's harder when I'm right. And I'm right that I could be a friend to you.

I have a second reason why the two of us should meet. I didn't tell you what it was first thing, but I'll tell it to you now.

Have you ever had a memory that could've been a dream? You know, a thing that might have happened, except you can't be sure.

I have one of those of you, but it's not of you exactly. It's of 1962, and a trip to Gram's at Christmas, and a walk I took with Mom through the darkness to your house. We didn't go past your gate, we just stood quiet at your high fence staring at your big brick house lit up with winter moon and falling snow. "Someone special lives here, Reen," Mom whispered like a secret, then she took a letter from her pocket and left it in your box.

I thought that you were Santa and we'd walked to the North Pole. And I thought it for a long time after that. That's the crazy way that kids think when they're small.

Was that a memory or dream? Did Mom leave you a letter, Mr.

Marsworth? I admit that Christmas letter made me want to write you, too. And it made me want to meet that special man inside that house. It wasn't just the route that made me write you.

If Mom thought you were special then she'd want us to be friends. Don't you think I'm right?

A Good Deed visit once a week, and we could talk of Betsy Kelly. And maybe you can tell me what she wrote to you that night.

Hoping for a Yes Still,
Reenie Kelly

P.S. I can't inquire of Blanche Kelly, because Gram's the kind of gram who thinks a bored kid ought to clean. Sweep. Dust. Mop. Sort the junk drawer. Do the laundry. I'd rather bake you cookies than match socks.

P.P.S. I'm so glad you wholeheartedly "concur" about Billy and the war. Hardly anyone concurs when it comes to Vietnam.

P.P.P.S. Do you support your Minnesota Senator for Peace Eugene McCarthy? Billy can't vote yet at eighteen, but he hopes if McCarthy wins for president he'll bring the soldiers home.

P.P.P.P.S. Please keep sending me new words like "concur" because I always like to learn.

Tuesday, June 18, 1968

Dear Miss Kelly,

I see you are a smart girl cursed with excess curiosity
and time. Have you visited our library on Colfax? What
about the beach? The children of Lake Liberty like to
swim there in the summer. Your route begins on Friday
morning; look to that.

    If you think it was a memory, then rest assured it
was. Although how much better to believe that you had
walked to the North Pole.

    A friend will come, Miss Kelly, one that is a child.

Sincerely,

H. W. Marsworth

H. W. Marsworth

Wednesday, June 19, 1968

Dear Mr. Marsworth,

You don't want me to be a nuisance so I won't, but just in case you're wondering, you don't have to be a Good Deed Project, or meet me face-to-face. Sometimes writing letters is the best way to be friends.

Have you ever had a pen pal? Was it Mom?

That's not a pesky question, you only have to answer yes or no.

I already have one pen pal, but I'm happy to have two. My pen pal is Army Pfc. Skip Nichols, from Baton Rouge, Louisiana. Skip's just twenty in April, and he's fighting for our country all the way in Vietnam. We don't always write about the war. Skip likes to hear about my school, or how I burned the pancakes, or Billy teaching me new chords on his guitar. I try to keep my letters funny, because our teacher, Mrs. Lamb, says when a soldier's in a hard time, our hard times never help. Skip is in a hard time in this war. He's written little things about the heat out in the jungle, and how he sees bombs in his dreams, and how sometimes when he's fighting he can't tell enemy from friend. He's never been a coward, but he's scared in Vietnam. Mostly he's pure homesick for his ma and pa, and his six brothers and sisters, all at home in Baton Rouge. And there's no jambalaya in the jungle. Or birthday cake. The soldiers spent Christmas all together, but Skip said it wasn't much.

At least once a week I write to Skip, and then I wait and

wait for letters, but I understand a busy soldier can't write often. First thing I did last week after I got settled in Gram's attic was sit down on my twin bed to tell my news to Skip. I didn't say how lost I felt driving out of Denton, or living in a new town, because my letters shouldn't be sad. Instead I said I'd have my own route in Lake Liberty, and every penny I'd be earning would be saved for Billy's school. I knew that part would make him happy. At the end of every letter, Skip says Billy shouldn't end up in Vietnam. If Skip had gone to college, he wouldn't be fighting now. (So the three of us, plus Billy, wholeheartedly concur!)

Skip's letters and all the other letters from our pen pals in the Fourth Platoon were the best part of fifth grade, and I wish that school hadn't ended so we could keep it up. We each had our own soldier, but when one kid got a letter, we listened as a class, and we learned how hard this war is through their words.

Once, when Lt. Gerald Walker lost his right leg in an ambush, his pen pal, tough guy Larry Palmer, ran out of the room. Then we all started crying, including Mrs. Lamb. That's how much we loved our soldiers, the whole Fourth Platoon was ours.

Every letter that they wrote us we pinned up to the board, including that sad letter about Gerald Walker's leg, and we hung them with their pictures, and whatever else they sent. The photo I liked best was the high school senior picture Skip mailed me last March. "Me before the Army," Skip printed on the back. Before he went away to war he looked a lot like Billy, or so many smiling boys in Billy's high school yearbook. I'll put his picture in this letter so you can see Skip for yourself. And here's a second one of Skip on his not-so-happy birthday. Skip's the dirty soldier with the cone hat on his head. The tall soldier on the right is Skip's best buddy Jackie Moon.

If you look closely at that picture, you can see that Jackie's holding the white turtle that he carved Skip as a gift. Skip says no one can make beauty out of soap like Jackie Moon. I wish you could've seen the dove Jackie carved for our class for Christmas.

I hope I haven't blabbered. I hope that you're not bored. What I really meant to tell you is a pen pal hears your feelings, and cares about your birthday, and how you looked in high school, and you don't need to be a homesick soldier to be a pen pal. You can be a shut-in, or a homesick kid alone.

What do you say to that idea, Mr. Marsworth? No meeting face-to-face. We won't even need postage, your milk box works just fine.

Special Delivery,
Reenie Kelly

P.S. Skip's favorite kind of candy is banana Turkish Taffy and grape Razzles. What's your favorite candy? Someday I might surprise you, Mr. Marsworth.

P.P.S. Pen pals or no pen pals, when my route starts Friday morning, you'll find your folded paper in the milk box by 6:15 a.m. You can answer before Friday, I'll come back and check your milk box, I don't mind.

P.P.P.S. Once you've had a look at Skip and Jackie, maybe you can leave the pictures in your box. I don't want to wait for Friday to get those keepsakes back. I'm sure you understand a keepsake, Mr. Marsworth.

P.P.P.P.S. I think Skip looks better clean and happy back in high school.

Thursday, June 20, 1968

Dear Miss Kelly,

A pen pal is a fine thing for a young man in the Army, and
I imagine those soldiers in the Fourth Platoon read your
loquacious correspondence with great joy. In that regard
alone, Pfc. Skip Nichols is a very lucky man.

I have returned your keepsakes promptly, as requested.
I agree, I prefer the photograph of Skip as a young senior
back in high school. War will age a boy, as I'm sure
you're well aware. Even grown men break down in war. What
boy should have to spend his birthday hunting for an
unknown enemy to kill? Or praying to be saved? Or praying
that another might be spared?

And now Lt. Gerald Walker must live without a leg.
Without a leg, Miss Kelly, and for what?

How will we claim victory when so much has been lost?
Not only for Americans, but for all the millions in the countries
ravaged by this war. The soldiers and civilians on all sides.

Please forgive me, dear Miss Kelly, as you can see
I'm not a proper pen pal for a child. I'm afraid my gloomy
letters would profoundly disappoint.

Best of luck tomorrow on the first day of your route.
How noble that you're working to save Billy from this war.

Sincerely,

H. W. Marsworth

H. W. Marsworth

Friday, June 21, 1968

Dear Mr. Marsworth,

Did you see me at your milk box dropping your <u>Tribune</u>???

Dare made us leave Gram's house at 4:30 in the morning, so we'd be the first to get our papers at the Dry-Rite drop on State. Dare says you get there late you end up short. Plus, he doesn't want to meet the other boys. (Dare doesn't want a friend here, except Float. He's just too mad about our move to make a friend.)

Can I tell you a small secret? It's really scary before daybreak on those dark streets all alone. The whole town fast asleep. A yard light now and then, but nothing more. Just my own fast heartbeat, and the thunk of papers landing on the steps. I thought of Skip on night patrol out in the jungle, a job he really hates, and how brave he has to be out in the night all by himself.

I'll get used to dew-soaked shoes, and the weight of all those papers, and the canvas sack slapping at my leg with every step, but I'm not sure how I'll get used to all that darkness.

If you're ever feeling friendly, I'd be happy for a hey. Look for me closer to 5:30, I'll be there before the sun.

> Mostly Brave This Morning,
> Reenie Kelly

P.S. If there is a problem with your Sunday paper, it won't be my fault. Your Sunday route belongs to someone else.

Sunday, June 23, 1968

Dear Mr. H. W. Marsworth of Lake Liberty!

You don't want to be my pen pal, but you wrote to the Tribune????

I guess the paper doesn't mind your gloomy letters. ☺ I don't mind them either, I really truly don't. There's plenty of gloomy news at Gram's house I could write.

"Mr. H. W. Marsworth of Lake Liberty?" Billy said to Gram, surprised. He was sitting at the table with a glass of morning milk and the Tribune. "He's right here in the paper."

"Where?" I said, and I edged in close to Billy to see your name in print. "That's Mr. Marsworth from my route!"

"You know him?" Billy said, like I should have told him sooner. "Have you met him face-to-face?"

"Well sort of. Not exactly. Why?"

"I've heard talk of him is all," Billy said. It was our Sunday morning slow time before Gram dragged us off to church. I was still lounging in my pj's, and Billy was in his faded jeans and T-shirt, his dark hair a sleepy mess. "Gossip at the station. You know how small towns are."

"You don't need to listen," Gram said. "Or read that letter either." Still, she hovered at his shoulder to read it for herself. All of us except for Dare were reading what you wrote. (Dare sticks to sports and funnies, that's why he's so dumb.)

"I think his letter's interesting," I said.

"Interesting?" Gram echoed. I didn't mind you wrote against

the war, but Gram sure did. "That's one word for it, Reen. Another would be rubbish. If Howard Marsworth doesn't love this country, he should leave it."

"He just disagrees with war," I said. "Folks do. He shouldn't have to leave this country over that."

"Even Bobby Kennedy thought the war was wrong," Billy said to settle Gram. All the Kellys love the Kennedys, and all our hearts are aching over Bobby being killed. I hope he's met Mom in heaven, because she sure loved him a lot. "If he'd lived and been elected, he would have worked for peace."

"Of course he'd work for peace," Gram said. "But he also served his country. Bobby, Jack, and Joe, all those boys fought in World War II. Joe Kennedy was killed doing his duty. They didn't write letters to the editor saying war is wrong. They served their county first. A letter is a coward's way—"

"Mr. Marsworth's not a coward," I said to take your side.

"You know who's not a coward?" Gram said. "Your pen pal Skip from Baton Rouge. Don't you think our soldiers deserve our full support?"

"Skip's not for this war either," I told Gram. Float gave a little whine the way he does when Gram's upset. "Our boys are getting killed in Vietnam."

"You don't have to tell me, Reen," Gram said. "They're dying for our country. They need us on their side."

"I am on their side." I tried to say it kindly, but Float let out a sickly howl.

"Stop arguing," Dare said. "You're bugging Float."

Gram disappeared into the kitchen, and I hoped that we were done, but she came back with sudsy, pink hands, and a lecture for us all.

"The Kellys love their country. Grandpa Kelly's youngest brother died in World War II. Your father was a soldier in Korea. He was nearly Billy's age when he enlisted. And Grandpa Kelly's nephew—"

"We know, Gram," Billy interrupted, but he said it sweet and calm. He grabbed hold of Gram's wet hand, and gave it a soft pat. "We're proud of all the Kelly soldiers. We really are."

"Men are fighting for our freedom," Gram said like she couldn't stop. She took her hand away from Billy, and propped it on her hip. "They didn't argue with their country, they didn't refuse to serve. They didn't stay home to write the paper. Or burn their draft cards like some boys are doing now."

"But are they fighting for 'our' freedom?" Billy asked. He didn't say it loud or angry, because even disagreeing, Billy's gentle. "Our men are dying in the thousands there, and nobody knows why. And the Vietnamese are dying. Or else they're made to suffer while their country is destroyed. Reports are coming in that we've killed women and children."

"Our soldiers wouldn't kill kids," I argued, because I had to stand up for Skip and all our pen pals. And I agree with Gram on one thing: the soldiers dying for their country need their country on their side. "Some just want to come home."

"Most," Billy said to me. "So why draft ten thousand more of us to fight against our will? To die in some strange country just like Mr. Marsworth says."

"Because that's how we beat the Nazis!" Gram snatched the paper from his hands, huffed into the kitchen, and shoved it in the trash.

"It's not the Nazis that we're fighting," Billy muttered. "This isn't World War II."

"We've still got to have an army." Dare dropped the funnies on Gram's carpet like he'd finally heard enough. "How else will we whomp 'em in a war?"

"You'll be in college come September," I said soft in Billy's ear. "You won't get sent to Vietnam. And I know it's not the Nazis, so you're right."

I don't know much about this war, but I know more than Dare. It's the Communists called the Viet Cong the U.S. troops are there to stop.

"Trouble will find Marsworth from that letter," Gram called out from the kitchen. "Trouble's going to come from this, just you mark my words."

No offense. I just thought you'd want to know we read your letter, and I bet other families read it, and argued like we did. No one can agree about this war, not even us. And I hope Gram isn't right that you'll have trouble.

Here's one thing to make you happy so we end on a good

note: I fished the <u>Tribune</u> from the trash to clip your letter
out for Billy, and I hid it in his wallet between pictures of
his sweetheart Beth and Mom. Someday he'll be surprised to
find it there, Mr. H. W. Marsworth of Lake Liberty. I would
have saved it for myself, but Billy needs it more. He's got
Dad and Gram and Dare and nearly all of Denton saying it's
disloyal to stand against this war. Mom stood against this war,
but she's not here for Billy now.

                              Your Reader,
                              Reenie Kelly

P.S. I wish Billy wasn't right about the thousands. Did you see
that front-page story about the soldier Kyle Smith? I can't bear
to read the news when our boys die, and still I did. He was
eighteen just like Billy, and his little sister Susan is eleven just
like me. The Smiths have other kids, but I keep thinking about
Susan, and all the Kyle things that are gone now from her life.
Maybe Kyle shared his records, or let her have the 45s she
listened to the most. Was he the kind of older brother that gave
up his favorite bear when she was born? Did he hold her on his
shoulders before she learned to walk? Did he do all the best-
big-brother things that Billy did for me? I don't ever want my
brother on the front page of the paper. Or Skip. Or any of our
pen pals. Not a single one.

Monday, June 24, 1968

Dear Mr. Marsworth,

Turns out Gram was right! Trouble came for you this morning before I even saw the sun.

Two boys riding Sting-Rays hurled eggs at your brick house. I was dropping papers down on Hillcrest when I saw them at your gate. They took off in the darkness, but I saw those two bikes plain and clear. Do you know two evil boys on souped-up Sting-Rays?

I'm afraid you've really got a mess there, Mr. Marsworth. I could come back this morning to hose those eggs off of your house. Or clean up all those broken shells on your front lawn. You don't have to pay me, I'm glad to lend a hand.

Maybe an old man that just wants peace shouldn't have written to the paper to say this war is wrong. Too many people read those letters, Mr. Marsworth. If you want to write against the war, you can write to me instead. I'm always here to listen to your letters. Mom didn't like the war, but she kept that in our house. If she'd written to the paper, we'd have gotten egged, or worse. Lots of kids in Denton had brothers, uncles, cousins, neighbors, fighting in this war.

Still, do you want Dare and me to find your eggers, Mr. Marsworth? We both love our country, but we don't want some town boys egging an old man. I know Billy would agree, but he's not going to want to scrap with kids. You want a couple scrappers, Dare and I will do that job. As Dad would say, you've got a right to your opinion, good or bad.

You got a hunch who they might be? One name will get us started, we'll hunt them down from there. When we played war down at the river, Dare was always drafted first. Dare Kelly has an even better nose for enemies than Float.

Your Avenger,
Reenie Kelly

P.S. Don't you have time to answer letters? I've already left a few. I know you're "napping at odd hours," but how long does a nap last? Ha-ha-ha!

Monday, June 24, 1968

Dear Mr. Marsworth,

I already found your eggers, and I didn't even have to look.

Two foulmouthed, filthy boys on souped-up Sting-Rays followed me down Hillcrest just after I'd left that last letter in your box. They cut me off when I was walking, so I couldn't step left or right.

"You got a paper route?" one said. He was a scrawny white-haired kid that the other kid called Rat. Pale skin. Beady little eyes. He looks just like a Rat, he really does. "We saw you out this morning."

"So what?" I was scared to be outnumbered, but the Kellys stand their ground.

"You took that route from Cutler," the pale Rat boy said.

Do you know these two? Pale Rat and scarred-up Cutler? Cutler in the camo pants and dog tags. Big white scar across his cheek. Another pink line along his head where he's had stitches. Gray bruises on his arms and face like all he does is fight.

I'm sure Cutler is a last name, because no mom would name her newborn baby Cutler.

"I've been in line to get a second route since May. Glen Taylor's should have gone to me." The kid named Cutler spit a loogie on my Keds. "Instead they gave it to a girl. Some hick girl from Misery. What are you, a women's libber? A girl can't work a route."

"It's Missouri," I said, tough. I don't know how they knew about Missouri, I guess the same small-town way Billy knew your name. That's how SMALL this stupid small town is.

"It's Misery to us." Rat sneered, and they both laughed.

"You guys egg that house this morning?" I asked Rat. I'm not a great big hulk like Dad or Dare, but I could beat that scrawny Rat kid if I fought him one-to-one.

"What are you, a cop?" Rat said, and I saw right then he did it. He didn't even bother saying no.

"Your hippie brother stole my brother's job at Casey's," Cutler said. "A Cutler works there every summer, but your brother stole the job."

"He's not a hippie." Billy's hair touches his ears and he likes to wear it shaggy, but he's never been a hippie. The only hippies back in Denton were longhairs on TV. "He's saving up for college. Is your brother doing that?"

"My brothers serve their country." Cutler scratched his bristled scalp then spit another loogie. "They ain't spineless draft dodgers too chicken for a war."

"Yeah," Rat said.

"What are you, the Yeah Man?" I asked Rat.

"Yeah," he said again, but this time he shoved his bike into my shin, backed up a couple inches, and rode over my foot. It hurt like heck, but I didn't flinch. Instead I grabbed him by the collar and shoved him and his Sting-Ray to the ground.

Tough guy Cutler dumped his bike and made a grab for me, and the three of us went at it, kicking, punching, slapping, until a woman down on Hillcrest screamed, "I'm going to call the cops."

Suddenly Cutler and his sidekick jumped back on their Sting-Rays and took off like the wind.

I didn't shed a tear, but I threw up on the street. Then I limped home to Gram's woods and spilled it all to Dare and Float. Turns out, Dare's already had his fill of those two boys. I guess they dogged him down on Main Street, calling him King Kong.

"I can't believe they hurt you, Reen." Dare shook his dirty head and jabbed his stick into the fire. Dare's tall and broad like Dad, he's taller now than Billy, with Dad's same freckled skin and straight, straw copper hair. He might be extra-large for a boy that's just thirteen, and he does wear size-sixteen husky pants, but he's nothing like King Kong. In Denton, kids admired Big Dare Kelly for his fairness and his size. He was big enough to be a bully, but he wasn't. "And Misery?" Dare said. "I ain't staying here for school come September."

"Me either," I agreed. Dare and I might bicker, but the Kellys keep the same side in a fight. "All for one," Dad always says, and so we are.

And all for one, Dare and I are scheming to get even with those boys. We're not telling Gram or Billy, because Dare and I agree we'd rather handle this ourselves. Billy just wants peace, and Gram won't want us scrapping in her town. We might write Dad in North Dakota once we've cleaned their clocks. It'll make Dad proud to know we set two bullies straight. He sure won't want them egging an old man.

I've got a welt around my neck, and I'm limping just a little, but even bruised and aching I'm proud I stood my ground. One girl against two boys and they didn't win! Skip will like this story. You might not like it much, but I thought you'd want to know those eggs will be revenged.

Please don't breathe a word of this to Gram. You tell Gram two boys tackled me, and I'll lose my route to Dare. Gram has old-fashioned notions about girls.

To Be Continued,
Reenie Kelly

Tuesday, June 25, 1968

Dear Miss Kelly,

One girl against two boys? Kicking, spitting, punching?
All of this over paper routes and eggs? Or Billy pumping gas?
Surely, the older Cutler sons aren't entitled to that job.

Those two boys were utterly uncivilized. I would
call the Cutler father, but I doubt he'd intervene. The
Cutlers have long terrorized this town. Young Steven
Cutler's father was a bully, and the apple didn't fall far.

Are you familiar with that adage? I believe it would
be apt for you as well. Your father was quick to join a
fight, and I'm afraid you might be, too. Didn't you say
you shoved that Rat boy to the ground? Yes, yes, after
the tire stunt, but still. What if you had turned the
other cheek? Walked home to Blanche Kelly's with your
temper still in check?

Forgive that second adage, but I'm at a loss for words.
Troubled and dumbfounded. Fistfighting on the street?

Please don't seek revenge. There is nothing you or
Dare can do to change what has been done. I don't care
about the eggs. You can walk away from insults, even
welts and bruises.

Might you practice peace? You're not too young for
that. Perhaps you should ask Billy if he would advise
revenge? One for all, as you would say.

Sincerely,

H. W. Marsworth

H. W. Marsworth

Tuesday, June 25, 1968

Dear Mr. Marsworth,

Good to hear from you AGAIN!!!!

I'm glad to practice peace, but when it comes to this, I can't. Not until we've taught those two boys they can't push us around. If they don't learn that lesson they'll be on us all the time. In Denton, kids didn't mess with Dare because they knew that he was tough. (We're both apples in your "adage." Thank you for that word.)

No offense, but when you LET bullies get the upper hand, they never quit.

Without Dare and me as allies, they'll egg your house again.

You're right, Billy Kelly's lived his whole life on the sweet side of the street. That's a good calm place for Billy, but it's not for Dare and me. (Or Dad!)

Don't worry, Mr. Marsworth, we won't lose.

Soon to Be Triumphant,
Reenie Kelly

P.S. We'll try to teach that lesson peacefully. How's that for a deal?

P.P.S. If your paper's late one morning, please don't complain to the Tribune. It won't happen twice, you have my word.

Wednesday, June 26, 1968

Dear Mr. Marsworth,

Here's a plate of sugar cookies so you'll know that I'm still kind, and if your paper's late tomorrow you won't be steaming mad.

I hope you like blue frosting. I hope you eat all six for lunch.

Dare and Float took my first hot dozen to the woods and ate them all. Float likes his unfrosted. Dare's too dumb to care.

I'm going to bring a bag down to the Conoco for Billy and his boss.

If two bullies try to steal them, maybe I'll turn the other cheek. ☺

Peacefully and Sincerely,
Reenie Kelly

31

Wednesday, June 26, 1968

Dear Miss Kelly,

I do hope you are sincere.

Between revenge and baking, baking would be best.

Your blue cookies are most welcome at my house.

                                 Sincerely,

                           H. W. Marsworth

                           H. W. Marsworth

Thursday, June 27, 1968

Dear Mr. Marsworth,

I know you warned against revenge, but this revenge was peaceful. As peaceful as it could be, so I hope that you'll be proud.

It took us a few days to hunt down Rat and Cutler near their paper drop on Main, but once we knew their schedule we hatched the perfect plan.

Five o'clock this morning we picked up our stack of papers, then we walked to Rash's Hardware to hide beside it in the dark. When the two of them hit Main Street, Dare ran out of the shadows and grabbed hold of Cutler's bike.

"You got a problem with my sister?" Dare growled in Cutler's face. Rat came to a skid, but he stayed back.

"You mean that ugly tomboy?" Cutler said like he was tough.

"Look who's talking, Scarface." Dare towered over Cutler, but Cutler didn't seem scared.

"She took his route," Rat said. "He was waiting for a second one once Glen Taylor quit."

"The Tribune hired us," I said. "Like Mr. Casey hired Billy. The Kellys are just better than you all."

"Misery and King Kong?" Cutler snorted. "And your chicken college brother?"

"Shut your trap." Dare squeezed Cutler in a headlock while I pulled out the can of Aero Shave to foam Cutler in the face. Cutler squirmed and cursed and spit, but we didn't stop.

"Cut it out," Rat called, but he didn't get in the middle. He just sat there on his Sting-Ray, scared of Aero Shave and us.

"You want to punch him, Reen?" Dare was foamy from the squirming, but he didn't seem to mind.

"Sure," I said, but instead of punching Cutler, I turned to foam Rat in the face. His whole scrawny face was white with foam.

"It's in my eyes," he screamed.

"Good," I said. "Maybe you'll go blind."

Dare pulled Cutler from the bike, then he pinned him to the wall of Rash's Hardware, and he told him if he hassled me again, he'd end up dead.

Then we picked up our two paper sacks and strolled off in the dark.

"You better watch your back," Cutler called behind us. Rat joined in with a weak "yeah," but neither of us turned.

"You, too," I yelled. "Don't cross the Kellys twice. And don't you mess with Mr. Marsworth."

Dare smacked me on the head like I was stupid. "You don't need to mention him. For once, just shut your mouth."

Doesn't that sound peaceful, Mr. Marsworth? Not a single fist? I could've had a punch, but I didn't take it. Dare didn't take one either.

I'm hoping all this peaceful makes you proud, because it sure wouldn't make Dad proud. Dad would say that one good punch will always prove a point.

Triumphant,
Reenie Kelly

P.S. I'm sorry your <u>Tribune</u> wasn't in the box by 6:15, but it wasn't much past 7:00, and I won't be late again. Thank you for not calling the <u>Tribune</u>.

And your mother,
young Miss Kelly?

What would your dear
mother say to this?

Friday, June 28, 1968

Dear Mr. Marsworth,

It was fun to find that little slip of paper in your box, even if I didn't much like the note. I thought that you'd be prouder of the Kellys' peaceful scheme. MY peaceful scheme. It took two days of begging, plus three dozen cookies, plus my sea-green cat's-eye marble I won from Mack McCoy, just to bribe Dare into using shaving foam instead of fists.

It won't happen twice, so this one time was worth some praise.

And you know what? If Mom were here, it might just make her proud.

Mom liked "ingenuity," and I was best at that. Billy was a pitcher all the way from Little League through high school, and Dare was Denton's All-Star pitcher three years in a row, but I couldn't be either one. (Football, baseball, basketball, PAPER ROUTES, Boy Scouts, etc. Don't even get me started on all that boys can do!) When I used to gripe to Mom, she said I was blessed with brains, not the nearly straight-A brain of Billy, but a brain that liked to think "outside the box." Ingenuity. Mom said my brain would take me farther than Dare or Billy ever dreamed.

So in answer to your question: Mom might just say, "Good job on the Aero Shave! I'm glad you skipped a punch."

Or . . . she might say that whole "turn the other cheek" thing, because it's true that was an adage that Mom liked.

Which leads me to a question: Just how well did you know Mom??? If she thought that you were special, and left a letter in your box, it makes me think the two of you were friends. I know Mom wasn't from here, but she came here every summer to a cottage on the lake. Did you meet Mom at that cottage? Did you know Mom when she was my age? Did she have ingenuity? I bet you that she did.

I asked Gram how you knew Mom and she said MYOB. Gram gets tired of my questions, so she tells me that a lot.

                              Waiting for Your Answer,
                              Reenie Kelly

P.S. Are you melting in this heat? I'm truly melting. Dare won't go with me to the beach because he hates everyone who lives here, especially the boys, and the beach is full of kids. (I guess another gang of town boys hassled Dare this morning. He didn't say much about it, but he's mad.) I tried to talk him into hose tag, but he doesn't want to play. I'm going out now with a bucket to toss water on his head!

P.P.S. I guess all of us are shut-ins, Mr. Marsworth.

Saturday, June 29, 1968

Dear Miss Kelly,

Are there not summer programs in Lake Liberty to
join? Have you visited our library? Summer reading
can be fun. The new woman on the corner has a
daughter near your age; I've seen that child in her
front yard doing cartwheels on the grass. Surely she
could use a playmate, too.

If none of those quite suit you, there's my cottage
on Gray's Bay. The house has long been locked, but the
two of you may swim on my shoreline undisturbed. Your
father loved to fish there as a boy. Perhaps a place to
play in safety would coax Dare from the woods.

Of course you'll need permission, so please ask
Blanche Kelly first. It's two miles or more from Main
Street, on Tuxedo, the first left past Becker's Bait
Shop. You'll see "Marsworth" on the marker. My cottage
and the shore are through those woods.

No doubt a healthy pastime would be best for all
concerned. Fewer fights and fewer letters will serve
both you children well.

There are better things to do with this brief
summer.

Sincerely,

H. W. Marsworth

H. W. Marsworth

Dear Mr. Marsworth,

A private cottage at Gray's Bay??? I can't believe it!!!! Thank you, thank you, thank you!!!!! It's the first I've seen Dare happy since we moved to this dumb town.

Dare already found a cane pole out in Gram's garage, with line and hooks left from the old days, and a rusted Folger's Coffee tin he's filled with dirt and worms.

When it comes to Dare and fishing, Dare does best with Dad. Billy can't bear to see a live thing captured, and I don't much like it either, so Sunday afternoons in Denton we stayed home while those two fished.

It's how the Reenie Billy Sunday Sundaes were invented. Billy scooped while I concocted toppings—melted peanut butter, marshmallows, grape jelly, crushed Oreos, raisins, Frosted Flakes, or Cap'n Crunch. Some of them were dreadful, but Billy always ate them, and we never once felt bad that Dare got time alone with Dad. (Well, maybe just a smidge.)

If you want a Sunday Sundae I could bring one to your house. ☺

So I won't fish at your cottage, but I'll be in that great blue water swimming in the sun. You ought to come down to Gray's Bay to spend the day with us.

We'll be there tomorrow in case you want to come.

Counting Down the Hours,
Reenie Kelly

P.S. If you're counting hours with me, we're at nineteen now. Gram's gone to Ladies Aid, and Billy's helping Mr. Casey, which means I've got a long dull day at Gram's all by myself. Don't you think on Sunday a family should stay home?

P.P.S. In case you don't remember, you didn't answer about Mom. I don't mean to be a nuisance, but my memory is good. I can't forget a question I want answered.

Dear Mr. Marsworth,

I did something that I shouldn't have, and it's night and I can't sleep. I can't sleep because my stomach's sick with worry, and there's no one else to talk to now, but you. I hope you'll listen and forgive me. I hope you'll say things will be fine. Asa Carver always told me, "Wait to worry," and every time he said it, my mind would ease a bit. Maybe you could say that to me now, or something else that calms a kid. I've said it to myself, but it didn't help.

First off, I need to tell you that I snooped through Billy's things. Billy hates a snoop, and I knew better than to do it, but Gram's house was gray and lonely, so I gave in to the urge to look under the cushion of Gram's couch. I knew Beth's letters would be tucked there, because that couch in Gram's small living room is all the private space that Billy has.

Beth and Billy have gone steady since Billy was thirteen, and I expected in her letters she'd be writing about love. "Kiss, kiss, kiss. I miss you so much, Billy. When should we get married???"

Why else would Beth drench them in perfume and Billy hide them?

I was right about the love, there was plenty of that there, but mostly there was talk of Vietnam, and how Billy can't give up on Mizzou in the fall. Beth said she'd heard Ace Turner was shot in Vietnam last week. He was two years ahead of Billy, an All-State pitcher, too, but now folks say Ace Turner might never walk again. Beth said if Billy went to war he could be next.

Beth has $180 saved, and she offered it to Billy. She said she'd give up college to keep Billy from the draft. "Mizzou is the only sure way you'll stay out of this war."

Beth's letters made it sound like Billy has dropped his dream for college, like he's given up on Mizzou because we don't have the money to pay for it this fall.

I KNOW we're short on money, but all of us are working, and every single cent I earn on my paper route is his. (It's not a lot, but I'll save every dime.) Dad went to North Dakota because that roadwork pays so well. Billy's working full-time. Gram has a full-time job at Brindle Drug. Isn't that enough to pay for college, Mr. Marsworth? How much could Mizzou cost?

Beth's letters were a worry, but her letters WEREN'T the worst of what I found. The worst thing was a letter from the Army urging Billy to enlist. A letter, and a bright brochure full of happy, clean-cut soldiers, boys in crisp, fresh uniforms that look nothing like my picture of Jackie Moon and Skip, or the photos of our pen pals tacked up on the board.

If the Army's after Billy, maybe they ought to show Skip dirty on his birthday, or Kyle Smith's sad family at his funeral, or Ace Turner in a wheelchair forever. They ought to show our Army pen pals, lonesome for their homes, or Lt. Gerald Walker without that leg he surely loved. Maybe they should show those wounded soldiers from Walter Cronkite's news. Or add in the rain and mud and snakes that Skip described.

Shouldn't they show that war to Billy and every other boy?

Whenever war was on the news, Mom would reach for Billy's hand. "Promise you won't go," she'd beg, and Billy always did. I'd like to do the same this minute, wake Billy from his sleep and beg him not to go to Vietnam. But if he wakes up to my crying, he'll know for sure I snooped.

Maybe I'll go out in the rain and talk to Dare.

No, I can't confess to Dare.

I know that you can't help me, Mr. Marsworth. Still, it helps to have you listen.

I guess you're like Dear Abby except that you're a man.

Sleepless in the Attic,
Reenie Kelly

P.S. Could you write back ASAP? Twice I've sent my troubles to Dear Abby, but she never writes me back.

P.P.S. Don't tell me to talk to Gram, she won't be ANY help.

Monday, July I, 1968

Dear Miss Kelly,

I am a far cry from Dear Abby, but I do not like to see a
child awake with worry in the night.

May I suggest you share your heartfelt fears with
Billy? Could you tell him you're increasingly concerned
about this war? Or perhaps you might remind him that
your mother's dream of college is your dream for him as
well? Mizzou is the place for him this fall.

You don't need to tell him that you "snooped." As
you describe too clearly, you are well aware of war.

He must make his way to college at all costs.

In the meantime, please go play down at my
cottage. This war is always with us; your worry won't
change that.

And perhaps a nap this afternoon? A nap can help
with nerves.

Yours Kindly,

H. W. Marsworth

H. W. Marsworth

Monday, July 1, 1968

Dear Mr. Marsworth,

You wrote back ASAP! And thank you for that "kindly." That
one word helped a lot.

I just couldn't go to your cottage with Billy on my mind,
even though I hate to think that Dare will see it first.

Thanks to your good advice, I didn't wait to talk to Billy, instead
I walked down to the Conoco and asked if he could talk. He was busy
pumping gas and wiping down the windshields and checking air and oil,
but I waited. It's still strange to see my brother pumping gas. Nearly
straight-A Billy should be reading at his old desk, or flirting with Beth
Harvey, or sitting on Gram's front steps strumming his guitar. He
shouldn't be grease-stained in a uniform sweating in the sun.

"What's up, Pup?" he said, concerned. That's the nickname
Billy calls me when he's being double-sweet. I guess he read the
worry in my eyes.

"I just stopped in to say hey," I lied. "Dare went fishing at
the lake, but you know I hate to fish."

"We can't do a Sunday Sundae here," he said, stealing a
glance at Mr. Casey, but Mr. Casey had his top half slid beneath
a Ford. He couldn't see us chatting near the pumps. "That'll
have to wait until I'm home. And besides today is Monday."
Billy's sweaty curls were sticking to his forehead, and rings of
sweat spread underneath both arms. "Why don't I take you to
the Tastee for a sundae after work?"

46

"No, thanks," I said. "We need the money, Billy."

"A sundae's twenty cents, Reen. I can blow a couple dimes on my best sister."

"You shouldn't." I felt guilty and ashamed standing at that station with the truth of all my snooping weighing on my heart. "We need to save all that we're earning to get you to Mizzou."

"Twenty cents won't get me there." Billy looked over my shoulder like he was hoping for some cars. "I hate to break it to you, Reen, but college and a crunch cone aren't quite in the same league."

"I know," I said. "But you're going off to college, right? You're heading off to Mizzou like Mom wanted?"

The only answer I wanted him to give me was a YES. Instead I got, "We'll see." And if there's two words that I hate, those are the words. "We'll see" is just a sneaky way of mostly saying no. (And you know that I hate no.)

"You see this in the paper?" I pulled a clipping from my pocket and offered it to Billy. "'Three Minnesotans Killed in Vietnam.'"

Billy looked down at the newspaper, but he didn't take it from my hand. Instead he shook his head like he wished I'd left that headline back at Gram's. "Why'd you clip this, Reen? Please don't start obsessing on those soldiers like Mom did."

Every time a soldier's death was in the paper, Mom would point it out to Dad. "Another boy gone, Frank," she'd say, and then they'd say a prayer.

"They're boys," I said to Billy. "Boys with names," because

47

that's what Mom always said. "And these three were on the front of the Tribune."

"You don't need to read the paper, just to do that route. Most paperboys don't read it. Leave it on the doorstep, right where it belongs."

"Three more dead," I said. "I just don't ever want this story to be yours. I need you to be safe at Mizzou in the fall. You know college was Mom's dream for you."

"I know Mom's dream." He draped his arm across my shoulder, but I didn't mind the sweat.

"So you're going?" I insisted. "You're going off to college like Mom wanted, and we'd planned. You won't enlist?"

"Reen." Billy sighed like he wanted me to drop it, but I couldn't.

"Dad's in North Dakota earning good money building roads. And Gram has her job at Brindle Drug. And Dare and I have papers, and I'll give you every cent."

"We're flat broke," Billy said. "We can't live at Gram's forever. When Dad comes home from North Dakota there won't even be room. The money Dad is earning already goes to bills."

"I know," I said, because once your family's bankrupt there's always talk of bills.

"Dad still owes tens of thousands to Mom's doctors. We don't even have a house." Billy ran his rag over his forehead, and left a streak of grease. A truck was signaling on Broadway, pulling into Casey's, and heading for the pump. "We've got until

September," Billy said. "We don't need to talk about this now."

"We do," I said. "Now that you're eighteen you could get drafted. You hate this war."

"So does Skip. And lots of guys they're drafting. And even some that are enlisting, trying to beat the draft."

"Don't sign up for the Army. Promise me you won't."

"You've got to hit the road, Pup," he said, forcing a weak smile. "Go off and be a kid while you still can."

And that's the worst part of this story, because Billy Kelly never ever makes a promise he won't keep. And when I asked him for that promise, he just said to hit the road.

Now I really need Dear Abby. I really truly do.

> Desperate,
> Reenie Kelly

Monday, July 1, 1968

Dear Mr. Marsworth,

It's nearly dark, and I've already left one letter, but I'm going to walk this over so you'll know how things turned out. I hope you'll check your milk box before morning. I hope you'll peek out of those curtains to see me at the gate. I hope one little clang won't be too much.

Just in case you planned to say it, I already talked to Gram. I did it during dishes when I had Gram to myself. (Shouldn't boys have to do dishes? Yes, they should!!!!) Anyway, I didn't pussyfoot around because that doesn't work with Gram, I just said Billy HAD to be in college come September, or else he could get drafted like everybody else.

"He could," Gram said. "It happens." She said it plain and flat like a cold fact we couldn't fix. I know Gram loves her grandkids in the gruff way that Gram loves, but how can she love Billy and not be scared he could get sent to Vietnam? "Billy owes his country service, the same as every healthy boy his age. Your dad and Uncle Will were on the front lines in Korea. Grandpa Kelly's brother—"

"I know," I said. "But Billy—"

"The young men of our country have a duty."

"But we're talking about BILLY. BILLY KELLY." I set my cloth down on the counter and stepped back from the sink. I wasn't staying in that kitchen with a heart as hard as Gram's. Gram's gray-haired and wrinkled, but she's not cuddly or soft like other grams. "Boys are dying in this war," I said. "You want Billy dying, too?"

"Don't be cruel." Gram frowned like she was hurt. "No one wants Billy harmed. No one. But isn't every soldier a Billy to his family? Don't you think so, Reen?"

"No," I said. "Not every boy is Billy. We only have ONE Billy, and I don't want him dead."

"Not everyone is dying," Gram said. "Soldiers do survive. And freedom isn't free. You can't love this country and not fight."

"But we're not fighting for this country. And we're already free."

"Don't you think that's selfish, Reen?" Gram said, trying to sound patient. "What if we'd said the same in World War II? When all those Jews were killed."

"I don't know," I said, because I don't. Except I know for sure this isn't World War II. Or the Civil War. Or the Revolutionary War, when we threw those chests of tea into the harbor. That war was right in Boston. We fought that war for us.

I can't say why we're at war in Vietnam, and Skip can't exactly either. Billy doesn't have an answer, and all Gram says is "liberty and freedom." Even Mrs. Lamb couldn't say for sure what we're trying to win in Vietnam.

I know nobody attacked us, so it isn't like Pearl Harbor.

I HATE this war. I hate everyone who made it. I hate the

Army and their letter. I hate Rat and Cutler and this entire stupid world. I even hate Gram just a little for what she said tonight. "Isn't every soldier a Billy to his family?"

NO! NOT EVERY BOY IS BILLY!!!!!

Billy is MY BILLY. He's been my watcher and my teacher since the day that I was born. In every picture in my baby book, I'm held in Billy's arms. "Maureen sure loves her oldest brother," Mom wrote under "Baby's First Month." And right under "Baby's First Word," Mom entered "Ba, for Billy."

If Gram doesn't understand that, she doesn't have a heart.

I'm writing Skip this minute because I know he'll understand.

Still Desperate,
Reenie Kelly

Tuesday, July 2, 1968

Dear Miss Kelly,

Please don't give up hope for Billy, and please don't
hate this world.

I admit, there are days when it is easier to hate
it than to love it, but there is beauty to be had here,
and happiness ahead. In the main, I'm afraid Blanche
Kelly is quite right. Every family loves the boy they
might be losing, and every family grieves when that
beloved boy is gone. I believe you know that, too.

What better reason do we need to work toward
peace on earth?

Perhaps for now, we should make sure Billy gets
to college. Surely there are scholarships for a nearly
straight-A student who can pitch and play guitar. The
university's Office of Financial Aid should help. I know
the Kellys won't take charity, but a scholarship is
earned. It wouldn't be charity, Miss Kelly, not at all.

Have you been down to the cottage? That should
cheer you some.

Sincerely,

H. W. Marsworth

H. W. Marsworth

Tuesday, July 2, 1968

Dear Mr. Marsworth,

Thank you, thank you, thank you!!!!

I'm glad to hear Financial Aid can help.

I'm going to find the money, I swear to you I am. Cross my heart and hope to die, I'll keep my brother from this war.

Do you know how much Mizzou might cost?

Billy says it doesn't matter when you're bankrupt.

Dad's bankrupt, Mr. Marsworth, but I'm not.

You got any work down at that cottage? We're going in an hour once I drop this in your box.

I'll collect this week, and Dare will do the same, but I know that's not enough to pay for Billy's school. I hope that I make twice the tips as Dare.

> For Hire,
> Reenie Kelly

P.S. Could you come to Gram's on Thursday to celebrate the Fourth? Fried fish. Rhubarb cake. Gram's creamy coleslaw. Aunt Kate and Uncle Slim are driving down from Willmar with their twins. I'm sure we could make room for a neighbor at Gram's house. ☺ Wouldn't you like to meet the Kelly kids?

P.P.S. I'm glad you're good at letters, because Skip hasn't sent one yet. Once a week Dad writes a "family letter," even though every week we each send letters of our own. (Even Dare writes Dad.) And Dad always says the same thing: "Be good. Don't make Gram mad. Stay out of trouble, Dare and Reen. Help Gram around the house. Have fun in Lake Liberty. Glad things are going well at Casey's for you, Billy. Wish I could be with you kids. Working day and night, I love you, Dad." It's that last line I like best. Short and sweet, but at least Dad sends his love.

Wednesday, July 3, 196

Dear Mr. Marsworth?????

You didn't leave a letter ☹, and this morning I was ambushed in the lot beside your house. ☹ ☹ ☹!

The first BB hit me in the ribs, and the next one hit my leg. "Go back to Misery," Cutler shouted from the tree, and Rat echoed down a yeah, then they both laughed.

When another BB hit me, I broke Dad's rule and ran. I couldn't stand my ground against a gun.

Please don't say that I deserve this from the Aero Shave last week. A foaming isn't shooting, I wouldn't shoot a kid.

Dare won't say that I deserve this, but he won't agree to Aero Shave this time for our revenge. This time he'll want to get those boys back good.

Please write to me this morning! I really truly need a letter from a friend!

Hunted,
Reenie Kelly

P.S. Forget it, Mr. Marsworth. I'm not going to leave this letter, because you'll tell Gram that I was shot. Then Gram will make me give my route to Dare. I'm not telling Dare now either, because he'll say the same as Gram. He'll say a route is no place for a girl. And he'll blab it all to Billy, and they'll all be on one side. Never mind. I'll write you something else.

Wednesday, July 3, 1968

Dear Mr. Marsworth,

It's two days in a row you haven't written.

You didn't answer my last question: Can you join us for the Fourth? Or are you going to be with family? I guess I hope you are. I sure wish Dad could come home for the Fourth.

I can't write too much this morning because I'm having a rough day. You probably wonder how a kid can have a rough day before the daylight, but believe me this kid can.

On a happy note, Dare and I both love your cottage! We wish the Kellys had a cottage just like yours to call our own. (Well, without the eggs, and mud, and boarded windows. Did you know that kids have wrecked your cottage? I hate the kids in this town, and you should hate them, too.)

We have chores before our party so we can't go back today. I'm scrubbing Gram's cracked toilet and dreaming of your shore. It was a perfect, peaceful place to swim with Dare. I wish that I could live there. I wish today could start again.

If you're alone tomorrow, could you please, please, please, please come?

I'll check back this afternoon, and hope you'll leave a YES.

Your Friend,
Reenie Kelly

Wednesday, July 3, 196̃

Dear Mr. Marsworth,

THREE TIMES today between my chores, I checked your milk box. You aren't answering my letters, should I take that as a NO? Have I turned into a nuisance? Don't you like me anymore? Did I do something to offend you? Are you mad I clanged that bell?

I can't look forward to tomorrow if you hate me, Mr. Marsworth.

Is this all because I told you we were broke?

We are broke, that's the truth. I know money should be private, and I'll keep ours private now. I won't say another word about the bills we have to pay. Or even Billy's college. I'm already busy solving Mizzou for myself. (Ingenuity, remember?)

And if you don't want to talk about the war, I promise you, I won't.

Is there another subject that might have made you mad? I wish I had my letters here to look.

If we're both at the parade could we please just say hello? You know I'm the freckled redhead dropping your Tribune. Do you have a little picture of yourself you could leave inside your box?

I want to know you when I see you, Mr. Marsworth.

I think you'll like me more in person, I really truly do. I'm better than my letters, I don't really write that well.

Your Friend Still,
Reenie Kelly

58

Wednesday, July 3, 1968

Dear Miss Kelly,

My apologies, but I'm afraid the Kelly picnic
isn't the place for me just now. It's a holiday for
families, and I'm happy you'll have yours.

It was kind of you to offer. I hope your
day is grand.

Sincerely,

H. W. Marsworth

H. W. Marsworth

P.S. As to the matter of your letters: less frequent
and exhaustive might be a worthy goal.

Thursday, July 4, 1968

Dear Mr. Marsworth,

Did you see me at your gate at 5:30 this morning? Did you see that rubbery, raw chicken Cutler hung up on your fence? A flag stabbed through its skin. A rusted steak knife in its leg. Ketchup slimed over the skin like it was blood.

I cut it down to help you, and I'm going to KILL those kids.

I know Rat and Cutler did it, Mr. Marsworth. Last night at Piggly Wiggly I saw Rat and Cutler scheming near the meat, making bawking sounds and clucking when I passed them in the store. What boys would shop for chicken, Mr. Marsworth?

"Chick, chick, chicken," they called, laughing, but Gram put on her scolding face and told them to grow up. (It'd be better if I'd said it. No kid wants a gram to fight her fights.)

I know they bought that chicken, because they left it on your fence.

Don't you worry, Mr. Marsworth, your enemies are ours. Dare and I made sure that slimy chicken went back where it belongs.

607 Grimes. That's the Cutlers' grimy corner house next to the school. (I found his address in the phone book while Gram was still asleep.)

I hope the Cutlers find that chicken on the steps with their Tribune.

I guess your letter to the paper caused the chicken AND the eggs. The mud smeared on your cottage. Or maybe they just hate you, the way they just hate Dare and me.

Kids can hate you for no reason, Mr. Marsworth.

Don't worry, we'll protect you, and we'll protect your cottage, too. No one's going to hurt you with the Kellys on your side.

Your Ally,
Reenie Kelly

P.S. My holiday is horrid and it's barely 8 a.m. Now I have to go to that parade, and think about that slimy chicken hanging from your fence. If we see Rat and Cutler, we plan to cream them both.

P.P.S. I wish you would have answered YES, I really do.

P.P.P.S. Is this too frequent and exhaustive? I tried to keep it short.

Thursday, July 4, 1968

Dear Mr. Marsworth,

Did you stay home from the parade? I wish I had!

The first bad thing was Main Street with that row of fancy tables set back from the crowd—Army, Navy, Air Force, and Marines—and soldiers giving out free stuff like pens and stickers. Every table that we stopped at urged Billy to enlist while Uncle Slim nodded in agreement, and Dare asked a hundred questions like he was ready to join now.

"You don't want to lose your chance to make a choice," those soldiers said to Billy, and they sounded so convincing with their promises of training, and a college education when Billy's service time was done, and the chance to choose a trade and travel, I couldn't leave Billy for a second for fear he might enlist. If they'd taken Dare at thirteen, he'd be enlisted now. He ate up every word those soldiers said.

"Don't do it," I told Billy when we'd walked off from the Marines. (All the soldiers seemed like good men, and they made me think of Skip, but I don't want my brother in this war.) "It's college that you want."

"You don't have to tell me, Reen," Billy said, but I could see these soldiers had him thinking that enlisting might be best.

"It doesn't mean that Billy will miss college," Uncle Slim said. He put his big hand on my head like I was six years old.

"But if he could get a desk job by enlisting it might keep him out of combat. They say he's safer signing up than getting drafted. Better chance of learning a trade he really wants. Not every kid gets sent to the front lines."

"Skip didn't get a desk job," I corrected Uncle Slim. "He's right there in the fighting, and in every letter that he sends me he says Billy should stay home."

"Well, was he drafted?" Uncle Slim asked, like I wouldn't know the difference, but I did.

"Yes," I said. "But not all the soldiers have been drafted, and they're fighting in the jungle just like Skip. Lt. Gerald Walker lost his leg."

"Okay, okay," Uncle Slim said. "That's enough of that talk, Reen."

"Well, it's true," I said. "Lots of boys are dying, Uncle Slim."

"Reen's always the expert," Dare said with a shove.

"There's no good choice without some money," Billy said, discouraged. He looked up at Uncle Slim like he was asking him for help, and his big brown eyes were sadder than I'd seen them in a while. Sadder than the day we left Beth Harvey waving in our yard. "If I'm too broke to go to college what else can I do except enlist or risk the draft?"

"I'm afraid that might be it, son." Uncle Slim tucked Billy close against him, the same way Dad does to us all.

"We're not too broke for college," I said, before we all

gave up. "We'll get the money, Billy. I swear to you we will. Ingenuity, remember?"

"Sure," Billy said, like he wished he could believe it. "I guess if anyone can save me, it's you, Pup."

The second terrible thing was the parade. Not the marching band, or floats, or the veterans with their flags, or the firemen throwing candy to the crowd, or the man on stilts dressed up like Uncle Sam, but the young soldier in a wheelchair with a cardboard sign that said SEND OUR SOLDIERS HOME, and the two hippie girls behind him who chanted "U.S. out of Vietnam! Peace now!" If you ask me, those three had a right to their opinion, but the town folks started booing, and telling them to leave. The younger kids threw candy, and nobody said, "stop."

"PLEASE STOP!" I finally screamed, because I couldn't just stand there on the sidelines doing nothing.

"Reenie Kelly!" Gram said, angry, then she grabbed me by the elbow to pull me from the crowd.

It's a good thing you skipped our picnic, because Gram said I'd made a "spectacle," and Slim and Kate left early because the twins were out of sorts, and Gram burned Dare's precious fish, and Dare wouldn't go to the fireworks just in case Dad called. In the end, we spread a sheet out on Gram's lawn and watched a few bright edges fizzle in the sky. Billy fell asleep before they'd finished, and Gram got tired of mosquitoes and went inside to bed. I kept thinking of that wounded soldier in the wheelchair and Skip in Vietnam.

"Well, those fireworks were crap," Dare said into the darkness. Snoring Float was stretched beside him with his ear against Dare's heart.

"The whole day was," I said. "All of it, beginning with that chicken."

"Yep," Dare said. "And Dad didn't even call."

It was a no-good Fourth from start to finish, Mr. Marsworth.

I could add on more, but I don't want to be exhaustive.

Unhappy Independence,
Reenie Kelly

P.S. You didn't tell me Cutler's father was the sheriff!!! Or that I'd have to see Cutler and his brothers riding on that sheriff's float like big shots. I guess we shouldn't have left that bloody chicken at Sheriff Cutler's door.

Friday, July 5, 1968

Okay, Mr. Marsworth,

All I do is hope for answers—from you, Skip, Dad, Mizzou's Office of Financial Aid. Can't you find a minute to write a letter to a friend?

That's right, Mr. Marsworth. I took your good advice and wrote the Office of Financial Aid at Mizzou by myself, and so far I haven't told a single soul, but you. Do you think Mizzou will give the Kellys money, yes, or no? I did a great job on the letter, best penmanship and all, and I wrote just what you wrote me: "Surely there are scholarships for a nearly straight-A student who can pitch and play guitar." I told them we were bankrupt, that we'd lost our house in Denton paying for Mom's cancer, and we owed money still to doctors, but as soon as we had extra we'd pay back every dime they could give Billy. We wanted scholarships, not charity.

I said they had to hurry, because school would start soon, and if Billy wasn't at their college he'd have to face the draft. Or worse, he might enlist, and a boy with Billy's good heart was too gentle for this war. He's never even punched another kid. I said I was his sister, and I was twice as rough as him. I made sure they understood that the Kellys served their country, so none of us are cowards, but college would be best for Billy now.

Wouldn't you give Billy money if you ran Financial Aid and got a letter from his sister? I definitely would.

Aren't you happy with my scheme? I know you don't want Billy in this war.

All Fingers Crossed for Good News,
Reenie Kelly

P.S. The chicken landed on Gram's doorstep ☹. It was covered with black flies and reeking like a dead fish in the sun. If Float had found it first he could have died. Luckily I stashed it in Gram's trash, but when she caught a whiff of it, she scolded Dare and me.

Do you think Gram ought to blame us for that chicken?????

We didn't tell her how it happened, Dare just said some town kids hate us, and it was probably those two jerks that left it on her steps. "Don't be ridiculous, Dare Kelly," Gram said before she left for Brindle Drug. "You have to be a friend to have one. Go inside and take a shower, maybe that would help."
    I liked the part about the shower, but I kept that to myself. ☺ ☺ Dare AND Float could both use showers, I won't lie.

67

Saturday, July 6, 1968

Dear Miss Kelly,

Is "okay" a proper salutation? I think not.

Nevertheless, I shall respond to simply set the record straight.

I did not advise you to write the Office of Financial Aid. I know better than to tell a child to do this on her own. Please don't ever tell your brother or your father that I did. I doubt I'd be forgiven, and I don't wish an ounce of ill will between your house and mine.

Ingenuity is one thing, but imprudence is another, and while your loyalty is moving, you can't ask a public college to save Billy from the draft. Or any other boy. The draft exists to force our young to fight. Without it, many of our drafted soldiers might not serve, including Skip. A state college cannot be a haven from the draft.

Was that letter wise or foolish? Only time will tell. I shall hope you were convincing for Billy's sake and yours.

Finally, I absolutely do not need an ally in Lake Liberty. Have I made that clear? There is no war on my behalf you need to fight, no dispute that should involve you: chicken, eggs, or otherwise.

You are impetuous, Miss Kelly, a trait common to the young, but I cannot be a party to your schemes; I simply can't. Your actions day-to-day continue to astonish, but I am far too old for such surprises. I wish your lovely mother could supervise your days; if she were here she'd know what would be best.

I do not pretend to know what would be best for you, Miss Kelly, except perhaps a rest in correspondence for us now.

Do enjoy the cottage.

Sincerely,

H. W. Marsworth

H. W. Marsworth

Dear Mr. Marsworth,

A rest in correspondence?

You're right, you don't know what's best for an eleven-year-old kid. Do you have any children, Mr. Marsworth? If you did you might remember it's best for kids to have at least one friend in a mean town.

Plus, I have things I HAVE to tell you. Things YOU NEED TO KNOW.

If it's too much to write an answer, you go ahead and rest, but I'll still write.

I know you're mad I wrote to Mizzou, but I had to trust my instincts, it's what Mom would say to do if she were here. "Trust your instincts, Reen," Mom always said. "You've got a good head on your shoulders, you'll be fine."

I guess she probably said that because she knew someday I'd have to make all these hard decisions for myself.

Don't worry, Mr. Marsworth, I won't tell Dad or Billy, or any other Kelly I wrote Financial Aid because of you. Never ever ever. No one knows we write these letters, and no one ever will. And I didn't mean to blame you, I didn't expect you'd be so mad. Do you know how hard it is to be eleven? I don't think so.

That's all I'll say this morning, so you'll have time to nap.

But just so you're prepared—there's trouble at your cottage, I think you ought to know. That letter's coming later,

70

but if you find it too exhausting just rest a couple minutes until you're ready to read on. That's how I taught my ex-friend Mack McCoy to read <u>Go, Dog, Go</u> when we were six. A few words at a time, then he could rest.

Your Loyal Friend Still,
Reenie Kelly

P.S. I didn't mean to ask Mizzou to be a haven from the draft. I hope it won't mean trouble. I doubt Billy will forgive ME if I screwed up his college plan. Please don't ever tell him if I did.

Saturday, July 6, 1968

Dear Mr. Marsworth,

Did you get through my morning letter and take a good long nap?

This one might be exhaustive, so remember what I said. A few sentences, then rest. Z . . . z . . . zzzzz.

Are you resting now? I bet you are. I'm the only one awake still in Gram's house. I'll be resting once this letter's done.

Good or bad news first?

Dad prefers the good news, so I'll just start with that.

THE GOOD NEWS

We love your cottage, Mr. Marsworth, we really, truly do. Dare loves your big deep woods as much as Gram's. We've built a stick fort in the trees, and every day we eat lunch on your dock. Warm bologna sandwiches and pickles, and a jar of grape Kool-Aid we mix at Gram's. (Float even gets a sandwich.) My favorite thing is swimming, and playing water tag with Dare, and the two of us together, because that really is a first. Dare had too many friends in Denton to play with me alone, and I never will forget this first summer by ourselves.

THE BAD NEWS

Do you get down to that cottage, Mr. Marsworth? I don't think you do because it's gone to rack and ruin, and I can't understand how a perfectly fine house is left to rot. If the

Kellys had a house that nice, we'd keep it good as new. Did you board up those broken windows? Did you know the white paint peeled to the gray wood underneath? How long has it been since you've spent summers at that place? When we look through the front window, it's like the house has just been left. We can see the furniture's old-fashioned, and there's a fish calendar from 1950 hung above the couch. Someone left her knitting on a bench beside the door. Was there a Mrs. Marsworth, Mr. Marsworth? Gram said you live alone, so I'm afraid she must be gone.

Did you leave this place alone for eighteen years???

I think maybe you did, because it's covered in dried mud, and eggs, and scribbled, mean graffiti, and someone left a misspelled "TRATOR" sprayed across your porch. We've filled three garbage bags with trash left on your land: empty bottles, cigarette butts, candy wrappers, a pair of moldy socks and shoes. We even found a jacket in your woods. Dare thinks the vandals come at night, because it's all ours in the daytime, but I don't want them coming there at all. Is there any way to stop them? Could Sheriff Cutler help? Or is it his horrible demon son who sprayed that "TRATOR?"

(Yesterday, that horrible demon Cutler stole six papers from my route. Six customers complained to the Tribune, but I won't bother you with that.)

Is that "TRATOR" from that letter that you wrote to

the Tribune? The paint looks fresh to me. The mud and eggs are cracked and faded from the sun.

ONE LAST QUESTION, Please just answer YES OR NO. (It won't count as correspondence.)

We'd like to fix your cottage, maybe give it some fresh paint, especially that "TRATOR" on your porch. We priced the paint at Rash's Hardware, and we also need a couple brushes, so $8.00 ought to pay for our supplies. We might not paint the whole thing, but we'll clean up what we can. My color choice is lavender or green, but Dare wants to leave it white the way it was. You decide about the color, we know it's not our house.

Wouldn't you like to have it painted, Mr. Marsworth?

You don't have to pay us for our labor, although I'd sure like some summer work besides the route. Every penny saved is a penny for Mizzou. We'll need every penny if Financial Aid won't help.

Your Grateful Helper,
Reenie Kelly

P.S. An ally is a helper, but you don't like that word.

P.P.S. All the Kelly kids helped Dad paint our house in Denton, so you don't have to worry, we'll get the job done right!

Yes. Enclosed please find $10.00 for your effort. I will be happy to pay more. White paint should suffice.

Thank you, Mr. Marsworth!!!!!
White paint will be perfect.
See I can keep it short, the same as you.

Sincerely,
Reenie Kelly

P.S. We avenged those stolen newspapers,
but I won't tell you about that.

Tuesday, July 9, 1968

Dear Mr. Marsworth,

Just in case you're curious, Dare doesn't know about our letters,
he only knows you left a note about your cottage in the box.
Dare doesn't ask a lot of questions, if you had Dare for a pen pal
every letter would be short.

We've hauled water from the lake and scrubbed the caked
mud from your cottage, but the egg yolks are more stubborn,
because they've stained right through the paint. Dare thinks we
can paint over those dried yolks.

The BIGGEST news today is that Billy saw your cottage, and
I'm starting with the good news, because you'll see the end is bad.

Tonight just after supper, we took Billy to the cottage so he
could see this place we loved. (Actually, he drove us in Gram's
Plymouth, but the directions were all ours.) The minute we
pulled into the driveway, Billy pointed at your faded sign.

"Mr. Marsworth from the paper?" he said to us, confused.
"That man that wrote the letter? This property is his?"

"Don't worry," Dare said quickly. "We don't really know him.
He just hired us to clean it, because he's on Reenie's route."

"So you know him from your route, Reen?" Billy asked
in that same suspicious way he'd asked that day we read the
letter that you'd written the Tribune.

"Whatever gossip you've heard, Billy, none of it is true."
I could see him looking at the weeds, and the graffiti on your

cottage, and wondering to himself how the place had gone to ruin. "This town hates peace and anyone that stands for it, you saw that on the Fourth."

"Shut up with the peace," Dare said to me. "We built a cool stick fort, Billy. You want to see that first?"

"I guess Float's set for the lake," Billy said. Float was leaping through the water, barking for us all.

"First swim, then fort," I said. "Race you to the water." I yanked my shirt over my head, then tore off toward the lake. Every day I race Dare, and every day I win. Well, every day Float wins, but Dare always comes in third. He's oversized and strong, but he's not fast.

"Okay, okay," Billy called, but instead of running with us, he stepped onto your front porch to peer through those two windows, exactly like we did the first day we were here. I guess every Kelly wants to see what's left inside.

"Just ignore that 'TRATOR,'" I yelled up from the lake. "Dare and I are going to paint it."

Dare splashed a wall of water in my face. "Come on!" he called to Billy. "Don't leave me here with Reen. I already have to waste every livelong day with her."

That part hurt my feelings, but I like to write the truth. True friends tell the truth.

So here's a second truth and I hope it doesn't hurt your feelings, Mr. Marsworth.

Billy told us that Mr. Casey told him you refused to serve your country way back in World War I, and that folks say you went to federal prison as a traitor. And even after prison, you're not ashamed of what you did.

Is that story really true or is it gossip? Did Mr. Casey make it up?

Did you really go to prison, Mr. Marsworth?

I'd like you to write back quickly to say the answer's NO. I've never written to a prisoner, and I'm not sure I ought to now.

Billy said as long as we did work for you, they'd hate us in this town. "You two decide," he said. "Gram isn't going to like it, so I'd keep it to yourselves." He said that you're not dangerous, or bad in any way, but what you did against your country, even all those years ago, folks just can't forgive.

"He's like Muhammad Ali," Dare said. "Ali used to be the greatest, but they stripped him of his title for saying he wouldn't serve once he was called. He went from being a fighter folks admired to a coward."

"I don't know, Dare," Billy disagreed. "Maybe folks you knew in Denton called Ali a coward, maybe even Dad did, and people on TV, but plenty of good people admire what he's done."

"But what's that boxer got to do with Mr. Marsworth?" I asked Billy. I don't follow boxing like Dare does, and all I really care about is why you went to federal prison, and what crime you committed that folks hold against you still.

Billy drew a circle in the dirt while he was taking time to think. "Well, for one thing, they both refused to serve, Reen. And there are people in this country who can't forgive a man for that."

"But you don't want to serve," I said. "You don't."

"Lots of men don't want to serve," Billy said. "But it's another thing to go against your country. You go against your country, you're a traitor to most folks."

"Darn right," Dare said with a salute.

Could you help me, Mr. Marsworth? Did you REALLY go against your country?

Am I a pen pal with a man who went to prison?

Waiting for Your Story,
Reenie Kelly

Wednesday, July 10, 1968

Dear Miss Kelly,

Billy is quite right, I was imprisoned during WWI for treason.
It's true, I refused to serve my country in what we called
"the great war," or worse, "the war to end all wars," which
sadly it did not. I was unapologetic then, as I am now.

Has that made me a pariah in Lake Liberty? Many
times it has.

Will the town hold it against you if you befriend me
in some way? Yes, some probably will. In good conscience,
I have not sought your friendship.

Should you write letters to a former prisoner?
Perhaps not.

This is all the explanation I can offer to a child.

I am guilty of no crime, except that of following my
conscience when I took a stand for peace. Someday you will
decide if you believe that right or wrong. Clearly, Billy
has decided I was wrong.

As for that "boxer," young Miss Kelly: I believe
Muhammad Ali to be a man of moral courage in the matter of
the draft. His public fight against this war is a call for
greater justice. I consider him a champion far beyond the
world of boxing. I hope history will prove me to be right.

May I assume we have found reason now to rest?

Sincerely,

H. W. Marsworth

H. W. Marsworth

P.S. Did I not say to seek permission from your grandmother
before you went down to my cottage? I am certain that I did.

Thursday, July 11, 1968

Dear Mr. Marsworth,

Is that all you can tell me about prison?

I'm a kid, but I'm not dumb. Did they treat you like a criminal? Were you with murderers and kidnappers? Did they feed you bread and water? Were you locked up in a cell like the prisoners on TV?

I looked up World War I in Billy's Webster, and it was 1914—1918. That was fifty years ago! Should the two of us quit writing over a war that's dead and gone?

Why do people in Lake Liberty care about this now?????

Here's the one thing I keep thinking: If Mom knew you went to prison, she didn't mind. Or maybe she said you were special BECAUSE you went to prison instead of fighting in a war you thought was wrong. Did Mom know you went to prison, Mr. Marsworth?

As far back as I remember, Mom always hated war, even before Vietnam or Billy and the draft. When we played war at the river, it always made Mom sad.

"It's a terrible game," she said, but it was fun for me.

I know now war isn't fun. I know it from Skip's letters, and all the letters from our pen pals, and I know it from the paper, and Time and Life and Newsweek, and the news with Walter Cronkite, and lost sons like Kyle Smith. I know real people die, and maybe you didn't want to die way back in World War I.

If that's why you went to prison, I don't blame you, Mr. Marsworth.

Billy doesn't want to die in the war, and Skip doesn't want to either. Who ever wants to die???? I don't want anyone to die! Not you, or Skip or Billy, or anybody else. Mom didn't want to die. She would have stayed with us forever, if she could.

Why didn't you go to college to stay out of that war? You seem smart enough for college. You know more million-dollar words than Mrs. Lamb. Was your family bankrupt, too?

Billy HAS to go to college.

Prison isn't right for Billy Kelly, it's just not. And Dad would never let his sons choose prison over war.

Please send more explanation.

Your Friend Still,
Reenie Kelly

P.S. We're not giving up your cottage, because prison or no prison, we love that stretch of lake, and Dare and Float adore your woods, and we want to earn our money, and it's the only place we like in this whole town. Dare doesn't care who hates us just for giving you a hand.

P.P.S. I told Gram you let us swim down at your at your cottage, so don't be mad about that still. She said she'd "rather" we didn't help you, but she didn't say we "can't." Until Gram says we can't, then we still will.

P.P.P.S. If you think Ali's a champ still, I'm sure you must be right.

82

Friday, July 12, 1968

Dear Mr. Marsworth,

I await your explanation.
I await it every day.
I await you and Skip and Mizzou most of all.
In the meantime, we're about to mow the weeds,
but first we need a key to that old shed.

Hardworking,
Reenie Kelly

Dear Mr. Marsworth,

Thank you for that key and five more dollars! We both think
$5 is too much for a mowed lawn. We'll mow those weeds all
summer for $5.

Are you okay there in this heat?

Why does your house always look dark?

Do you ever have the lights on, Mr. Marsworth?

Do you know the Canes on Hillcrest? 501 Hillcrest. Mr.
Cane delivers milk.

This morning on my route, I saw one of their sons leaving
for the Army, at least I think it was the Army, because he
was dressed up like a soldier, and the whole family stood
outside in their pajamas hugging him good-bye. I tried to look
away while I dropped off their morning paper, because I knew
if it were Billy leaving, we'd want to be alone.

First thing I did at Gram's was rush to give a hug to Billy. I
don't usually hug him early mornings, but I couldn't help myself
today. I just had to feel my arms around his neck, and my head
against his heart, and how warm he is just waking up for work.

"You okay, Pup?" Billy asked me, and that was all it took
for me to cry.

"For goodness' sake," Gram said. "It's 6:30 in the morning.
What's got you worked up, Reen?"

"Nothing," I said, sobbing, because I couldn't explain to Gram or Billy that the Cane boy leaving for the Army was enough to break my heart.

It's hard to be eleven, Mr. Marsworth.

I wish Mom could be here.

Yours Truly,
Reenie Kelly

P.S. You can skip the explanation about prison if you want. I don't need an explanation to stay friends. I don't want to lose you as a friend.

Sunday, July 14, 1968

Dear Mr. Marsworth,

There's something I didn't tell you because I hoped you'd be surprised.

I planted those marigold seeds down at your cottage. Now you'll have a little garden right beside your porch.

"Something beautiful and blooming might be solace for your soul."

Do you remember when you wrote that back in June? We've been friends now for four weeks. I hope you'll say you're still my friend.

I hope you'll come to see your flowers when they're grown.

True Blue,
Reenie Kelly

Monday, July 15, 1968

Dear Mr. Marsworth,

You won't believe what Rat and Cutler did this morning in the rain!

They pinned me to the wet grass and shoved worms down my shirt. Rat smashed them in my hair while Cutler dropped them on my face.

I'm not lying, Mr. Marsworth.

I've been in the shower twice and I still feel every slimy worm.

I just want to SCREAM and so I will.

Can you hear me, Mr. Marsworth? That's how loud I'm screaming at Gram's house.

Tortured,
Reenie Kelly

Dear Silent Mr. Marsworth,

Another empty milk box after everything I've said?

Tears and worms and flowers, and you won't even write?

I don't care about that prison, I swear to you I don't.

I've decided there's a song you have to hear: "I Am a Rock," by Simon and Garfunkel. Do you know it, Mr. Marsworth? Did you hear it on The Smothers Brothers Comedy Hour?

It's a song about a person walled off from the world, a person sort of like a shut-in behind a tall black fence, a man who wants to be rock or island so he won't hurt anymore.

Is that you, Mr. Marsworth? Are you done with love and friendship like the sad man in this song?

You probably don't think a kid could understand that feeling, but I can. I understood it back in fourth grade when Mom was dying, and I'd fall asleep to Billy singing that sad song on his side of our wall. All of us were islands, even Billy, because when you're as sad as we were, you're sad all by yourself.

The year Mom died of cancer was the same bad year I got ditched by my best friend Mack McCoy. Even with Mom dying, he ditched me out at recess to play sports with the boys. When I'd ask if I could join in, he'd say, "No girls allowed." From ages four to ten, Mack and I had practically been twins. Everything we did we did together. I taught him how to read, and he taught me to play marbles, and we shot snakes down by the river, and found bottles at the dump. Maybe he didn't want a friend whose mom had cancer (it's not contagious, but some kids acted like it was) or maybe he'd outgrown having a girl for a best friend. (Billy said it happens.) I asked Mack a hundred times, but he wouldn't tell me.

I was so much like an island, I'd replay that record, Billy's record really, and I'd pretend I was a rock so all the hurt would disappear.

That's how it was until I met Asa Carver, and I got Skip for a pen pal, and I stopped feeling so alone because I finally had two friends.

You can be my good friend, Mr. Marsworth. You can answer when I write you, and tell me if you're sad.

You don't have to be an island in that big house all alone.

And I don't have to be an island in this town, if I have you.

> Not an Island,
> Reenie Kelly

P.S. I'm going to drop off Billy's 45 so you can hear it for yourself. It's a little scratched from too much wear, but it still works. I'll drop it off at noon, but you'll need to get it from the milk box right away or it will warp. RIGHT AWAY! Billy won't be happy if I wreck his 45.

Tuesday, July 16, 1968

Dear Mr. Marsworth,

Here it is! Please listen to each word, so you understand it all. It's sort of like a poem, but not a poem. Even Mrs. Lamb loves Simon and Garfunkel. "Sound of Silence" is her favorite. I bet you'd like that, too. In Vietnam, Skip says, our troops love "Homeward Bound." That's the same song Billy sings when he's lonesome for Beth Harvey, and it makes me think of Denton and the whole life that we left.

Please answer when you've heard "I Am a Rock."
Please tell me if you liked it, yes or no.
You'll have to listen more than once to understand it all.

Your Friend,
Reenie Kelly

Dear Miss Kelly,

If I ever was an island, you have landed on my shore.
One can't long be an island with Miss Kelly in the world.

Yes, I understood the painful lyrics very well.

Of course, I am disheartened that such sorrow spoke
to you, but then you are no ordinary child.

And you have shared no ordinary song.

Am I a rock? I can assure you, dear Miss Kelly,
I have cried more than a rock. And while I might seem
to you an island, the fence around my house has not
sheltered me from sorrow, nor have you been sheltered
by your youth. I know you've suffered deeply; I know
you suffer still. Letter after letter, on every page I
hear your heart. Of course I do not wish to be another
Mack McCoy.

You are right: the song is lovely, lovely like a
poem, and so much more than mindless rock and roll.
Not every song should be shoo-bop shoo-bop. It brought
to mind a work that you should read: "No Man Is an
Island," by John Donne. Although the piece is in fact a
meditation, you might consider it "sort of like a poem"
much like your song. I memorized this version as a

child, and perhaps you will as well. Surely, you are smart enough. You can comprehend a metaphor better than most minds. Perhaps Billy will enjoy the poem as well. If I remember right, your mother loved fine poems.

The page is marked. The book is yours to keep.

I see now my brief hiatus can't continue without increasing your distress, but please know I can't keep pace with your rate of correspondence, and please try not to misinterpret nor disregard my words. ("Advice. Permission.") Read carefully, Miss Kelly.

Finally, expect some interludes of silence while this former island rests. "No offense," as you would say; I am quite old.

Sincerely,

H. W. Marsworth

H. W. Marsworth

No Man Is an Island

No man is an island

Entire of itself;

Every man is a piece of the Continent,

A part of the main.

If a clod be washed away by the sea,

Europe is the less

As well as if a promontory were

As well as if a manor of thy friend's

Or of thine own were;

Any man's death diminishes me,

Because I am involved in Mankind;

And therefore never send to know for whom the bell tolls;

It tolls for thee.

John Donne (1572–1631)

Wednesday, July 17, 1968

Dear Mr. Marsworth,

THANK YOU! THANK YOU! THANK YOU!

You're not a thing like Mack McCoy, don't you worry
about that. Mack McCoy would never read a poem. And he
wouldn't use million-dollar words like "interlude" or "hiatus!"

My own book from Howard Marsworth! And there's your
very name on the inside of the cover, it's that same fancy
signature on every letter that you sign. Do you use fountain ink?
Is that why your cursive looks old-fashioned? Did you really own
this old-time book as a young boy? No wonder you grew up to
be so smart! Kids today wouldn't read a book like this, but I
sure will.

I'll keep your gift forever, my first gift from my friend.
Oops, I meant to say my second. I still count the seeds. But a
real book of old-time poetry, no one ever gave me that.

I'll read every word, even if I'm slow to understand it. I
understand the poem's beginning: No one is alone. Not you, or
me. But the "clod" and then the "promontory"? I borrowed
Billy's dictionary, but I didn't show him your book. Right now,
I'd rather keep it to myself. Dare has Float, and Billy has Beth
Harvey. I have Skip and Mr. Marsworth. No one else has that.

You're right, Mom was crazy about poems. She loved
William Shakespeare, and Elizabeth Barrett Browning,
and sometimes Emily Dickinson, whose poems were more like

puzzles. When Mom got too sick to read, I'd sit beside her bed and try my best, but only Billy understood the way Shakespeare ought to sound. Dare found a book of limericks, and those would make Mom laugh. I wish she could be here to read these poems.

Mom would be so proud to see me with John Donne.

> No Kid Is an Island,
> Reenie Kelly

P.S. *Promontory. A high point of land or rock that juts out into a large body of water.

P.P.S. *Clod. A lump or mass especially of earth or clay.

P.P.P.S. The bell outside your house, it clangs for thee. Do you think John Donne meant "clang" when he wrote "toll"?

P.P.P.P.S. *Hiatus = Rest. Interlude = Break. You might not know this, Mr. Marsworth, but I look up your words.

P.P.P.P.P.S. We've had trouble with your mower so your lawn still isn't cut, but your front porch wall is mostly painted, and every trace of that red "TRATOR" has finally disappeared.

Wednesday, July 17, 1968

Dear Mr. Marsworth,

Before I go to sleep, I have to make one small confession, because friends should tell the truth, and so I will.

Yesterday at noon, I was perched up in the oak tree in the lot across the street from your brick house. Sometimes I like to sit up there in case you come outside. (I'd just like a glimpse of my good friend.)

Anyway, I wasn't really spying (Billy hates it when I spy on him with Beth), but I couldn't help but notice a man that couldn't be YOU took Billy's record from your box. At least, I don't think he could be you, unless you have a mop of shaggy blond hair, and you look closer to someone Billy's age, than Gram's.

Is there someone else besides you in that house? Your grandson or your son? Remember when I asked if you had children? You didn't answer that yet, either. (I remember what I ask.)

I don't want a long-haired stranger reading what I wrote. I don't mind Skip sharing my letters with the soldiers because those men are our pen pals, but I only wanted YOU to read my words. Plus there's things I've told you, I hope you'll never tell another soul.

Are you really in that brick house, Mr. Marsworth? Are you really Mr. Marsworth, or is there another man inside there pretending to be you???

Really Reenie Kelly,
Reenie Kelly

Thursday, July 18, 1968

Dear Miss Kelly,

I'm afraid your wild imagination has been wasted on my
days.

For better or for worse, I am really Mr. Marsworth.
The man you spied——and I'd rather you didn't spy like
Nancy Drew——is employed as my assistant, Carl Grace.
He brought your record to me, but I listened to it in
a room behind closed doors. Well, Clyde may have heard
it, too, but Clyde's a cat of honor. He won't tell a soul.

I can promise that your words are safe with me. My
silence and my sentences——those have been my own.

I am pleased John Donne has found a good home in
your hands. The clod and promontory are metaphors as
well. No man is an island. That image matters most.

Please don't labor at the cottage. Today it's 95
and sunny; put your cottage chores aside and take
a swim.

Sincerely,

H. W. Marsworth

H. W. Marsworth

Thursday, July 18, 1968

Dear Mr. Marsworth!!!!!!

Skip finally sent a letter, and I thought you'd want to see
it!!!!! I wish I could read it to you now, just the way I stood
up near the blackboard to read Skip's words to my class. I'd
read his letter, then I'd tack it on our wall. But there are
things inside this letter I can't tell Billy YET. Things like how I
wrote to Mizzou mostly, and my Rat-and-Cutler war.

You can read it all you want, because I think that it's
important, and someone else should hear how Skip feels in this
war. Some parts I'll tell to Billy, some I won't.

Doesn't Skip sound sweet, and scared, and done in by the
war? Doesn't he sound eager to come home?

Your Pen Pal,
Reenie Kelly

Hey there Reenie Kelly,

I'm sorry it took weeks to answer all those letters, but
a guy at war can't write like a young kid. I've got all
my friends and family writing, too. The only good part
of this war is getting mail, so keep those letters coming
even when I don't quick write you back.

So let's see where should I start? I'm glad you're
with your gram, or mawmaw as I call mine, because even
if your gram gets crabby, family is the best. No one loves
you like your family, that's for sure. I bet when school
starts you'll make a great big batch of friends. Dare, too.
Come September you'll be singing a new tune.

Don't give too much attention to those boys.
Best way to lose a bully is ignore him, didn't your
mama teach you that? It sounds to me like they're
just trying to mark their turf, making sure that
you and Dare know who's the boss. It's the same way
here, except with mortars and rockets, and people
dying for a turf war, which makes you see how
stupid a thing like fighting is. Especially with kids.
Not to say you're stupid, but you've got too much
upstairs to waste your time on those two boys.

I hope that don't sound mean, but if it does I'll
tell you something nice: I'm sure proud you wrote to

Mizzou, and I hope the **$$$$** comes for Billy before he's drafted or enlists. You ought to get a medal for Best Sister in the World. Don't ever tell my little sisters, but they didn't do a thing to keep me from this war. 'Course they didn't have a clue how it would be, and I didn't either. One thing a grunt learns early, it's nothing like the movies, that's for sure.

Now about that second pen pal, I'm not one bit jealous. It sure hasn't kept you from sending me lots of letters, ha-ha-ha. I bet he looks forward to your stories same as me. If I ever get to be an old man, which don't seem likely here, I hope a girl like Reenie Kelly will be assigned my route.

You ARE the first papergirl any of us know, and I'm all for equal rights as long as they don't draft girls for this war. I don't want to think you'd end up here. The women serving here won't ever be the same. No one will, and that's the truth.

The other day, I watched some young kids playing in the rain, and I thought of you and Dare down at the cottage, and how kids across the whole world really are the same. Maybe everybody is, I'll never know.

It's hard to fill a letter when there's nothing that I've seen or done these last few weeks I'm proud to tell.

I should be proud to serve my country, but I'm not. If I ever make it home, I won't touch another gun.

Oh, I almost forgot that thing you asked me:

No, I'm not mad your old-man pen pal wrote the paper saying war is wrong. And I'm glad those kids showed up at that parade to march for peace. Some guys feel betrayed by the protestors back at home, but I'm not one. It's up to all of you to help us now. We're here doing the fighting, you get us soldiers home. And keep more boys from coming, your brother Billy at the top.

If they run out of soldiers, the war will have to end.

Pray for me, Reenie Kelly. I always need your prayers.

> Your Favorite Pen Pal,
> Skip

P.S. You see why I don't write more often? I can't be fun and funny anymore.

P.P.S. I almost forgot to thank you for the Life magazine you sent when Bobby Kennedy was killed. It sure made us sad to see him on the cover running down a beach with that black dog. First Dr. King gunned down in Memphis, and now it's Bobby. It's hard to know what we're defending when good men are killed at home. When we got the news on Bobby, Jackie Moon led a little service just like he did when Dr. King was killed. Jackie's not a real-life preacher, but he could be. He's not shy with songs and prayers, and he sure knows how to sing. No instruments or nothing, just the sound of Jackie trying to give us hope with those old hymns.

P.P.P.S. I'm sorry that the world is such a mess for a young kid.

Thursday, July 18, 1968

Dear Miss Kelly,

Yes, I would say Skip sounds "done in." It's a terrible
task we're asking from a boy as kind as Skip, or any
feeling human being ravaged by a war. Whatever I can
do to bring our soldiers home, I will. Today I'll write
the president again, our senators and congressmen,
although I doubt change will be swift. One old man in
Lake Liberty can hardly end a war.

Still, every voice for peace must speak and
speak again.

Isn't that what Dr. Martin Luther King and Robert
Kennedy would want?

As long as I am living, a better world will be
my work.

Sincerely,

H. W. Marsworth

H.W. Marsworth

P.S. Here is my copy of Life magazine from April. If
you didn't send Skip this issue when Dr. King was
killed, please send it now. I've included an envelope
and postage. If there is extra cost involved, please let
me know. At my age I have few heroes, but Dr. King is
one. I hope someday you make a study of the good that
man has done.

Thursday, July 18, 1968

Dear Mr. Marsworth,

Thank you for that magazine for Skip. I'm sorry I didn't send him one in April, but I know he'll like it now, and I bet he'll double-like it when I tell him it's from you!

Before Dr. King was killed, I didn't know much about him, but Mrs. Lamb said he was a great man with a dream of equal rights and freedom for his people, and he hoped someday his children wouldn't be judged by the color of their skin. She read some of his speech about that dream, and she told us we should grow up to help his dream come true.

That same cover of <u>Life</u> magazine was taped up to the wall in Billy's room in Denton.

I want a better world, too, Mr. Marsworth. I don't know how to get it, but maybe I can learn.

I don't want this world to stay a mess.

Wondering What to Do Next,
Reenie Kelly

P.S. I just wrote my OWN letter to the president asking him to end the war and send Skip home. Would you mail it with your letter? I keep thinking of the sad sound of Skip's words, and how he said he's not proud of what he's doing, so there's not much he can write. What exactly did Skip mean when he said that?

P.P.S. Mizzou can drag their feet—it's been two long weeks since I've written—but no matter what they tell me, Billy can't go to this war.

July 18, 1968

Dear President Johnson,

You probably get a lot of letters about war, because now there's 500,000 troops in Vietnam, and that's a lot of soldiers, with a lot of families worried that their boy might not come home. I live in Minnesota, and already just this summer, the paper's printed stories about five boys that have died in Vietnam. There could be more, but I can't bear to look. All five of them have families, and when someone in your family dies, every day you live without them you feel a little lost.

Has someone in your family ever died?

If they did, you'd know how bad these soldiers' families feel to lose their sons, and if you know how bad they're feeling, don't you want to end this war? I have a friend in Vietnam who doesn't want to fight, but he was forced to be a soldier in the draft. Don't you think that draft you have is wrong? I mean, if a boy wants to be a soldier, let him pick. You're not drafting any girls. Why should it be different for the boys? Do you believe in sex equality? I do.

You'll probably say just what my brother Billy says, without the draft nobody would fight. So if nobody would fight we wouldn't have wars. Or we'd have smaller wars. And wouldn't that be a good thing? It seems to me it would.

I'm not against all wars, and the Kellys love our country. I understand the Revolutionary War gave us our freedom, and the Civil War kept us all one country and freed the slaves, and World War II helped save the Jews, and my dad fought in Korea although he never did say why, but I'm not sure what we're doing in this war in Vietnam. I don't think the Communists will conquer the whole world.

I'm sorry if I'm wrong about this war. If you could please explain it better, that might help.

In the meantime, I'd like to see you end it. Send ALL our soldiers home starting with Army Pfc. Skip Nichols, and all the soldiers in the Fourth Platoon before one of them is killed.

And STOP THE DRAFT ASAP so no more U.S. boys get sent against their conscience. Not everyone's a fighter, let the fighters volunteer.

                    Yours Truly,
                    Maureen Kelly of Lake Liberty,
                    Minnesota, U.S.A.

P.S. Please answer if you can.

Thursday, July 18, 1968

Dear Miss Kelly,

You will be pleased to know your letter has been
posted. I wish every child in America would write
against this war. No one speaks the truth quite
like a child. No one speaks the truth quite like
Miss Kelly, I should add.

    If you'd like, please tell Skip he will be in my
prayers this very evening, and every evening after
that. Skip, and Billy, and all our dear young men,
and every other soul touched by this war. This world
can't have too many of our prayers.

                 Sincerely,

              H. W. Marsworth

              H. W. Marsworth

Friday, July 19, 1968

Dear Mr. Marsworth,

I told Skip about your prayers, but maybe you could say one for me, too. I could use a prayer in this dumb town!!!

I know the war is so much worse than my dumb trouble with these boys, but I'm tired of being hunted, I really truly am. I've been beaten up, and wormed, and shot at from a tree, and this morning Rat and Cutler tackled me on Vallacher, then ran off with my sack. I found it down on Maple, but my papers were all gone. I had to tiptoe into Gram's to get my money for the paper box to replace the nine I lost. That's money from my savings I've kept for Billy's school.

I haven't bought a bite of candy this whole summer, I haven't seen a movie, I haven't bought a Mr. Freeze or Popsicle even when Dare did. Now twice I've paid for papers those two swiped.

They roughed me up before they left me, and by the time I'd finally delivered my last paper, I'd made up my mind I needed help from Dare. When you're one girl against two boys you need a scrappy brother.

The only good part of this story is Dare beat Cutler bloody down at Weber Park—bloody nose at least—and I'm proud I had Rat facedown at home plate eating dirt. That skinny twerp can't fight alone to save his soul.

I hope you'll understand we HAD to do it, Mr. Marsworth. These morning sneak attacks have got to stop. Please don't say to give up on the route. Dare wouldn't ever quit his route, and

I won't either. That's part of being equal, and it's equal that I want. If you tell Gram she'll call Sheriff Cutler, and calling Sheriff Cutler will only make things worse.

We gave peace a chance, we really did. Shaving cream. Snatching back my papers. Dropping that dead chicken outside the Cutlers' door.

Talking with our fists was all that we had left.

I don't mean to disappoint you, Mr. Marsworth. I want a better world, but a better world won't come without a fight.

You won't like this letter, so I'm not going to send it. There's not a grown-up in the world that likes to hear about kids' fights. Even Skip said they were stupid.

Good-bye, Mr. Marsworth, this <u>True Confessions</u> letter isn't really going in your box. I'm going to grab a clean page, and write one that you'll like.

Friday, July 19, 1968

Dear Mr. Marsworth,

That's nice about the praying, and I told Skip that you would.

You can pray for me, too, if you want. I'd be happy for some prayers.

Peace can't always be the only way to make things better. I just thought you ought to know that, in case you believed it was. Sometimes you turn the other cheek, and you get punched.

We're on our way down to the cottage. Did I get a chance to tell you how much we like your shed? It's like an old-fashioned antique shop packed full of dusty mysteries. Questions will be coming. You know how much I love an answer, Mr. Marsworth. ☺

Your Friend,
Reenie Kelly

Friday, July 19, 1968

Dear Mr. Marsworth,

Please don't think I'm nosy (or I should say WE'RE NOSY, because even dumb Dare Kelly likes the stuff inside your shed) but I can't help but wonder about the old days at your cottage, the years you must have come here, and if you had a family, and if you have one still, and if you do, why are you alone in that big house with that assistant? (By the way, I would make a great assistant, if you ever want my help!!!!)

We've been friends since June, and there's a lot I still don't know. (Like how well did you know Mom???? Hint, hint, hint.)

Here's some of what I'm wondering, and I hope you'll answer at least a couple questions, but if anything's TOO personal, just tell me to GET LOST. (Please don't REALLY tell me to get lost!) Or we could have a fair trade if you want. My questions for your questions, even-steven.

1. Who owned that baseball mitt on the hook inside your shed? (Dare thinks a boy once lived here, but a girl could have a mitt. I have a mitt.)

2. Who owned that blue scooter in the rafters of the shed? It's a pretty cool scooter, and Dare thinks it might still work.

3. Who owned that flowered garden glove? Why is there only one? (It's too small to be a man's glove, Mr. Marsworth.)

4. Are you the one who liked to fish? Dare's sure keen on that old tackle box he found up on your shelf. Would you

mind if he borrowed an old-time, wooden bobber from
that box to catch more fish? You can tell us no.

5. What is Brandenbrook exactly? And why is that red
pennant tacked up to the wall? Dare swears that it's
a team, but I'm not sure.

6. Are you an artist, Mr. Marsworth? I have a hunch you
are. I love all those cottage paintings, and I'm sorry
they're covered now with dust. I'll take one for my room
if they're just going to go to waste. They look exactly like
the lake looks when the sun hits it just right. White and
green and blue. And I love the winter paintings. Is that
the way the lake will look six months from now?

I hope these questions aren't too nosy. You can say MYOB like
Gram does, but I'm hoping you don't.

Just Curious,
Reenie Kelly

P.S. Have a happy weekend. On Sunday, Billy's coming to
the cottage to help Dare fix your mower!!!! That'll be our
first time for a FULL day at the lake, just the three of us
together swimming in the sun. I'm packing up a picnic, and
we're going after church. When I drop your Monday paper,
you'll get the full report.

Dear Mr. Marsworth,

The Office of Financial Aid said no. ☹ ☹
    Mizzou said they won't help.
    I waited all these days to get a no???
    It's worse than that, but I can't write another word or else I'll cry, and I've cried my share already.
    Did you hear me out there clanging? Just once I wish you could come outside when I need you. I don't want to write this letter.

                        Reenie Kelly

Saturday, July 20, 1968

Dear Mr. Marsworth,

Here's the story I couldn't write in my last letter, but I'm too sad for sleeping so I'll tell it to you now. Billy knows that I wrote Mizzou. After all these days of making sure I got the mail while Gram and Billy were at work, Mizzou's letter came for me while I was at the store with Gram.

Billy got it and he read it even though it was addressed to "Reenie Kelly."

"I'd like a word with Reen," he said to Gram when we pulled into the driveway, and I could hear in that short sentence he was mad.

"Something wrong?" Gram asked, because she could hear it, too.

"Let's take a walk," he said to me, and we left Gram to carry groceries while we headed for the hill. Billy always helps with groceries, but that's how mad he was.

"What is it?" I asked worried. I thought it was my fight with Rat and Cutler, or my snooping in his things, but when he pulled the Mizzou envelope from his pocket, I didn't have to wonder anymore.

"Financial Aid?" he said. "You wrote my college, Reen?"

"Did they say yes?" I asked, reaching for the envelope. (I feel stupid I had hope still, Mr. Marsworth, but I did. All that mattered at that minute was the hope that they could help.) "Are they giving you a scholarship? Is there more money for this fall?"

"No," Billy said. "They aren't. You had no business, Reen."

He shook his head the same way Dad does when he's

disgusted. Or disappointed. Or fed up with my "stupidity." (Please don't be fed up, Mr. Marworth. You already told me I was wrong to write.) "Because you said we didn't have money for your college," I told Billy. "That day down at the Conoco. And you and Uncle Slim said the same thing on the Fourth. And all that talk about enlisting—"

"I'm not going to college, Reen," he said, and we stood there in Gram's street with my heart stopped in my chest. I swear to you it stopped. "I'd already withdrawn when you wrote."

"Withdrawn? Withdrawn from college, Billy?" (I told you it was terrible, Mr. Marsworth.) "But what about Mom's dream? And the draft? Don't you have to go to college to stay out of this war? Skip says to go to college."

"Can Skip send me the money? I don't think so. Our family's bankrupt, Reen. No matter what I earn this summer, it's not enough for tuition, room and board, books—all the costs of college. Plus, we're going to need a place to live when Dad comes home. I'm already sleeping on Gram's couch. You think Dare and Dad should be sleeping on Gram's floor when winter comes?"

"Dad and Dare can sleep up in Gram's attic," I said. "I'll take the couch. If you're at college, you won't need a bed."

"I WON'T be at college," Billy said like he might cry. "Why can't you get that through your head, Reen? I've already withdrawn."

"But the draft," I said. "You know how many people are dying in this war? It's dangerous in Vietnam. Skip says—"

"I know all about it, Reen," Billy said, and his big eyes were glistening with tears. "Don't tell me again about all the people dying. It doesn't help to hear it, it just doesn't. And don't write letters to my college, or any other place that's not your business. You're eleven. I'm eighteen. I'm the one who has to be a grown-up now. Go play down at that cottage."

"You have to go to college." I tried to take his hand, but he just brushed me off. "Mom's dream."

"Mom isn't here to help," he said, and both of us were crying, Billy less than me, but he still cried.

"Billy," I begged. "Don't give up this easy. Dad will find the money. Dare and I are saving—"

"For once just stop it, Reen," he said. "You can't make the whole world go the way you want."

Then he headed back toward Gram's without another word, even with me pleading and saying I was wrong. Once we'd reached the driveway, he climbed into Gram's Plymouth and took off.

"Well?" Gram said, stepping out the kitchen door with Dare and Float beside her. "What's eating Billy, Reen?"

"Did you know he gave up college?" I asked Gram. I was nearly screaming-crying, I was ready for a tantrum that's how mad I was.

"Gave up college?" stupid Dare said, baffled. "You mean he don't need the money that we're saving after all?"

"He didn't have any choice, Reen," Gram said. She wiped

her hands dry on her apron. "I'm sorry, college isn't something the Kellys can afford. Not this year, at least."

HE DIDN'T HAVE ANY CHOICE????????

I don't believe that, Mr. Marsworth.

I don't, and never ever will, not now and not until I die, and Mom wouldn't believe it either. Do you believe it, Mr. Marsworth? Please tell me it's not true. Please say there's something more that can be done.

If you loved Mom, you'd love her dream. I know you don't want Billy in this draft.

Your Wrecked Friend,
Reenie Kelly

P.S. Adding Part 2 to this story Sunday morning, before Mass. I'll drop this letter at your house when church is done.

Part 2: Billy woke me in Gram's attic in the middle of the night, to say that he was sorry, and he knew I only wrote to Mizzou because I thought it might help. Even in the darkness, I heard how sad he was.

"Lie down," I said to Billy, the way he used to say to me in Denton, and I handed him my pillow and my quilt so he'd have something soft beneath to curl up on the floor. It's what he always did for me all those nights in Denton when I went into his bedroom worried about Mom. Or all those nights I wished I had her still. I slept better on his hard floor just listening to his breath.

"We're going to get a plan," I said, tucking my hands beneath my cheek to make a pillow. "I've got ingenuity, remember?"

"This draft is bigger than that, Pup," he said. "I'm just one of thousands. Skip probably felt the same, and so did all those other pen pals serving with him now."

"He didn't have me as his sister," I told Billy. "He even said so in his letter. His sisters didn't do anything to help."

"They couldn't help him." Billy sighed. "And I'm afraid you can't help either. But I thank you for it, Pup, I really do. I'm sorry I was mean about that letter."

"You weren't," I said. "Don't worry." Then I whispered, "Go to sleep," which is exactly what he told me all those nights in Denton.

I had to add Part 2 so you'd know Billy didn't stay mad. I couldn't stand to have him mad at me for long. I'll check your milk box for an answer when we come home from the cottage.

Please say what I should do if Mizzou isn't going to help.

Hoping You Can Help Me,
Reenie Kelly

Sunday, July 2I, I968

Dear Miss Kelly,

Sunday is a day of rest, and rest is what I wish for you
today. All this constant worry is too much for a young
girl. I shall hope this very minute you're all down at my
cottage: sunning on the dock, or splashing in the lake, or
eating your fine picnic, warm bologna sandwiches and all.
I hope this summer Sunday, your brother Billy knows how
deeply he is loved.

I'm sorry your heartfelt letter to Financial Aid
failed to help Billy as you'd hoped, and I share your
great distress over his decision to withdraw from
Mizzou before funding could be found. I agree your
mother's dream for Billy's college must be honored. In
whatever small way I might assist, please rest assured
I will. Billy's safety in September weighs on my heart
as well.

For today, please be a child. Some Plan B is in
your future, I feel confident of that. You are not a
child short on plans.

Sincerely,

H. W. Marsworth

H. W. Marsworth

Dear Mr. Marsworth,

Thank you for that hope, and for sharing Mom's dream with me.
First thing tomorrow morning, I'll put on my "thinking cap," as
Mrs. Lamb would say. While Billy's working at the Conoco, I'll be
busy working on a scheme to save him from the draft.

We shared a good day at your cottage, even though the
cloud of Billy giving up on Mizzou hung over us all, including
dopey Dare who knows deep in his heart that Billy's not cut out
for war. For all of Dare's tough talk, I know deep down it's
college that he wants for Billy, too.

Billy made me triple swear I'd drop the subject for the day.
"Swear," he said, "or else I'm staying home."

So I didn't say ONE word about the draft, I really didn't.
Instead, I tried to make believe Billy was too young to go to war.
He was thirteen still, or fourteen. He was the kick-the-can-young
Billy, the boy who still played baseball with the neighbor kids at
night. I held on to that dream while the three of us cracked open
a watermelon and split it into fours so Float could have his share.
Billy picked out most of the seeds so Float wouldn't end up sick,
and we ate it all together stretched out on your dock.

We showed Billy all the work we'd done—scrubbing,
sanding, painting—and he helped Dare tune up your mower,
and he taught us how to use that scythe inside your shed to
clear the weeds before we mow. He agreed with us, a fresh

coat of colored paint on those old shutters would be nice. Dare likes black, and I like green, but Billy thought the best was cobalt blue. Would you like those shutters painted, Mr. Marsworth?

I had Billy look through your back window at that worn bear left on the pillow, the baseball on the dresser, the patchwork quilt over the twin bed. He studied that small room like he was looking for a clue. "We shouldn't be snooping, Reen," he said abruptly.

"I'm not snooping," I told Billy, and I wasn't.

That child's room, the bear, all the stuff inside your shed—the baseball mitt and scooter, the paintings and the garden glove, it's all right there for us to look at, Mr. Marsworth. I can't help that all these objects make me curious, I can't.

Anyway, except for that quick second when Billy said I was a snoop, I wish every summer day could be like this: watermelon endings, staying at your shore to swim under the stars, me tucked between my brothers on your dock, Billy saying that a man might walk up on the moon before too long.

Do you believe a man will walk up on the moon?

Still Looking for a Plan B,
Reenie Kelly

Monday, July 22, 1968

Dear Mr. Marsworth,

Did you read that story on the front page of the <u>Tribune</u>? It's the story of a St. Paul family divided by the war: one brother joined the Army, and the other brother objected to the draft. The brother who enlisted believes the war in Vietnam is right. The one against the draft believes it's wrong.

The father in the story was on the side of both his sons.

If this were Dare and Billy, I think Dad would take Dare's side. I know for sure Gram would. They'd both be proud that Dare enlisted just like Dad did at eighteen.

Were you a house divided during World War I? Was your family on your side? Did you get sent to federal prison while your brother went to war?

How long was your sentence during World War I? The peaceful brother in this story got five years in prison. FIVE YEARS! Plus he has to pay a $10,000 fine. Did they fine you all that money back in World War I? We couldn't pay $10,000! We can't even pay for Mizzou in the fall!

Five years would be too long for Billy in a prison. In five years, Billy would be twenty-three, and I'd be seventeen. Would Billy even know me when his prison time was done?

Was your time in prison terrible? I wish you'd answer that.

How come they never taught us this in school? We've learned some U.S. history, and we've learned about old wars, and we know the names of famous men that fought: George Washington, Robert E. Lee, Ullysses Grant. (Sorry if I spelled that strange name wrong.) But not a single teacher, not even Mrs. Lamb, said they sentenced peaceful men to prison during wars. She didn't even mention Muhammad Ali and he was in the news! I'm going to write to her this morning, to tell her that she should. We ought to learn about good men who objected to those wars.

Tomorrow, I'm sending Dad this story, so he can think about it, too. And I'm asking him why he let Billy give up on Mom's dream, and what he thinks of peaceful boys in prison, because if we don't get Billy money it's prison or the war. Dad ought to be afraid about this draft! He better not write back: "Be good for Gram. Don't give her any trouble. Say your prayers. Have fun."

I need more than that from Dad, I really do.

Determined,
Reenie Kelly

P.S. If you sit down with this story on the Tribune's front page, you'll see my first Plan B. We don't have $10,000, but at least I'm going to call the place that helped the older brother stand against the draft. Twin Cities Draft Information Center in Minneapolis. The story said they offer counsel and it's counsel that I need. Plus, I'm going to ask a counselor how to bring Skip

home from Vietnam. Cross your fingers for good counseling!!!
Stay tuned, Mr. Marsworth, a letter will be coming with
whatever I find out!!!!

Did this center help you back in World War 1?

Dear Miss Kelly,

Well, you are most certainly resourceful. I wish I
had a tenth of your sharp mind. Perhaps one day
they'll let you run the world.

I did not live in Minnesota during World War
I, but I know about the center and I know it serves
men well. No doubt a counselor from that center will
enlighten you this morning, but more importantly,
I hope Billy will seek their counsel on the draft. As
you read in the Tribune, the choice for peace or war
must be left to one's own conscience. You can't
object to Billy being drafted; Billy must object.

The path to peace is difficult; be prepared for
that, Miss Kelly.

It may well include a fine and prison; often
times it does.

I quite agree, Miss Kelly, beyond the generals
and explorers, the inventors and the villains, why
not teach the lives of peaceful men and women who
have stood against the wars? Or the peaceful men
and women who have made a stand against injustice of
all kinds? Perhaps someday every child in America
will know the work of Dr. King.

I send good wishes for Plan B, and in the
meantime I cast my vote for Billy's shutter choice
of cobalt blue. Please accept this $40 for future
service and supplies. You and Dare have earned this
and much more.

Sincerely,

H. W. Marsworth

H. W. Marsworth

P.S. I read the brothers' story with purring Clyde
asleep beside me on the couch, and I thought how
sweetly simple the life of Clyde must be. Not a
single thought of war disturbs his dreams. I'd wish
the same for you, Miss Kelly, but of course you are
much smarter than a cat.

Monday, July 22, 1968

Dear Mr. Marsworth,

I'm already smarter than I was in my last letter!

WHAT I LEARNED FROM KEITH THE COUNSELOR,
by Reenie Kelly

1. Billy has to call the Draft Information Center, or better yet he needs to go in person to be counseled, except it's all the way in Minneapolis, and we don't know that city, and I can't ask Gram to drive us to a place against the war. Do you know how to get to Minneapolis?

2. It's not too late for Billy to say that he won't fight, but it would be better if he'd been against the war in public so there's proof. A letter to the paper like you wrote. And he should have said he was a pacifist when he signed up for the draft.

3. There's a bunch of questions Billy has to answer, like is he against all killing, and would he defend his family if a murderer broke in, and how long has he been against all wars? He has to be against ALL wars, it can't just be the war in Vietnam.

4. It would help if we weren't Catholic, because I guess a few religions are just plain opposed to war. Mennonites and Quakers are the two that I wrote down. We didn't have those folks in Denton, not a one. Are you a Mennonite or

129

Quaker, Mr. Marsworth? The only Quakers that I've heard of are on the can of oats. Could Billy be a Quaker or would he need that goofy hair?

5. What else? Keith, the counselor at the center, said the same as you: Peace isn't easy. But, the sooner Billy stands for it, the better off he'll be. Once you're fighting in the war the way Skip is, then you're stuck. Or mostly stuck. Even if you hate it, and say you think it's wrong.

6. The thing Billy needs to be is a concionxx—oops I mean CONSCIENTIOUS (I had to use the Webster for that word) OBJECTOR. It means Billy would object to war based on his conscience, but first he has to get the draft board to believe he's really, truly, deeply, way down in his soul opposed to war. Or any kind of killing. Then he might get a peace job in the Army if he's drafted, or stay home in America and get assigned to peaceful service if the draft board is convinced. Or he might say he won't obey the draft at all because his conscience says he can't. (Is this what you were, Mr. Marsworth? It's what Muhammad Ali is now.)

7. Still, Keith said Billy's best option would be college. If not Mizzou, then a school we could afford, but even at a college, Billy has to stand against this war. Otherwise he could be drafted once his college years are done. (Do you think the war will last that long???)

WHAT I WONDER

1. How can we get to Minneapolis?
2. How to find a college our family can afford. Do you know another college, Mr. Marsworth?
3. How exactly did you end up in prison, and will Billy go there, too?
4. What will Billy say about the center? Does he deep down in his soul object to EVERY war? Would he defend our family if a murderer broke in?

On my way now to the library to learn more about this subject, but whatever you can tell me on conscientious objectors sure would help. We spent the last half of fifth grade learning how to research, and as long as I don't need to bother with those footnotes, I'll be fine.

I might even try to find another college while I'm at it, Mr. Marsworth.

Is Dare Kelly going to help me? No he's not. Dare's fine with weeds and painting, but he doesn't care for books. He's not a fan of peace, so for now I'll keep this subject to myself. (To myself, and you and Billy.)

Stay Tuned,
Reenie Kelly

P.S. Do you really think they'll let me run the world???????

P.P.S. THANK YOU so much for that money! I've never ever earned $40 in my life. We've got a coffee can marked BILLY stashed under my bed with all the money that you gave us minus our supplies, plus my earnings from my paper route. I can't pay for Billy's college, or a $10,000 fine, but every penny I deposit gives me hope.

Tuesday, July 23, 1968

Dear Miss Kelly,

As to your litany of questions:

Indeed, I am a Quaker, but I do not have "goofy hair." How unfortunate to be defined by breakfast oats. When you've exhausted current research, perhaps you'll broaden your impression of the Quakers.

Yes, I was a conscientious objector in World War I, but I would caution against using my example in future conversations with your brother. I'm not a man admired in Lake Liberty, and didn't Billy say himself that I was wrong? Let Muhammad Ali be the best example for you now.

Finally, if you're on the hunt for colleges for Billy, you might consider the one on that red pennant in the shed. Brandenbrook. (I, too, remember what you ask.) Their president, Dr. Roland Price, is a personal acquaintance, and he might have a scholarship for a nearly straight-A student as fine as Billy Kelly. What college doesn't need a boy to pitch and play guitar? Of course, time is of the essence, so if this option interests Billy, he should inquire soon.

In all of this, Miss Kelly, in each choice and conversation, you must follow your own dreams, honor your own conscience, make your own decisions as you've assured me that you do. As you

already know too well, the Kelly clan is fiercely
independent. I'm afraid my interference wouldn't
be welcomed. Might you find a way to suggest
Brandenbrook to Billy without mentioning the
"trator" so many here despise?

Can you agree to follow your own conscience,
young Miss Kelly? As you say, please answer yes
or no.

Sincerely,

H. W. Marsworth

H. W. Marsworth

Tuesday, July 23, 1968

Dear Mr. Marsworth,

Yes! I'll decide things for myself, I always do. I've got a good head on my shoulders. I'll get things figured out. (Whatever hints you give me, I'll keep quiet.)

Do you know what I like best about my route? Opening your milk box to a letter left inside!!! Days that you don't write, I do feel sad. I don't mind coming back to check for letters any time of day, but a first-thing-bright-and-early-morning letter is the best!!!!

Brandenbrook????

I'll go back to the library when it opens up at 10:00. Yesterday I went for my first visit, but crabby Mrs. Strait from 207 Hillcrest (and later those monsters Rat and Cutler) made me wish I'd stayed at Gram's. Why does everybody hate me in this town??? (I might not be a "trator," but when it comes to being hated, you and I are two peas in a pod.)

Anyway, yesterday I found ONE book in the library about conscientious objectors, and it was way up on a dusty top shelf in Adults. A very tip-top shelf. The pretty librarian Miss Peabody had to climb up on a ladder to pull the old book down.

"Will you be reading this?" Miss Peabody asked as she set it on the counter. "You know it's not for children?"

"It's for my older brother." I only told that small lie so she'd let me check it out.

"The Kelly boy who works at Casey's Conoco?" There was crabby Mrs. Strait with her BIG NOSE stuck in my business. Her arms were full of romance paperbacks, but she was busy asking questions about my one boring book. "Your brother wants to read The Conscientious Objector? Why exactly would a Kelly boy read a book like that?"

"Well, I don't know," Miss Peabody said softly. "People should be free to read—"

"Shouldn't that book be banned?" Mrs. Strait said too loudly for a library. "The kids today don't need books about objecting. We've already got those draft dodgers marching on the streets against this war. All those dirty hippies with them. Kids like that are cowards plain and simple."

"Well," Miss Peabody said, like she wasn't going to argue, but she didn't really agree.

"Not Ali," I said. (I don't like frumpy Mrs. Strait with her hair pinned up in curlers, and those angry painted eyebrows like two frowns over her face. Plus, she's never tipped me once.) "Ali couldn't be a coward, he's a boxer. He's a champion. He fights."

"That boxer is the worst of them," she said. "And you can tell your brother I said that. Or I'll tell him myself next time he pumps my gas. And your grandmother, Blanche Kelly? Did she approve this book?"

"Don't ask," I said, reaching for the book. The last thing I needed was Gram discovering my Plan B before I'd even talked to Billy. "Billy's not against the draft, he's really not. It's research for his college, for a paper."

"In the summer?" She arched those frowny eyebrows. "Now I've heard it all. We don't need another draft dodger—"

"He's not," I said.

Then I rushed to write my name down on the card, and guess whose name was just a few lines above mine? Betsy Brighton! I swear it, Mr. Marsworth. In 1949 Mom checked out The Conscientious Objector, by Walter Kellogg! I could almost feel her when I held it in my hands.

Do you know why Mom read it in 1949? Was that when Dad went to Korea? Because Mom didn't have a brother to keep out of that war.

I wish she'd left a note inside, you know one of those little scraps of paper you sometimes find in books? Wouldn't that be a miracle???

I saved the best for last because I knew you'd be surprised!!! Betsy Brighton and her daughter reading the same book!!!

So far the book looks old and boring, with little tiny print, and dull language from the old days, mostly military stuff, but if Mom read it once, then I can, too.

Tomorrow, I'll go back to research Brandenbrook, and hope Mrs. Strait stays home to clip her shrubs. (She's always clipping shrubs.) Do you think she'll blab to Gram and Billy? Fingers crossed she won't. Shouldn't a library be private?

Yes it should!

Betsy Brighton's Reader Daughter,
Reenie Kelly

P.S. Oh, I almost forgot to tell the worst: Rat and Cutler saw me on the street on my way home, and they started chanting "Misery," then Cutler snatched that book by Walter Kellogg and called the Kellys cowards, and he took off on his Sting-Ray, before he circled back to throw that book right at my face. That's right, Mr. Marsworth, Rat and Cutler strike again! No matter what we do, they never quit. We try to teach them lessons, peaceful and not peaceful, but those two never learn. Another lesson is in order, but you don't have to know.

Wednesday, July 24, I968

Dear Miss Kelly,

In all your ingenuity, might you find a way to strike
a temporary truce with those two boys? Each time you
and Dare teach them a lesson, they teach one in return.
Children fight, I understand that, but I would like this
trouble with these bullies to be done.

How amazing that your mother signed that same
card long ago. Even as a young girl, your mother was
inclined toward peace like Billy, but I hope she never
read that awful book. Please don't read it either. In
fact, kindly throw that dreadful book into the trash.
I will gladly pay the fine to have it gone.

If an old man's memory serves, I recall the
author was a soldier with a deep disdain for peace.
That book he wrote about the World War I objectors
slandered many of the men who refused to fight that
war. Objectors at that time were beaten, starved,
imprisoned, even killed, and yet that book by Walter
Kellogg turned a blind eye to those atrocities.

It wasn't until World War II that humane treatment
for objectors was achieved by the Society of Friends.
In fact, those Quakers with the "goofy hair" won the
Nobel Prize for Peace for their work during the war.

As our library has failed, the Draft Information Center in the city would be the best place for advice. I hope Billy will consider a visit before long. The work they do is quite heroic; he might be impressed. Their city office has been bombed, but they didn't quit. I would call that courage.

Please give up Walter Kellogg, and do not pursue more "lessons" for those boys. Go back to John Donne. "No Man Is an Island." Perhaps those boys would like a copy; there are lessons for us all in those good words.

Sincerely,

H. W. Marsworth

H. W. Marsworth

Wednesday, July 24, 1968

Dear Mr. Marsworth,

The one book on objectors and you don't want me to
read it? Or anybody ever? Even though Mom did?

How can any kid in this dumb town learn how to
object? Not every kid can drive to Minneapolis to find help.

And I'm not giving Rat and Cutler a copy of that poem!
My conscience says I can't. Those two would never understand
a John Donne poem! And I can't throw out a book. I'm
surprised you even asked that, Mom never ever would. (You
see I ALWAYS follow my own conscience, Mr. Marsworth!)

Did you read this morning's paper? Two more Minnesotans
died this week in Vietnam. Lt. Harrison E. Wellman Jr., 25, and
Pfc. Jeffrey Overton, 20. Jeffrey was a Pfc. like Skip, and the
paper said he'd only been in Vietnam two months. Harrison for
four months. Harrison left a brother and a sister just like Billy
would. I don't want to ever read William Kelly has been killed. To
see Mom's name in the obituaries was sadder than you know.

Two months. Four months. That's all the time it took
for those two soldiers to be killed. I wish I had a way to
bring Skip home. Every day he's fighting is a day that he
could die. I don't know if he's near Quang Tri or Dak To
where these two men were killed. Skip never says exactly
where he is, but I'll ask in my next letter. I hope it's
someplace safer, fingers crossed.

This week I'm getting Billy to that center, I definitely AM. (Please pray that it's not bombed again while we're inside!!!) And in the meantime, I'm going to the library to find out about Brandenbrook. Encyclopedia under B is where I'll start.

Dare bought the cobalt blue paint for $2.49. It cost more because it needed to be mixed. We'll start on your fresh shutters sometime this afternoon. You sure you want to pay us all that money, Mr. Marsworth? (It's a lot more than we're earning, even Dare says it's too much.) We're both so happy at that cottage, we don't need a single cent to make it good as new.

More Later,
Reenie Kelly

P.S. Could you also pray for Harrison and Jeffrey, and their families left behind, and say a couple extra prayers for Skip, and I will, too, because nothing but our prayers can help them now. Maybe I should write the president again.

Wednesday, July 24, 1968

Dear Mr. Marsworth,

That book spy Mrs. Strait went into Brindle Drug and told
Gram about the book! Then she drove down to the Conoco "to
have a word" with Mr. Casey, who "had a word" with Billy,
and now I'm in hot water just for checking out that book. One
book! It isn't even on the side of the objectors!

I told Gram and Billy the author was a soldier, not
someone against war, but neither of them cared. Gram said I
disgraced the Kellys just by checking out that book, and Billy
said I shouldn't have lied to the librarian. He was embarrassed
to be blamed, and more embarrassed to be scolded by his boss.

"What's wrong with you?" Gram glared into my eyes
like I'd gone nuts. She'd barged in from a storm and she was
sopping wet with rain, but she was too busy being mad at me
to even grab a towel. "How'd you hear about this subject,
Reenie Kelly? From that serviceman you're writing?"

"It wasn't Skip," I said. I didn't want Gram to say we
couldn't be pen pals. "I read it in the paper. That front-page
story of two brothers divided on the war."

"You keep your nose out of that paper." Gram scooped
the paper off the table and smashed it in the trash.
"There's nothing in that paper fit for kids to read."

"The funnies," Dare tried to joke to calm Gram's temper.

143

He and Float had come inside in case of a tornado, but Dare was in a hurry to leave now.

"Let me see that book, Reen," Billy said.

It was right on Gram's buffet waiting to go back.

"It's against objectors," I said, handing it to Billy. "It says that they were wrong in World War 1."

"World War 1?" Gram said, confused. "And how is that your business? If you want to read a book, stick to ones for kids."

"Mom checked it out," I said to Billy, while he stood there soaking wet, flipping through the pages. "In 1949. Betsy Brighton. Her name was on the card."

"She did?" Dare said, closing in near Billy to have his own quick look.

"You sure about that, Reen?" Billy stopped his paging and gave me a long look, and I saw a hint of anger leave his eyes. "Mom's name was on the card?"

"I don't believe it," Gram said. "What would your mother care of conscientious—" Gram stumbled on the word.

"Objectors," I said, glad to know a word that Gram didn't know. "Conscientious objectors. They're men who stand for peace."

"I don't need a definition," Gram said, reaching for the book. "We've already got one objector in this town. Now give that book to me, I'll bring it back. Who finds trouble at the library? Your father won't be happy, I can tell you that."

"It's just a boring book," Dare said. "It's not like a dirty magazine, Gram. Reen didn't even read it. We've been playing cards all day."

"You watch your tongue, Dare Kelly. Dirty magazine!" Gram huffed. "I better not find dirty magazines out in that tent. And I don't want to hear that Billy—"

"You won't," Billy said, because he knew where Gram was heading. She was on her way to saying Billy couldn't object. "I won't shame the Kellys."

"Your father would be furious," Gram said above the thunder. "And I could never show my face—"

"To who?" I said. "That old crab Mrs. Strait? Who cares about Lake Liberty, when it's Billy we should care about right now? Two more Minnesota boys were killed in Vietnam. Wouldn't you rather have him living and objecting, than dying in that war?"

"Reenie!" Dare pressed his dirty hand over my mouth, but I didn't stop.

"I mean it!" I said, pushing off Dare's hand. "You're all just acting stupid!"

Then I ran out of Gram's house even with the rain and lightning, and I would have run to your house, but you never ever come out for that bell. I was nearly to the bottom of the hill when Billy drove up in Gram's Plymouth.

"Get in," he said, and he sounded twice as angry as he'd been about Mizzou. "I'm not going to chase you down this road, and you don't want to stay out in a storm, you're scared of storms."

I got in, but I didn't speak, and Billy didn't speak either, we didn't say a single word until he parked down by the beach, and we sat there in more quiet watching the rain beat against Gram's windshield.

"You've got to stop this, Reen," he said. "If I get called for Vietnam—"

"You will," I said, "I know it. You'll get drafted, and you'll die just like Mom did."

"Come on," he said. He pressed my slimy face into his chest, tears and snot and rain, but he didn't care. "You can't think like that, Reen."

"What else can I think?" I said. "You know that boys are dying."

"They are," he said. "But that doesn't mean I will. We've got Mom up in heaven to keep me safe on earth. I can't buy time with college. I don't want to go to prison for objecting to the draft. You read that story, Reen. Five years in prison? Even a man as famous as Ali might go to prison. And you remember that book by Dr. Spock Mom always read. Well, they've sentenced Dr. Spock to prison for his work against the draft. A famous pediatrician, Reen."

"Prison might not happen," I said. And then I told him about the Draft Information Center in Minneapolis, and how on Saturday we could drive into the city to see the counselor, Keith. "We'll tell Gram we're going to the Art Institute," I said. "Because it's right down the street so it's the truth. And we can go there when we're finished at the center. I've never seen a real museum. I could navigate the way Dare always does for Dad. Or Dare can navigate."

"Dare going to see art? Float too?" Billy laughed, and all the dirt and grease from Casey's seemed to disappear. "Of all your wild ideas, Reen, this one is the worst."

"The counselor said he'd help you, Billy. If you wouldn't murder an intruder, and if you're against all wars, and a bunch of other questions, you might not have to fight."

"You mean like Mr. Marsworth?" Billy said. "That man who owns that cottage where you and Dare play all the time? You think Gram wants 'traitor' spray-painted on her house? Or mud and eggs smeared on her windows? You think that's what Dad wants from his son?"

"Just talk to them please, Billy. Saturday. We'll drive into the city. You don't even have to lie to Gram. I'll do all the talking."

"I don't think so, Reen." Billy laughed again, and it made my heart so happy to hear his easy laugh. "I think Gram's heard all the talking she wants to hear from you right now."

Okay, so I won't do the talking, Mr. Marsworth, but maybe Billy will. He didn't flat out say no about that center! He just listed all the reasons Dad and Gram would be ashamed if he refused to serve. Kelly pride and courage were right there at the top. But it's not Dad or Gram who could be killed in Vietnam.

I'm sorry you got tangled in a letter that's too long. My next one will be shorter, because I know that's what you want, but today I thought you better hear it ALL. The good parts and the bad parts, and the best part of my story, when Billy didn't say no. He didn't say no, so I'll hope for a yes. At least he didn't say "we'll see," because you know I HATE "we'll see." (Please don't ever write that, Mr. Marsworth.)

So this is what I'm hoping: YES YES YES YES YES YES YES YES YES YES YES YES YES YES YES YES YES.

Yes Believer,
Reenie Kelly

P.S. When you see this too-long letter, please don't throw it in the trash. In fact, I better write that on the top.

Dear Mr. Marsworth,

You know how much I like a morning letter in your box. (Hint, hint, hint.)

Have you forgotten all the people I don't hear from, Mr. Marsworth?

Skip. (Too busy fighting.)

Dad. (Too busy working.)

Mrs. Lamb. (Too busy? I don't know with what. Are teachers busy in the summer? What do teachers do when they're not teaching kids at school?)

President Lyndon Johnson. (Too busy with America and war.)

If you're too busy, Mr. Marsworth, maybe you could tell me what a shut-in does all day? Is Carl Grace still your assistant? Aren't you free to answer letters with an assistant doing chores? If I had an assistant, I'd never scrub another toilet at Gram's house. Or sweep the kitchen every morning. Or do laundry in Gram's dungeon. Imagine all the letters I could write!

Could you please tell me ASAP what you think about Billy and the center? Do you believe my Plan B is going to work? And what about Gram's temper over one dumb book? Will Keith the Counselor rescue Billy? Is the art museum cool?

That's five quick questions you could answer, Mr. Marsworth!

Just so you know I do more than wait for letters, here's my Thursday schedule:

Nine o'clock I'll call the Draft Information Center to make Billy an appointment just in case I get that YES, at 9:30 I'll finish up the letter I've been working on for Skip, at 10:00 I'm stopping by the library to find out about that college that you like. Brandenbrook. Dare and Float are coming with me, so we can go straight to the cottage, but don't worry, Mr. Marsworth, Dare won't research a word. Bet you ten bucks, Dare will skip the library to wait outside with Float. (If Rat and Cutler try to stalk me, at least I'll be with Dare.)

FINALLY, we're going to end up at your cottage, and when I'm sick of batting at Dare's pitches so he can keep his curve ball tight, I'm going to sit down at your dock, and write you every fact I learned about that name on the red pennant. Brandenbrook. I hope you're right. I hope that college has the money to help Billy get to school.

Write me when you're able, Mr. Marsworth.

I'll be back at 4:00 to check your milk box. Signing off to call Keith the Counselor now.

Practicing My Patience,
Reenie Kelly

Thursday, July 25, 1968

Dear Miss Kelly,

From time to time even an old shut-in has
appointments he must keep.

When it comes to steadfast siblings you are
incomparable. What a lucky thing for Billy to have
you in his life. If anyone can urge Billy toward
that center it is you.

Shall I assume you've reconciled with your
grandmother and returned that worthless book?
However much you disagree regarding Billy, please
do not doubt her love. Many loving, decent families
believe duty to our country must come first. Of
course a stand for peace is also a duty to our
county, but very few can see how that is so.

Wars have always ravaged families, and this one is
no different. In the end, despite your disagreements,
love must be remembered. Love is all.

Sincerely,

H. W. Marsworth

H. W. Marsworth

P.S. The Minneapolis Institute of Art is quite "cool," as
you would say. Many years ago, I went there often. The
world beyond a small town like Lake Liberty is vast. In
my opinion, a trip into the city would be grand.

Thursday, July 25, 1968

Dear Mr. Marsworth,

THERE ISN'T PEACE AND LOVE IN LAKE LIBERTY FOR US!!!

All our weeks of hard work at the cottage are destroyed!!! There's a big red blotchy "commie" painted on the wall of your front porch!!! That same wall we painted white!!! And a horrible mess of egg yolk splattered on your windows. All our sanding, painting, scrubbing went to waste! You didn't even get to see your cottage all fixed up.

Someone did this, Mr. Marsworth, and someone's going to PAY. If you don't call Sheriff Cutler, then I will. He ought to know one of the vandals is probably his own son.

You've wasted all your money, and we've wasted all our time, and after all that wasting, your cottage looks like crap. (You might not like that word, but it's exactly what Dare said, and it's the truth.)

I wish I could stop there, but the bad news just gets worse.

Before we'd even finished supper, a friend of Uncle Slim's knocked on Gram's door. Do you know a man named Clay McCardle who grew up in Lake Liberty? He's a recruiter for the Air Force, and his mother's in Gram's bridge club, and he drove from St. Paul to Lake Liberty to talk Billy into signing up right now. Travel. Planes. Adventure. Training on the job. College money when his Air Force time is done. Money for a house when he gets married. "I hear you have a sweetheart in Missouri," he said to Billy. "I bet she'd like a house. And we need good men like you. Smart men who can lead. You get called up in the draft you'll be a grunt."

While Clay McCardle bragged about the Air Force, Gram served him rhubarb pie and poured fresh coffee in his cup. Dare fired off his questions like he was ready to enlist, and mostly Billy listened in the polite way Billy does.

"Will you take me at sixteen?" Dare asked. He looked big enough, and tough enough, with his bulky freckled arms and rough red face, and that filthy, torn T-shirt too small for his wide chest. Between giant Dare and slender Billy, if I were looking for a soldier, Dare would be my pick. But I didn't want Dare enlisting either. I know Dare can be a dope, but I don't want him in this war. "If I get my dad to sign, can I quit school? Will I get to work on bombers?"

"High school first, then Air Force," Clay McCardle said to Dare, and the pie swirled in my stomach when I realized that five years from now, Dare could volunteer for the war in Vietnam.

"U.S. planes have been shot down, Dare," I said. "You ought to read the headlines once. And we're killing people with those bombs. People who deserve to live like us."

"Hush now, Reen." Gram squeezed my wrist to give a warning, but I pulled my arm away.

"We'll need our best to win this war," Clay McCardle said to Billy, and I could tell he didn't like talking to a girl. "And son"—he

paused—"you don't want to lose your chance to make a choice."
It was the same thing those soldiers said to Uncle Slim and Billy
on the Fourth. Like enlisting was the safest choice that Billy could
make now. "You let them send you in the draft, you won't have a
say in your assignment. You could well see the worst of it."

"Billy's never been up in a plane," I said. Clay McCardle could
ignore me, but I wasn't giving up. "And it's college that he wants."

"Reen," Billy said, embarrassed. "You don't need to speak
for me."

"Or anyone," Gram added.

"Well, someone does," I said. "Your only choice can't be the
Air Force."

"Reen can't keep her mouth shut," Dare blurted like a big
shot. He gave me a hard shove, but I stayed put. "Go on in and
do those dishes. He's not here to talk to you."

"Dare." Billy rolled his eyes, disgusted.

Clay McCardle cleared his throat. He nudged his empty plate
like he was done. "Best pie in the county," he told Gram. "You're
sure doing God's work taking care of three young kids for a whole
summer. I bet you'll be relieved when Frank comes home."

"I do my best," Gram said. "But you can see it isn't easy
at my age."

"I surely see that, Blanche." Clay McCardle turned again
to Billy, and handed him a card. "You're a man now, son. You
call me anytime. You're in a tough spot here, and I can help.

Your uncle Slim is worried you'll get taken in the draft. And remember, four years down the road your college will be covered. A young man in the Air Force can go far. You could have a bright career ahead."

"No, thanks," I said, but Billy took that card. (If he can't argue with Clay McCardle, he sure can't fight a war.) "It isn't what Mom wanted for her son. And Billy doesn't want it either."

"Your sister's quick with her opinions," Clay McCardle said to Billy, but he still wouldn't look at me.

"She means well." Billy sighed. We'd been at that table for an hour and he'd barely said two words to Clay McCardle.

"Just ignore her, Clay," Gram said. "Sometimes Reen's too big for her britches. Doesn't matter what the subject is, Reen puts in her two cents."

"You don't have to tell me, Blanche." He stood up from the table, and patted at my head like I was Float.

"I'm not a dog," I said. "And I don't want my brother—"

"I got my own bigmouth girl at home," Clay McCardle said to Gram. "Sally's thirteen now and snotty as a hankie. All mouth."

"I'm more than mouth," I said, because I am. Then I looked straight at Billy. "And you should take my side," I said. "Because I'm always taking yours. And you should stand up for Mom's dream, because I am."

"Come on, Reen," he said, but I walked off from the table, and ran up Gram's attic steps.

That's all I have to say now, Mr. Marsworth.

1. I AM MORE THAN MOUTH.
2. Vandals wrecked your cottage.
3. Uncle Slim sent in the Air Force.
4. Billy didn't defend me, and he didn't defend
   Mom's dream. I know he's not a fighter, but he
   needs to be one now.

Not Snotty as a Hankie,
Reenie Kelly

P.S. Oh, and by the way . . . Brandenbrook's for QUAKERS, and it's in PENNSYLVANIA, which is nearly to New York! A Pennsylvania Quaker college for a Catholic from Missouri who lives in Minnesota??? Don't you think you should have said that from the start???

P.P.S. I'm sorry I wrote that, Mr. Marsworth. I'm still mad at Clay McCardle, and Uncle Slim, and Gram, and Dare, and Billy, too, and I want Billy off in college, but not in PENNSYLVANIA.

P.P.P.S. Saturday is nearly here, and I still don't have a YES from Billy.

Dear Miss Kelly,

Please don't waste your sorrow on my cottage. It's a shell of what it once was, let it go. Perhaps you'll understand now why I've left the place to ruin. This wouldn't be the first time someone painted "commie" on my porch.

Your good work wasn't wasted, because good work never is.

More alarming in my mind is Clay McCardle at your house. Do you think Billy was persuaded to enlist?

Yes, Brandenbrook is nearly to New York, and yes, it was founded by the Quakers, but neither of those things needs to be an obstacle just now. First, Billy has to have an interest, and then he must apply. It will be August all too soon, and right now you have the Air Force knocking on your door, and I'm afraid Plan B appears uncertain. I wouldn't delay on Brandenbrook, would you?

Will the Quakers take a Catholic? Yes, they will.

If you continue with your research, you might find that Brandenbrook fits Billy Kelly like a glove.

Sincerely,

H. W. Marsworth

H. W. Marsworth

P.S. Absolutely do not contact Sheriff Cutler about my cottage, young Miss Kelly. Unfortunately, law and justice are not always synonymous.

Dear Mr. Marsworth,

Happy Friday morning!!! Look what Billy left while I was on
my route!!!!

Don't give up on my Plan B, it's coming true!!!!

I'm running to the Conoco to give Billy a hug!!

Hey Pup,

Want to see the Minneapolis Institute of Art? Gram
agrees you need some culture, and Dare could use
some, too. If you're not booked tomorrow morning,
let's go into Minneapolis. Gram says you and Dare
need baths before a trip to a museum, and Dare
better get a haircut. Gram says Dare can't go to a
museum with that mop of filthy hair.

You two get that done today so we can go.

Have a great day.

Love you,
Billy

Friday, July 26, 1968

Dear Mr. Marsworth,

I can only write a minute, because I want to run this over
before Gram gets home from work.

Guess what??? Dare let me cut his hair and it looks terrible,
ha-ha-ha. He wasn't even mad, because he wants to look his worst.
If kids weren't scared of him before, they'll be scared now!

Billy says we're leaving at 8:30 in the morning, and Dare's
already griping about leaving Float behind. (Not to mention
having to go to a museum!) But Dare won't miss a chance to
do his navigator job. Dare is always in the front seat reading
maps for Dad.

Wait until Dare finds out our first stop isn't even the
museum! If he's mad we're at the Draft Information Center
he can fume out in Gram's car.

Can they help us at the center? I sure hope so.

In the meantime, wish us luck!

Family Barber,
Reenie Kelly

P.S. We couldn't make it to the cottage, but we're never
going to quit. If the sheriff won't bring justice, then we will.
We're going to tack up the two more NO TRESPASSING signs
Dare bought at Rash's Hardware.

P.P.S. I continued with my research while Dare went to buy the signs. Brandenbrook College. Founded by the Quakers, alias: the Religious Society of Friends. (That Society of Friends name FITS YOU like a glove.) Your religion stands for peace, and Brandenbrook does, too. Did you know Billy can study music at that college if he wants? It's a college just for men, so I guess when I'm eighteen, I won't get to go. That's okay, I wouldn't leave my family to move to Pennsylvania, and if Billy says the same thing, please don't be surprised. He'll probably say that Pennsylvania is too far. The Kellys stick together, that's why we're all with Gram. Do the Quakers have a closer college, Mr. Marsworth? Is there one in Minnesota?

Just in case they don't, I have that address in my pocket, and according to the atlas, it's almost 1,160 miles far from Gram's. 1,160 miles??? How would we see Billy? How would he come home?

Saturday, July 27, 1968

Dear Mr. Marsworth,

I have a hundred thousand million trillion things I want to write, but I'm too beat to tell them to you now.

The big city makes you sleepy, have you ever noticed that?

I'll write you in the morning, I promise that I will.

Until tomorrow, Mr. Marsworth . . . zzzzzzzzzz.

Tomorrow: Sunday morning, 4:30 a.m. to be exact.

Good morning, Mr. Marsworth!

I'm up at the crack of dawn because I can't sleep past 4:30, and for once I'm happy I don't have a Sunday route. I'd rather be in bed writing to you. (Well, that's not EXACTLY true. I'd rather talk in person, and I HOPE someday we will.)

Please grab a cup of coffee because this letter might be long.

Okay, so Billy borrowed a map from Mr. Casey, and Dare got us to the city telling Billy where to turn, but when we pulled up to the center, Dare was stumped.

"This ain't no art museum," he said, and Billy had to tell him we were meeting someone first.

"At the Draft Information Center?" Dare said, concerned. "Are you already signing up for war? Can't you wait a little bit?"

"Not signing up today," Billy said. He rubbed his hands over

162

his face like he does when he gets nervous, and I was nervous, too. I really was. "Information mission only."

"I don't get what you're saying." Dare threw the map in the backseat, and we climbed out of the car. "We drove all this way for some museum and the draft? I knew this trip was screwy from the start. Don't they got baseball in this city like St. Louis? Can't we catch a Twins game while we're here?"

"You don't have to come inside," I said to Dare.

"Oh no, he does." Billy reached up to squeeze Dare's shoulder. Dare may be taller now than Billy, but Billy is the brother we've admired all our lives—even Gram and Dad admire Billy—and I knew Billy wasn't ready to lose our love over this draft. "I need Dare to hear this, too. 'All for one,' remember, Reen? The Kellys have to stay on the same side."

"Hear what?" Dare asked. City cars were rushing past, and the strangers on the sidewalk and the sirens and the skyscrapers in the distance made me feel too far from home.

"Let's just go in to see Keith." I grabbed hold of Billy's other wrist, and pulled him toward the door. "Dare can hear it all when we're inside."

"Keep an open mind, Dare," Billy said, with his hand still on Dare's shoulder, "Please just hear them out. We're not deciding anything. And you, too, Reen—"

"I know," I said, and then we went inside.

First thing we saw were posters about peace, and framed

pictures of protestors, and stories from the newspaper tacked up on a board, and STOP WAR NOW signs stacked against the wall. Two shaggy, bearded hippies were working at their desks, and I hoped one wasn't Keith, because I knew Dare wouldn't want a hippie talking Billy out of war. The only hippies back in Denton were the marchers on TV, and every time Dad saw them, he'd turn the TV off.

"I bet you're Reenie Kelly." The blond one in the PEACE T-shirt flashed me a big smile. He stood and shook our hands before I even answered yes. "I'm Keith," he said to Dare and Billy, and he seemed fine for a hippie, he truly did.

"Sit," he said, as he dragged three chairs to his desk. "So your sister filled me in," he said to Billy. He leaned back in his chair and put his hands behind his head. "You're eighteen years old, and registered, but now you don't want to fight in Vietnam. You hope to find some way out of this draft, is that correct?"

"Well, I'm not as sure of that as Reen," Billy said with a shy smile.

"Find a way out of the draft?" Dare said, alarmed. "But you can't do that, Billy. You might not be as tough as Dad or me, but you'll still serve. The Kellys ain't afraid to fight."

"No," Billy said, embarrassed, his tan cheeks burning pink. "I am. I am afraid to fight, Dare. And I don't want to kill—"

"Even Skip's afraid," I said to Dare. "And he's a soldier. Boys can be afraid."

"There's nothing wrong with fear," Keith said to Billy.

"You don't need to be ashamed. Heck, I don't want to die in Vietnam. We all should be afraid."

"Scared or not, the Kellys serve their country," Dare said, and he sounded gruff like Dad does when he's "had it up to here."

"But maybe Billy's different," I said quickly. "Let him make his mind up for himself."

"Can you just listen, Dare and Reen?" Billy said, so the two of us wouldn't bicker anymore. "I came here to learn, and so should you." He wiped his palms over his jeans and swallowed hard. "So what exactly are my choices?" he asked Keith. "That's what I need to know."

"You can't go to college, right?" Keith asked. "Is that definitely out? Reenie told me you were going, but then you didn't have the money, so you decided to withdraw. I'm sure you know that college is one way out of this war. At least until you finish, they'll draft you after that. But the young guys that they're drafting, those are mostly poor kids. Not all the guys, of course, but plenty of them are."

"I can't afford to go to college," Billy said, impatient. "So what other things—?"

"Well," Keith said. "There's Canada. If you can get across the border. Of course, you'd be a fugitive, which means you can't come home."

"Canada?" My heart was in my stomach, and I knew that Dare's was, too. "Billy can't run away to Canada."

"A fugitive?" Dare added. "You think Dad would want a Kelly running from the law?"

"No. I don't think I could do that," Billy said. "I can't leave my family. So is the only option prison and a $10,000 fine?"

"Like that story in the paper," I said.

"Hard to say," Keith said sadly. "We have lawyers volunteering, but no one knows for sure what will happen with these cases. But first things first—you'd have to file C.O. status if you're hoping to object."

"Conscientious objector," I told Dare, because Billy knew already. "That's where Billy says his conscience objects to the war in Vietnam."

"I know what it means," Dare said. "You ain't the big shot here."

"So what I know from your bright sister"—Keith interrupted, and I was glad Dare had a chance to hear a stranger call me bright—"is that you weren't raised a pacifist, and you're not opposed to war based on your religion, and you don't have a public history of speaking out against the draft."

"I guess Reen covered all the bases," Billy said. "I sure don't have a public history—"

"But Billy doesn't fight," I said. "He never has. Not even as a kid. And he didn't play with BB guns like we did. And he didn't hunt or fish with Dad. Could he write to the <u>Tribune</u>? Does the paper count as public?"

"The <u>Tribune</u> would be a start," Keith said.

"A letter to the paper," Billy said. "Does it have to be that public? I'm concerned about my family. My grandmother. She lives in a small town."

"All of us!" Dare said. "You want people spraying 'commie' on Gram's house? You want to be like Old Man Marsworth? Chickens hung up on your gate?"

"No," Billy said. "I don't want that, Dare."

"Well, C.O.s aren't exactly popular," Keith said to Billy. "Get ready for that, man. And you should have a public record, especially if you didn't indicate your C.O. status when you registered. That would've been the time."

"He didn't know about it then," I said. "But he does now. You said it's not too late."

"Or is it?" Billy asked, like he wasn't sure of what he wanted, yes or no.

"It's not," Keith said to Billy. "But this is up to you, not your sister. You take on Uncle Sam it means a fight. A long, hard public fight just like Ali's. So you'll have to fight for something—war or peace—you'll have to fight. And someone painting 'commie' is the least of what might happen. Draft resisters are generally despised, you must know that from Ali."

"Billy knows that," Dare said. "We all do. All of Denton hates him now."

"You know I don't," Billy said to Dare. "At least he's following his conscience."

"Yeah," I said. "And we don't care if they paint 'commie,' if Billy's safe with us. I bet Skip would rather face graffiti than those bombs in Vietnam."

"Would he rather be in prison?" Dare's freckled face was burning red. "Like Alcatraz? San Quentin? Because that's where Ali is headed, and Billy will be, too. You think prison will be fun, Reen?"

"No one thinks that, Dare." Billy tugged the collar of his shirt like just this talk of prison made it hard for him to breathe. "I'm not sure I'm strong enough for prison," he told Keith. "Or the shame I'll bring my family. My dad—"

"It might not come to prison." Keith pulled some papers from his file drawer and handed them to Billy. "Certainly not Alcatraz. Let's all just take this one step at a time."

Okay, I have to take a break now, Mr. Marsworth. I need two bowls of Sugar Smacks before I write another word. Are you ready for more coffee? Go ahead and help yourself.

Stay tuned, Mr. Marsworth. Chapter Two is still ahead.

Chapter Two: The Art Museum, etc., etc.

All of us were rattled after we'd said good-bye to Keith. Billy had a list of things he'd have to answer if he decided to object. Like, what does he believe? And why? And when did he first believe it? And who gave him the training to be against a war? What religion is he? Is there someone specific in that church that taught Billy war was wrong? (None of the priests at Holy Family back in Denton taught us that.) It was a list too long to write, but if I can borrow it from Billy, I'll let you have a look. Or maybe you already know the questions that they ask? Stuff on self-defense, or fighting for your family if your family was attacked. How long has he been a pacifist? Is he against the use of force no matter what?

Did you have to answer all these questions during WWI? Or was it enough to be Quaker, because Keith said being raised in a religion against war would really help. I said we'd learned the Ten Commandments, and shouldn't "Thou shalt not kill" be good enough?

It turns out that it isn't, Mr. Marsworth.

Anyway, all of us had too much on our minds to visit a museum, but Billy made us do it so our trip wouldn't be a lie. We saw a bunch of paintings, and naked statues, and old tapestries, and fancy antique furniture, and we wandered all those quiet rooms like everybody else. (I guess no one likes to talk in a museum.)

When Billy finally let us leave, we found a leafy park, and spread our lunch under a tree, and when a whiskered man stopped to say that he was hungry, Billy handed him his sandwich, plus a dollar from his wallet for more food.

"You're a good guy, Billy," Dare said when the man had walked away. "You've been the best kid in our family, best grades, best at baseball, best at music, always good to me and Reen, but you stand against your country, no one else will see you're good. They'll think of us as cowards."

"Just me." Billy hung his head like he didn't want to be a coward. "But if you think you'd be ashamed if I object—"

"We won't," I said. "We just want you living."

"Maybe you, Reen," Billy said, and he waited to hear Dare say that's what he wanted, too. "But I'm not sure that's enough for Dare."

"Of course I want you living." Dare tore off a hunk of sandwich and handed it to Billy. "But a traitor to your country? You want to live like that? You think we shouldn't have fought back after Japan attacked? You think we should've let the Nazis keep on killing the Jews? If that's what you believe, then go ahead. But someone has to fight like Dad did in Korea, and those soldiers are my heroes, not the cowards that object. If you want to be a coward—"

"He doesn't," I said. "Billy's not a coward. Didn't you hear what Keith said? Billy has to fight for peace. It's going to take a lot of courage to stand up against this war. Maybe peace is just as brave."

"Ask Dad," Dare said. "He'll tell you that it's bull—"

Billy turned his face up toward the sun like he was studying the sky. "I know the men who serve their country are heroic, I won't argue with you, Dare. And I wish I had Dad's courage, but I don't. Or even Skip's. Or any of the guys in Vietnam right now. But I don't want to kill, I really don't, or fight a war that could be wrong. I guess I'm more like Mom, or Mr.—" Billy looked at me like he was thinking of your name, but he couldn't bring himself to say it.

"You're exactly like Mom, Billy," I said, squeezing his warm hand. "You look like Mom. You think like Mom. You have all the good of Mom inside your heart. Mom didn't want you in this war. Don't you think it'd make her proud to see you fight for peace?"

"Maybe." Billy nodded.

"Okay, okay, done with that," Dare said, standing up abruptly, because talking about Mom is too much for Dare to take. "Let's finish this fiasco and get home."

We didn't go straight home like Dare wanted, instead we drove downtown to see the skyscrapers, and walk the busy streets, and wander through that fancy department store called Dayton's where Mom took us to see Santa on that same Christmas trip to Minnesota when I stood outside your house. Dare asked to see Met Stadium, but it wasn't near downtown.

We did all that without more talk of war or what Billy might do next. Instead, we walked those city streets for hours because Billy said he was tired of Lake Liberty, and Casey's Conoco, and Gram's house, and the three of us might never have a city day again.

"I got to hope so." Dare shoved Billy's shoulder like he was halfway between serious and fun. "You and scheming Reen won't trick me twice."

Okay, that's all I can tell you, Mr. Marsworth, because it's nearly nine o'clock now, and we have to go to Mass. Wouldn't it be AMAZING if Father Gleason stood up on the altar and spoke against the war? And wouldn't it be STUPENDOUS if he said Catholic boys couldn't kill?

I know I'm just imagining, but maybe someday, Mr. Marsworth.

When I get home from St. Patrick's, I'll walk this too-long letter to your house.

City-Slicker Schemer,
Reenie Kelly

Monday, July 29, 1968

Dear Miss Kelly,

May I make a small confession?

Yesterday, Clyde and I eagerly awaited your news of
Minneapolis, and while we didn't expect this morning's missive,
we welcomed every word. (I hope you don't mind, there are
days Clyde likes to hear how young Miss Kelly fares.)

I am pleased to learn that Billy might object. Not so
many years ago, I counseled boys like Billy, and Keith is
right, he has a fight ahead. Although the extensive list of
questions may overwhelm, I trust Billy has the answers in
his heart. One can't long stay a secret to the self.

And Brandenbrook, Miss Kelly? Have you broached that
subject yet with Billy? Time is of the essence if he wishes
to apply. Remember, the draft would be deferred just as
Keith counseled, and your mother's dream for college would
come true. Do not count the miles, but instead the days and
years we could keep Billy safe from harm.

Sincerely,

H. W. Marsworth

H. W. Marsworth

P.S. I see Disney's Blackbeard's Ghost is playing at the
Lakeview. Perhaps a Monday matinee would be fun for you and
Dare? A small break from the troubles of this world. Please
don't save this money for your Rescue Billy Fund. I will
gladly give to that as well.

173

Monday, July 29, 1968

Dear Mr. Marsworth!!!!

May I make a small confession? There isn't anybody nicer in
Lake Liberty than YOU! Not a single soul!!! I wish you'd come
with us to Blackbeard's Ghost!!!!

I told Dare it was a tip. I hope that you don't mind. Dare
wishes he'd picked Hillcrest when we split up our streets. No
one on Dare's route would tip five bucks.

If you get the urge to join us, we'll be there at 1:00.
We're buying buttered popcorn, a king-sized Coke, and licorice.
If there's any money left, I'm buying candy for Guess Who.
Do you like Junior Mints? Mom always loved a box of Junior
Mints. Listen for your bell, because you won't want a melted
chocolate mess inside your box.

Your Good Friend,
Reenie Kelly

P.S. Don't you love the smell of buttered movie popcorn?????
Maybe I should leave some buttered popcorn in your box.

Monday, July 29, 1968

Dear Mr. Marsworth,

I didn't get to buy you candy, or have fun at <u>Blackbeard's Ghost</u> the way you wanted, because Rat and Cutler ruined it by attacking us with Milk Duds once the theater went dark. We tried to just ignore it, and twice we changed our seats, but when they hit Dare's head with a hard one, he tore up to the balcony, and dumped our king-sized cup of Coke over them both. I did the same with our warm popcorn, even though it went to waste. ☹

Some mother ran to get the usher, and the owner made us leave. US!!!!

We were the victims, Mr. Marsworth, but no one seemed to care. We couldn't even buy a second buttered popcorn for the road. Never mind your Junior Mints. The owner shoved us out the front door, and said we couldn't come back.

I know you stand for peace, but we couldn't put up with Milk Duds bouncing like hard rocks against our heads, even if it meant we lost our chance at <u>Blackbeard's Ghost</u>.

Dare says next time he'll knock out Cutler's teeth, and if we're not gone by September, Dad's going to have two school dropouts on his hands. I don't want to leave you in Lake Liberty, but I WON'T go to school with these kids.

Still Craving Buttered Popcorn,
Reenie Kelly

Monday, July 29, 1968

Dear Mr. Marsworth,

In a million trillion years, you'll never ever guess who showed
up at Gram's house just after supper! That bully, Sheriff
Cutler, with his rotten, scar-faced dressed-in-camo kid, and
that pale yeah-man Rat. Cross my heart and hope to die—all
three of them stood right in Gram's hot kitchen, calling Dare
and me delinquents, and telling lies to Gram.

Sheriff Cutler said we're lucky he didn't arrest us for assault.
Assault?

"Heck no. That was self-defense," Dare argued right away,
but Gram didn't want to hear it. As far as Gram's concerned,
Dare had no business dumping Coke on someone's head.

"Wesley Morgan called me from the Lakeview." Sheriff
Cutler hooked his thumbs over his belt like he was tough.
"But this wouldn't be the first complaint I've had about
these kids." The sheriff has the same flat block face as his
mean kid, the same shaved head, those same cold steel eyes,
and the minute he walked into Gram's kitchen, Float hid
under Gram's table like he was scared. "I hear these two are
stealing papers," he told Gram. "And I know they've taken
Steven's. He's had angry customers calling with complaints. A
man wants to wake up to his morning paper, that's his right.
We don't need two Missouri hoodlums wreaking havoc in this
town."

"Hoodlums?" Gram said, shocked. "Dare and Reen are hardly hoodlums."

"Those two are the hoodlums." I nodded toward his scabby kid and white-haired Rat. "Those two have swiped MY papers. They've tackled me. Shoved worms down my shirt. Fought me two-to-one for no good reason. Why don't you ask about the chicken on Mr. Marsworth's fence? The eggs." (I didn't tell about the BBs because Gram would end my route. Ooops! CROSS THAT OUT: I just remembered you don't know about the BBs!)

"Well, aren't you full of spit and vinegar." The sheriff sneered at me while his rotten kid and Rat just stood there smug.

"Did you two rough up a girl?" Billy said to them, disgusted.

"I got them straightened out," Dare bragged to Billy. "Don't you worry about that."

"Why didn't you tell me, Reen?" Gram said, like not telling was my fault.

"We weren't going to snitch like these two punks," Dare said. "Me and Reen fight our own battles."

"Could someone please enlighten me?" Gram said, flustered. "Why am I the last to know?"

"They've been dogging us since we moved to this dumb town," Dare said to the sheriff. "You want to send someone to juvie, start with them. They're out for me and Reen, and that's the truth."

"Not just us," I said. "They've done their share to Mr. Marsworth."

"Old Man Marsworth?" Sheriff Cutler turned his sharp gaze from Dare to me, and I was sorry that I'd opened my big mouth. "What's he to you, girl?"

"He's on my paper route," I said. "I caught Rat and Steven throwing eggs at Mr. Marsworth's house."

"That's crap," Steven interrupted, but Sheriff Cutler slammed him with a backhand right into Gram's wall. (I hate to say this, Mr. Marsworth, but for one teeny-weeny second I hoped he wasn't hurt. I've never seen a father hit his kid that hard or fast. Dad's never even spanked us and he's lost his temper lots.)

"You watch your mouth," he said. Steven slouched against Gram's wall, a little out of reach, and Rat tried to steal a couple sneaky steps out of Gram's kitchen.

"Oh for heaven's sake," Gram scolded, like she was fed up with us all, including Sheriff Cutler for hitting his own son. (Gram's not a spanker either.) "This is kid stuff, Stu. Let them work it out. I raised three boys as a widow, and I didn't butt into their fights. If memory serves, you and Frank had your share of scraps."

"Most Frank started, like these two," the sheriff said. "And now we've got another Kelly tied up with Old Man Marsworth."

"Tied up with Old Man Marsworth?" I asked Gram, but she didn't answer. (Was he talking about Mom?)

"He's on Reen's paper route," Gram said. "She's not tied up with anyone."

"I'll talk to Dare and Reen." Billy opened Gram's door wide, but no one moved.

"You'll talk?" Sheriff Cutler glared at Billy. "I hear you're hiding from the draft board. You're living in Lake Liberty, trying to dodge the draft."

"No sir," Billy said. Flies were swarming through the door, but Billy held it open. "I'm working full-time down at Casey's, living with my gram."

"I know where you work," he said. "A boy your age ought to enlist." He dropped his right hand to his holster, and pinned Billy in a stare so mean I saw how brave Billy would have to be to stand against the draft in front of a man like Sheriff Cutler. Braver than I was, I'll tell you that. I just wanted Sheriff Cutler to get out of Gram's house. "My two oldest boys are serving," he told Billy. "Buster will follow his two brothers when he's done with senior year. And yet, you're at Casey's wiping windshields when you could be in Vietnam. You think that's fair to my two sons? You too good to do your duty?"

"No," Billy said, and for once I didn't jump in to argue about Billy and that war. (I hope you're not disappointed, Mr. Marsworth. I just couldn't argue with a man as mean as Sheriff Cutler.)

Sheriff Cutler rapped his fist on Billy's chest like he was knocking at a door. "You get that letter from the draft board, you better plan to go." He clicked his tongue against his teeth.

"We don't need another Howard Marsworth in this town. I know good men on that draft board. They'll see to it you're called."

Gram pointed toward the door. "You've had your say now, Stu. I'll take care of my family, you take care of yours."

"I could've charged you with assault," he said again to Dare. "You ever touch my kid again—" He grabbed hold of Dare's old T-shirt, but then he let it go. "Get out to the squad car," he ordered Rat and Cutler, and they cowered out of Gram's door like two scared dogs. "You're a great big ape like Frank," he said to Dare, but then he turned again to Billy, pulled a Camel from his pocket, and lit it in Gram's kitchen like he was staying put all night. "But you . . ." He waved his cigarette at Billy. "You don't look much like a Kelly."

"Good-bye, Stu," Gram said, pointing toward her door.

"You ought to let Frank know they're on the wrong side of the law," he said to Gram. "All three of them as far as I can tell. I'm sure he'd hate to see his kids in jail."

In jail, Mr. Marsworth?

And will he really tell the draft board to send Billy off to war?

Gram's calling up the stairs so I guess I've got to go. Dare and I are probably grounded, but at least I'll get to leave to do my route.

Not Guilty,
Reenie Kelly

P.S. Tied up with Old Man Marsworth??????

Wednesday, July 3I, I968

Dear Miss Kelly,

How I wish I had a time machine to take back <u>Blackbeard's</u>
<u>Ghost</u>. I never could have guessed the harm a matinee might
bring. Please steer clear of Sheriff Cutler. I would advise
the same of Rat and Steven.

I know well the fear you felt with a man like Sheriff
Cutler, and I understand the desire to stay silent when
you're scared, but if Billy stands against this draft,
moral courage will be called for on all fronts. There will
be other men like Sheriff Cutler, other times you are
afraid to say what you believe.

And yet, perhaps your fighting spirit will finally
serve you well.

Better to take a stand for peace, than to fight a
couple bullies with warm popcorn.

In the matter of the draft board: time is of the
essence. August I arrives tomorrow; in September college
classes will begin. Is there a chance he's written to
Brandenbrook? Any chance at all?

Sincerely,

H. W. Marsworth

H. W. Marsworth

July 31, 1968

Dear Mr. Marsworth,

I wanted you to see this. I guess I don't know why. It's too
sad for me to read alone.

Jackie Moon from Mississippi was killed in Vietnam.

You can keep Skip's letter. I don't want it in Gram's house.

Hey there, Reenie Kelly,

We're coming up on August, so I thought I better write. Thanks for sending all those letters, and cutting out those comics, but I thought I ought to tell you I don't laugh at Beetle Bailey anymore. The Army isn't funny, you can take my word on that. Billy won't be laughing in the Army, so I hope you've found a way to keep him home.

I've had a few good days, and by good I mean I'm living. A week or so ago we took some heavy fire, and lots of guys were hit, but the worst for me was losing Jackie Moon. You know he was my best pal since I landed in this place, and I won't find another like him in this life. You remember that pretty soap dove he sent your class at Christmas? Or that tape he made of folk songs he'd learned as a kid? I'm glad you've got a little bit of Jackie to remember. I have the birthday turtle that he carved for me, but I'd give anything to hear that tape of Jackie singing now. He always had a song when I was scared. "Joke, or song, or verse, what'll it be?" he always asked me.

I still expect to hear that question, but instead I'm left with my bad nerves, and a space where Jackie Moon once was.

Lieutenant Kohl sent the news to Mrs. Lamb so

she can break it to his pen pal. I sure hope you never get a letter saying that I'm dead.

I won't tell you how it is here because this killing's not for kids, I'll just say it's hard as hell to be a soldier in this war. And worse to wonder why you're living, on a day your buddy's dead.

You keep Billy from the Army, little sister. I guess it's good you got that old man Mr. Marsworth on your side. If Billy gets into that Quaker school, tell him he should go. Aren't you close to Canada? Maybe he should run. To tell the truth, I'd take prison now. I don't mind if he objects to serving, I sure don't.

If I make it out alive, I'll come to see that cottage and we'll all go for a swim. That's the kind of dream I like to have here. You and Dare and Billy, and that pretty, private shore. Gram and her peach pie. Float racing to the lake and beating you and Dare. Keep sending me those stories, I like to get your news.

Say hey to all the Kellys from your friend Skip in Vietnam. I hope folks know I'm fighting for their freedom, or for something, I'm not sure. I just want folks to know that I'm still here.

                              Your Friend in the Army,
                              Skip

Wednesday, July 3I, I968

Oh my dear Miss Kelly,

I am truly, terribly sorry. Sorry for Jackie Moon,
and everyone who'd hoped he would come home from
Vietnam. And for you of course, and young Skip,
whose heart is ravaged by this war.

You're right. You should not be alone with this
hard letter.

Please go out to the woods to sit with Dare. Or go
down to the cottage, where the two of you are safe.

I wish that I were stronger, you need a strong,
young friend.

In Sympathy,

H. W. Marsworth

H. W. Marsworth

Wednesday, July 31, 1968

Dear Mr. Marsworth,

I don't need a strong, young friend, I really don't. Dare is young and strong, but he won't do me any good when I'm this sad.

You're the only friend I'd like to talk to, Mr. Marsworth. Can you see me in the oak tree in the lot across the street? I'm here waiting for a friend if you'll just come.

Why don't I ever ever get to see you, Mr. Marsworth? Why does your assistant carry in my letters and walk yours to the box? Aren't you well enough to walk outside yourself?

Please, please say that you're not sick.

It would be too sad to have you sick.

I can't stand another sadness, I just can't.

Jackie Moon. Jackie Moon. Do you think there's any chance Mom will meet him up in heaven, or are there just too many millions up in heaven for Mom to meet them all? Do you think God meets them all?

I hate thinking about heaven.

I'm going to the Conoco to see Billy Kelly living. I just want to see him pumping gas.

                              Brokenhearted,
                              Reenie Kelly

Friday, August 2, 1968

Dear Mr. Marsworth,

Did you send a girl named Moira to Gram's house? That cartwheel girl from California you mentioned back in June. The one from 349 Hillcrest who was gone to San Francisco for July. Well, this morning she just showed up on Gram's steps.

"You looking for a friend?" she asked. "Someone told my mom you were new to town the same as me this summer."

I don't need another friend, I truly don't. The only friend I really want is you. I don't think a barefoot girl in a yarn poncho can cheer me up from Skip's sad letter, or the death of Jackie Moon, or help me find a quick way to keep Billy from this war.

She's an only child, Mr. Marsworth. An only child with a California accent, and crooked bottom teeth, and a frizzy mop of hair, and she knows nothing about brothers, and she likes to knit and sew and make strange ponchos. Her dad lives in California, and her mom works here as a lawyer, which means she's on her own this August just like us. She offered us free snow cones because she has her own machine, but we didn't have a lot to show off except for Float. All the cool toys we owned we sold in Denton.

Dare liked her right away because she kissed Float's filthy nose, and oohed over Dare's tent, and drank a cup of wood-smoked Sanka even though it tastes like dirt. Float napped right in her lap, a thing he only does with Dare.

All in all she seems okay, but I don't need another friend. She'll never be a better friend than you.

I wouldn't mind a summer snow cone, BUT I don't want her at your cottage, and Dare already told her she could hang out down there with us.

That cottage is for US and NO ONE ELSE.

Dare can go without me. I think I'll just stay home. I can tell already it's Dare she likes best.

Please say that you didn't send her to Gram's house.

Odd Girl Out Now,
Reenie Kelly

P.S. I'm staying home to work on Billy's letter to the paper so he can have a public record of objecting to the draft the way Keith said. I'm not going to lose my brother like Skip lost Jackie Moon. Don't worry, I won't send it. And I'll let Billy change whatever words he wants when he comes home.

P.P.S. And what about the Kelly-Marsworth tie the sheriff mentioned? Gram won't give an answer, but of course Gram never does. You had a Kelly friend before me, that much I know for sure. Did he mean Betsy Kelly? I have a hunch he did.

Friday, August 2, 1968

Dear Miss Kelly,

An unexpected friend is one of fate's great gifts.

Don't turn away an unexpected friend.

Who taught me that, Miss Kelly? I believe it
would be you.

Sincerely,

H. W. Marsworth

H. W. Marsworth

Friday, August 2, 1968

Dear Mr. Marsworth,

Did I really teach you something??? You're so smart and wise with your million-dollar words, and adages, and poems, and metaphors like "no man is an island," I thought every lesson in our letters came from you. Knowing that I taught you one small lesson makes me proud.

I guess that means you're right about the unexpected friend, or I was right when I chose you, whatever way it works. So I'll give a chance to Moira, and I'll try not to be jealous if it's Dare she really likes. (Everyone in Denton liked Dare more.)

The truth is, I'm just blue, sitting in Gram's attic, feeling sorry for myself while they have fun.

You know what??? I'm going to take your good advice and walk out to your cottage, even though I hate that long, hot walk alone.

Your Sometimes Teacher,
Reenie Kelly

P.S. I didn't get far on this first draft of Billy's letter. Go ahead and mark it up with your red pen like Mrs. Lamb.

Dear Minneapolis <u>Tribune</u> Opinion Section,

I am an eighteen-year-old boy who believes the government is wrong to force young men to fight in Vietnam. The draft takes away our chance to follow our own conscience, and if my conscience disagrees with killing the people in that country, the draft just doesn't care. Every boy that's called is forced to go. Even one that's never killed a living thing, except maybe some insects, and I don't think an insect really counts. Otherwise, all my life I've tried to be a peaceful kid.

As far as my religion, I believe the Ten Commandments, and I've always lived them all including "Thou shalt not kill." I'd have to break that good commandment if I'm sent to Vietnam. I'm not against any of the soldiers fighting for our country because I know that they're all brave, I just don't have it in me to be a hero in a war.

I hope I can do service work at home.

William Kelly
Lake Liberty, Minnesota

Saturday, August 3, 1968

Dear Miss Kelly,

Please leave this public declaration to your brother.
This is a letter he must write in his own words. (Just as
you must write in your own words.)

But what of Brandenbrook? I find you strangely
silent on the subject of that school. (I, too, remember
what I ask.) Did you ever talk to Billy? Did he write to
Dr. Price?

This summer will be gone soon. Please don't be
deterred by Pennsylvania: a train or bus or plane
could bring him home. Holidays and summers you'd have
him here with you.

Sincerely,

H. W. Marsworth

H. W. Marsworth

Sunday, August 4, 1968

Dear Mr. Marsworth,

You don't have to worry about me writing the <u>Tribune</u>.
Somehow Billy did it. Between pumping gas at Casey's and
writing back to Beth and taking Gram for groceries and helping
Dare practice his pitch, and working on my swing, and trying to
coach us both on making peace with Rat and Cutler, he wrote his
letter to the paper, and he woke me up past midnight because he
wanted me to be the first to hear the words he wrote.

Me. His one and only loyal little sister.

It was 100 percent better, no, 200 percent better than
the one I gave to you, and I hope someday I'll write as well as
Billy. (If I get a chance to steal it, I'll let you have a look.)

It was brave and strong and sure, stronger than the way he
sounds in person. He said he had to put his conscience before his
country so he couldn't fight in Vietnam.

"You're sure?" I whispered in the darkness when he came
to those last words. He was on the edge of my twin bed lit up
by a little patch of moon, and even in the shadows, I could tell
he was afraid.

"I guess I have to be." He closed his hands into a steeple, and
dropped his head against them like a prayer. "If I want out of
this war, I have to say that I won't serve. It's not enough to hope
I won't get called. The draft board has my name—"

I laid my hand on Billy's back to give him comfort, and I

wished I was older, and I wished it could be me, not him, to stand against this war.

"But Dad and Gram," he said. "I know they'll be ashamed. They won't want a coward—and getting sent to prison—" Billy's voice broke in the darkness. "And Dare will be embarrassed to have me as his brother. Even Beth. She doesn't want a felon for a boyfriend, that's for sure."

"Did she say that?" I asked Billy. "After all these years of going steady, shouldn't Beth be on your side? She doesn't want you dying in that war."

"Well, she's not for prison either." Billy cleared his throat. "She won't stay with me for that."

"We will," I said. "You'll always have us, Billy."

"If they print this in the paper, you'll have ten times the trouble you have now in this small town. And Gram will suffer, too. And Dad when he comes home from North Dakota."

"We're tough enough," I said, even if I wasn't really certain that we'd all take Billy's side. (Did your family take your side in World War 1? Did you have to write the paper?)

"I'll probably lose my job at Casey's. And you know we need the money, every dime I earn. Maybe Gram will lose her job at Brindle Drug. And we'll never get a house. Or earn enough to move our family back to Denton like Dare wants. And Beth," he said again.

"Is there another way besides that letter to the paper?" I asked, because to tell the truth, I didn't much like the list of trouble moving through his mind, and I still don't like it now, writing you my worries when it's nearly 2:00 a.m.

Isn't there a better way to get out of this war?

Maybe he ought to wait to send it? I wonder if he should.

Did you suffer all this worry way back in World War I?

Billy's Sleepless Sister,
Reenie Kelly

Monday, August 5, 1968

Dear Mr. Marsworth,

You left a letter in your box for Billy Kelly, but not for me???

Or maybe your assistant did, because it's not your watery blue cursive on the outside of that envelope. (I know exactly how you write.)

But why would Carl Grace address an envelope to Billy? Why would you?

Did you tell about our letters? Billy doesn't know we're sort of pen pals.

Did you tell him all the secret stuff I've shared about the draft? I hope not. Billy likes to keep his private business to himself.

Did you tell him about Brandenbrook??? You don't need to do that, because I talked to him already, and he said a private East Coast college was a thing we couldn't afford. He didn't believe about the scholarship, he didn't. And he said it was too late to even try.

I would have told you sooner, but—

Well, never mind right now.

Right now I have this envelope from your milk box addressed to Billy Kelly, and I'm not sure I should deliver it.

I'd rather know what's in it, before Billy finds out first.

I could steam it open. Dare used to steam his grades before Dad saw them, but I'd rather you just tell me what you wrote. Or what Carl Grace wrote Billy.

Impatient for an Answer,

Reenie Kelly

P.S. WRITE BACK ASAP!

Monday, August 5, 1968

Dear Miss Kelly,

Rest assured your summer stories are quite safe
inside my home.

The envelope you mention is a note from Carl
Grace, a Brandenbrook alumnus, urging Billy to
apply. They're acquainted from the Conoco where
Carl Grace buys gas, and he believes as I do, that
Billy is a fine fit for that school.

Perhaps a kind note from an alumnus will
be the encouragement Billy needs to write to
Brandenbrook himself. It is August 5, Miss Kelly,
and if Billy hopes to be considered he'll have to
contact Dr. Roland Price at once.

That is essentially the content of letter,
paraphrased of course. No need to steam for curiosity;
no dark secrets have been leaked.

Let us hope together he applies.

Sincerely,

H. W. Marsworth

H. W. Marsworth

Dear Mr. Marsworth,

I DO hope it with you! In fact, I've already hoped so hard ("May I make a small confession?") that I went ahead and wrote to Dr. Roland Price myself. ("Time is of the essence." You said that.)

I'm covering my ears in case you're yelling at me now. Do you storm around your house when you get mad? I'm afraid you're really mad. Our friendship almost ended from that letter I sent Mizzou, and I don't want to lose our friendship now.

Please please please don't hate me, Mr. Marsworth. I would've told you sooner, except I knew you wouldn't approve of me pretending to be Billy when I wrote to Dr. Price. I'm just not as good as you are, Mr. Marsworth. If there's a problem I can fix, I have to fix it. When Billy said my college scheme was crazy—my craziest so far—I wrote to Dr. Price to prove him wrong.

And my letter was stupendous. It really, truly was. It wasn't like that crummy letter I wrote to the Tribune. I used the library's thesaurus, and every word I wrote showed Billy at his best. "Assiduous. Scholarly. Compassionate. Endowed."

"No man is an island," I added at the end. Billy hasn't read John Donne, but that quote made him sound smart.

If Billy writes them now, my scheme will fail! They already have one letter, a second letter wouldn't make sense. Can't we wait for Dr. Roland Price to write us back? He might say Billy has the scholarship, my letter was that good.

And if he does, I SAVED THE DAY!
WE SAVED THE DAY!

If it wasn't for your good advice, I never would have written, and we wouldn't have a single hope of saving Billy from this war, or court, or prison, or leaving us for Canada.

You know I have to follow my own conscience, Mr. Marsworth, and I have to help my brother in whatever way I can.

Please Don't Hate Me,
Reenie Kelly

P.S. Skip would say I did the right thing. I'll bet you that he would. Did you see this morning's headline? "B 525 Drops 25,000 Tons of Bombs." How many people will we kill with all those bombs?

P.P.S. I'm heading to the cottage with Dare and Snow Cone (Dare's nickname for her now), but I'll check for your reply on my way home. Please don't make me wait forever to hear how mad you are.

P.P.P.S. Please don't be so mad you never write.

Monday, August 5, 1968

Dear Miss Kelly,

There are days you do exhaust, and this is one. A younger, sharper mind might have guessed at your charade. How did I not suspect what you have done?

You are correct: I thoroughly disapprove of you pretending to be Billy, but worse, you played a childish prank on a man whom I admire, the one man I hoped might offer Billy admission into college before fall. Quite likely Dr. Roland Price recognized the writing of a child, and promptly put your letter in the trash, where it belongs. However clever your young letter, I doubt it met the standards a college president expects.

In your rush to save your brother, you may have done more harm than good.

You are slow to learn your lessons, yet I am slower still. At all turns with you, Miss Kelly, nothing should surprise.

Here is a word to research in the thesaurus: "irrepressible." Several more words: "imprudent, malapert, unyielding." Self-restraint, Miss Kelly; please learn to practice that.

H. W. Marsworth
H. W. Marsworth

P.S. Please return the letter meant for Billy to my box.

Monday, August 5, 1968

Dear Mr. Marsworth,

No "sincerely"??? Not even one kind word?

PLEASE don't say I did more harm than good.
I wouldn't harm Billy Kelly, not in a thousand, trillion
years. And you don't have to call me all those names, you
really don't. You've already told me LOUD and CLEAR that
I was wrong.

I'm going to make it right, I swear I am.

Will Carl Grace tell Billy? Please, please say he won't. I
don't want him at the Conoco blabbing my mistake.

Remorseful,
Reenie Kelly

Dear Mr. Marsworth,

Here's the letter of apology I wrote Dr. Roland Price, and I'm sorry to you, too, I hope you know that in your heart. You're my best friend in Lake Liberty. I shouldn't have pulled a prank on someone you admire. (I didn't think it was a prank, I really didn't.)

If this letter isn't good, I'll do another draft. Cross out anything you hate, I won't feel bad.

Please leave it in your milk box, I'll pick it up tomorrow morning on my route. Right now I have to get down to the cottage because Dare and Snow Cone left this morning, and I promised Dare I'd help him build a tree stand in your woods. Dare says we need a lookout, just in case THEY come.

> Hoping You'll Forgive Me,
> Reenie Kelly

P.S. Please write back to say you're still my friend.

Monday, August 5, 1968

Dear Dr. Price,

My name is Maureen Kelly, and I live in Lake Liberty,
Minnesota, where I am the sister of William Kelly, and a very
good friend of Mr. H. W. Marsworth. Mr. H. W. Marsworth
suggested to me that my brother William Kelly should apply
to Brandenbrook, but William said it was too late to write
a college for this year. He also thought he'd never get a
scholarship, and we can't afford a private school way off in
Pennsylvania, or even a public school in Missouri.

William is almost always right, but so is Mr. H. W.
Marsworth, so I thought there might be hope for William to
somehow be a student at your school like Mr. Marsworth said.
William's not a Quaker, but he does believe in peace. And
even though I don't want him all the way in Pennsylvania, I'd
let him move that far if Mom's dream for William to attend
college could come true.

Unfortunately, I might have done more harm than good
when I wrote to you pretending to be William. Did you already
read my "fake" William Kelly letter? Did you throw it in the
trash because William didn't sound smart enough to go to your
fine school?

William writes a whole lot better than an almost-sixth-
grade girl. I swear to you he does. He's the smartest in our
family, and he would have stayed a straight-A student if

Mom's cancer hadn't happened. It's hard to concentrate on school when you're sad, it really is.

Please don't let my fake letter damage William's chance of getting into Brandenbrook IF he ever does apply. (I can't promise William will, but your alumnus Carl Grace also thinks he should.) He deserves a scholarship, he does! If the esteemed Mr. H. W. Marsworth believes Billy would do well there, I hope you'll trust his good word and give Billy one more chance.

In Sincere Apology,
Maureen Elizabeth Kelly

Dear Good Friend Mr. Marsworth,

You didn't even read my letter to Dr. Roland Price. I was sad to open up your box in morning darkness and see my letter sitting there without a mark or a single word from you.

Please read ASAP, and let me know if it's good enough to send, or else I won't.

I want to fix things up so Carl Grace can write to Billy, and I need Billy in that college because things are getting worse.

That's right, Mr. Marsworth, you're not the only one who's livid. Gram and Dare are livid. ("Livid" was Gram's word, but Dare is livid, too.) They were livid during supper, when Billy read aloud the letter that he planned to send to the <u>Tribune</u>.

"I want you to be forewarned," he said, when he'd finished with the reading. He looked from Dare, to Gram, then me, and I did my silent best to let him know how proud I was. "I didn't want to mail it until you all knew what I wrote."

"Mail it?" Gram dropped her fork against her plate like she was already done with dinner. "You can't send THAT to the <u>Tribune</u>."

"Did you ask Dad if you could write that?" Dare said. "You think he wants that crap in the <u>Tribune</u>? You think he wants his own son saying he won't serve?"

"It isn't up to Dad, Dare." Billy said it calm, but strong. "It won't be Dad that's sent to Vietnam. I have to have a public record—"

"A public record," Gram said, shocked. She got up and shut the windows, every single one, then she closed the curtains, and locked the kitchen door, to make sure this conversation stayed a secret in our house. "A public record that you've gone against the government?" Gram's old face was white with worry, and I could see a terrible tremble moving through her hands. "Are you crazy, Billy Kelly? Do you want to go to prison, because that's right where you'll end up."

"He knows that," Dare said, angry. "He knows he'll go to prison, he knows what folks will say. But Reenie and her big mouth has him set against this draft."

"It isn't Reen, Dare," Billy said, before I had a chance to speak. He had the same scared look as Gram, except a whole lot younger, and I wondered if we'd all still be a family once this war was done. "It's me. It's me acting alone. I have to follow my own conscience on this war."

"And that's what Mom believed," I said to take his side.

"To go against the government?" Gram laid her shaky hand over her heart. "To write a letter to the paper for Lake Liberty to read? Or, every town that's taking the Tribune? Do you know you're hurting veterans? And families whose sons are dying for us, Billy. Grandmothers and mothers."

"I'm not against those families," Billy said. "Or their sons. I'm against the draft for me. And I'm against the U.S. forcing boys to fight. Our men are dying in a war that isn't ours. And we're destroying someone's country. Killing strangers."

"Of course we're killing strangers," Dare said. His filthy, freckled face was red with rage. That's how mad he was. "They're our enemies."

"Not mine," Billy said. "I don't know a soul from Vietnam. And I'm supposed to kill them? I can't even make sense of this war or why we're there."

"I've always loved you, Billy." Gram leaned her weight on Billy's chair like she'd lost her strength to stand. "I intend to love you still, but the Kellys serve their country. They do. Unless you don't want to be a Kelly—"

"Gram," I interrupted. I didn't want her saying Billy wouldn't be family if he wrote against this war. "Why can't the Kellys stand with Billy? Why can't we take his side against the draft? You and Dad and Dare. If Mom were here, she'd be on Billy's side. And she'd want us to stand with him."

"Well, she isn't here now, Reen." Gram said it like a fact that I'd forgotten. "So that leaves the shame to me. I'm the one who has to watch my good name be destroyed."

"I don't want to hurt my family—," Billy started, but Gram just waved her hand to make him stop.

"Well, you will," Dare said like he might cry. He crumpled Billy's letter in his fist and threw it to the floor. "You send that to the paper, we'll be cowards."

Isn't this enough to make you write me, Mr. Marsworth? This war is wrecking our whole family. We're cracked right down the middle, and Dad doesn't even know.

I don't need another person mad.

Writing from a House Divided,
Reenie Kelly

P.S. Please don't hold a grudge against me. Dare and Gram hardly have a word to say now, and the cold silence in the Kelly house makes me feel alone.

P.P.S. I wish Billy was in college, and he'd never have to write to the Tribune.

P.P.P.S. Does he HAVE to mail that letter to the paper? Isn't there another way to be against this war?

Tuesday, August 6, 1968

Dear Mr. Marsworth,

I just left that letter and discovered that your paper is still
sitting in your box. Your paper, and my letter to Dr. Roland
Price. It's already after ten o'clock. In a summer full of
papers, you've never left your paper once. Did you hear me out
there ringing? Why didn't you bring it in???

Please write back ASAP and say that you're not sick.
Are you okay alone inside that house?
Is Carl Grace there with you?

Your True Friend,
Reenie Kelly

Dear Mr. Marsworth,

I stayed home from the cottage just to check your box, and my letters and your paper are still there.

Please say that you're not sick.

Please say you haven't disappeared like Asa Carver. One day I knocked on his back door and he'd been moved off to St. Louis by his son.

Please say you're inside sleeping. Please say you had to nap because you're old.

Worried,
Reenie Kelly

P.S. I'm going to wait up in that oak tree just in case you come outside. And where is your assistant, Mr. Marsworth?????

Tuesday, August 6, 1968

Dear Mr. Marsworth,

I sat up in that tree until my legs were nearly numb, then I gave up on my "worry watch" and came home to Gram's house. I hope tomorrow morning all my letters will be gone. I hope tonight you come out for your paper, and take my letters, too.

I guess you could be napping, but would you nap for one whole day?

Mom napped all the time when she was sick. Please say that you're not sick.

Sick with Worry,
Reenie Kelly

P.S. Snow Cone found something important at the cottage, but I don't want to ask about it now, in case you're sick.

P.P.S. Here's some news you'll like: Snow Cone and her dad joined a G.I. march for peace in San Francisco, and she said hundreds of soldiers want our troops sent home. "You don't have to be a hippie," she told Dare, "or a coward to say this war is wrong. Our own soldiers marched against it." I guess you sent a good friend after all.

Wednesday, August 7, 1968

Dear Mr. Marsworth,

Please please please say that you're okay. Are you too weak to walk out to the milk box and bring the papers in? Or did you go away on Tuesday? If you went away, where exactly did you go? When other customers are traveling they put a stop on the Tribune. Shouldn't you have put a stop on your Tribune?

Dare says two papers not picked up doesn't mean a thing, he says his customers leave papers on the doorstep all the time. (Dare's too dumb to worry, but at least he's talking to me now.)

In my heart, I don't believe you'd go away without a word.

Waiting for Your Letter,
Reenie Kelly

CONFIDENTIAL DELIVERY!!! FOR MR. MARSWORTH ONLY

Dear Mr. Marsworth,

So your assistant, Carl Grace, said you "went off for a rest." He came outside while I was clanging and ordered me to stop.

I don't trust him for a minute, Mr. Marsworth. (Isn't he too old for that long hair? And those silly granny glasses?) Wouldn't a GOOD assistant tell me where you went?

Why would that be a secret, Mr. Marsworth???

I said I was Reenie Kelly, your loyal summer pen pal, Billy Kelly's sister, and he ought to bring your papers in before some spider starts to spin a web in sports. Then I opened up your milk box, and handed him my letters and your <u>Tribunes</u> through the fence.

"Don't read any of my letters," I said. "Those are Mr. Marsworth's only." (I hope he doesn't read what I wrote Dr. Roland Price.) "Top secret."

"I understand." He nudged his granny glasses up his nose like he was nervous. "I'll see to it he gets them."

"Where is he on his rest? Is he near enough to visit?"

"He isn't up to visitors." (If this were Alfred Hitchcock, I'd know that Carl Grace had you hostage in that house. Are you in there bound and gagged? Would Sheriff Cutler even help you if I called?)

I don't trust him, Mr. Marsworth, I just don't. I can't trust a person who won't tell me where you've gone.

If you REALLY get my letters, send me one good clue, so I can be sure it isn't Carl Grace reading what I wrote.

And please please please just tell me where you are.

Your Good Friend,
Reenie Kelly

Thursday, August 8, 1968

Dear Miss Kelly,

Rest has been advised, and so I rest.
I shall hope for Billy's letter to be
printed in the paper, and I shall send a
prayer of courage for you all. He has done
a brave thing; he will need you to be brave.
The clue per your request: For whom
does the bell toll?

Sincerely,

H. W. Marsworth

Friday, August 9, 1968

Dear Mr. Marsworth,

It's you!! It's really you!!! It's not your watery blue pen, but I recognize your fancy flowing cursive.

And the answer would be "THEE"! The bell "tolls for THEE"!!!!!! That's the final line from John Donne's poem. I know that part by heart. When I'm clanging at your gate, I'm tolling for thee, too.

Where are you resting, Mr. Marsworth? If you're close enough for Carl Grace to visit, I'm sure you can't be far. Wouldn't you like a visit from a good friend while you rest?

Please say that you're not sick. "Rest" was what Mom did when she was sick. And your letter sure was short. When will you be back in your brick house?

I'll be brave with Billy, don't you worry about that.

True Blue,
Reenie Kelly

P.S. I made this paper chain from the Tribune to cheer you up. Mom loved happy decorations while she rested. She adored the tissue paper garden I made while she was sick. I could do the same for you. When you come home to Hillcrest, could you hang the paper chain out on your gate as a signal you've returned? I'll be on the lookout, Mr. Marsworth!!!

P.P.S. Please tell me when you're well enough to answer one small question. There's a MAJOR cottage mystery I need your help to solve. Snow Cone has a theory, but I need to know from YOU.

P.P.P.S. I mailed Dr. Roland Price my letter, and I hope it does the trick. Could creepy-but-maybe-sort-of-okay Carl Grace go to the Conoco and talk to Billy about Brandenbrook? Do you still want me to deliver that letter Carl Grace wrote Billy? I have it hidden in Gram's attic, you just say the word.

P.P.P.P.S. While we were gone down to the cottage, someone left a paper bag of dog poop in Dare's tent. (SOMEONE = YOU KNOW WHO.) The place stinks to high heaven, and now Dare has to sleep under the stars. Float, too. They've been devoured by mosquitoes, but Dare's too mad about his pup tent to sleep inside Gram's house. He won't let those bullies force him from the woods.

P.P.P.P.P.S. Ooops, I shouldn't end with trouble. A letter should be cheery when the receiver might be sick. (We learned that from Mrs. Lamb.) Do you remember those marigold seeds you gave me back in June? Well, they're growing at your cottage! Bright green stalks are rising from the dirt. A garden will be blooming for you soon! Will you come down to see them? We could have a picnic on your porch!!

Friday, August 9, 1968

Dear Mr. Marsworth,

I'm not really going to send this letter to you now, not because you might be sick, but because I know the thing I did was wrong. And you would say it's wrong. I'm just writing you to get it off my chest.

I'll pretend that you forgive me. Or God forgives me. Or maybe Mom forgives me up in heaven, or Dad in North Dakota would forgive me if he knew, but Dare says Dad would take our side. Either way, I want my guilty conscience to be clear.

We did it for revenge, but it was wrong. It was really Dare's idea, but I helped.

I didn't have to follow Dare, but I still did.

I didn't want to be a chicken, especially to Dare. I hate to be a chicken.

Today we found Rat and Cutler's souped-up Sting-Rays at the beach and stuck a dozen carpet tacks into their tires until we heard a little hiss. Hiss. Hiss. Hiss. Snow Cone didn't want to help, but she stood watch.

The dog poop they tossed into Dare's tent was worse than what we did. Everything they've done to us is worse than four flat tires.

Still I know we shouldn't have done it, and I feel a little sick.

I told Gram I had the flu, and she sent me up to bed with ginger ale and old saltines. The truth is, I'm scared down to my knees what Sheriff Cutler might do next.

I wish that I could change it, but I can't.

Delinquent,
Reenie Kelly

P.S. This part might be the worst . . . Dare found the pack of carpet tacks inside your shed.

P.P.S. I am SINCERELY TRULY TERRIBLY ABSOLUTELY DEEP-DOWN SORRY, Mr. Marsworth.

P.P.P.S. I'm writing a new letter so you'll NEVER know the rotten truth of Reenie Kelly.

Friday, August 9, 1968

Dear Mr. Marsworth,

I'm in bed with some dumb sickness, but I'm sure tomorrow morning I'll wake up good as new. Are you almost good as new?

Guess what? I'm teaching Snow Cone how to swim! She's learned to hold her breath and put her face into the water, and tomorrow she's promised to go under by herself.

Dare likes to put her on his back and pretend that he's a dolphin, and the three of us play Marco Polo in the shallow end with Float. I bet you know Float always finds us first.

Snow Cone loves your cottage just like we do. The shutters are all painted cobalt blue. Billy's driving out on Sunday to see the work we've done.

He mailed his letter to the paper, and every day that they don't print it, I can tell Gram is relieved. Dare, too. Things are ALMOST back to normal at our house. I think everybody's wishing the draft just disappears. Some days that war seems so far away it can't be real, and I wonder how a thing that far can wreck so many lives.

Is that a selfish thing to say while Skip's in Vietnam?

Did Carl Grace go to the Conoco? He can talk to Billy now. Dr. Roland Price should have my letter.

> Good Night, Sweet Dreams,
> Your True Friend,
> Reenie Kelly

Saturday, August 10, 1968

Dear Mr. Marsworth,

Could you please just send one letter, one little tiny note so I know that you're okay? Carl Grace can leave it in your box. I know he takes my letters, because every day they're gone.

The worst part of every morning is opening your milk box. It used to be the best part of my route.

Can't you just write a few words while you rest?

Lonely for Your Letters,
Reenie Kelly

Saturday, August 10, 1968

Dear Mr. Marsworth!!!!

Hold on to your hat!!!!!

Brandenbrook wrote Billy!!!!

A great big silver envelope addressed to William Kelly was delivered to Gram's house!!!!!

We all waited while he opened it, all three of us gathered around Billy on Gram's old saggy couch. My heart was pounding in my ears with fear and hope.

"What is it?" Gram asked, but she let Billy read the letter while I flipped through the shiny catalog with bright college boys like Billy leaning against trees, or entering brick buildings, or laughing on the lawn. Boys playing baseball. Boys reading great big books. You were right, Brandenbrook fits Billy like a glove.

"What's it say?" I said, when Billy finished with the letter. I was praying Dr. Roland Price didn't tell him what I wrote.

"I guess I've been recommended to their college," Billy said, confused. He turned the letter over like he was looking for a clue, then he looked at the silver envelope again.

"That's great!" I could've jumped with joy, but I stayed put.

"Recommended you for what?" Gram took the letter from his hand, and Dare snatched away the catalog, and Billy caught me with his eyes, but I just gave a shrug.

"That's amazing!" I said, grinning. "Someone must've known you were a nearly straight-A student."

Gram peered down at the envelope and frowned. "I hate to say this, Billy, but there must be some mistake. Why would a school in Pennsylvania write to you? William Kelly in Lake Liberty?"

"Pennsylvania?" Dare chimed in. "You mean you'd get to see the Bucs play at Forbes Field? Ain't Pennsylvania way off by New York?"

"It is." Gram snatched the catalog from Dare. "Don't talk so dumb, Dare Kelly."

"Brandenbrook?" Dare said. "Ain't that the name on that old red pennant in—?" I kicked him in the shin before he said another word. (I didn't want Gram to think about you now.)

"This school sure looks expensive," Gram said like she was sad. "I wish there was a way—"

"Didn't he say there was a scholarship?" I leaned closer to the letter still in Billy's hand. "Yep," I said, pointing to the print. "Right there. 'Scholarships available.'"

"And what about the rest of his expenses?" Gram said. "College costs a pretty penny."

I took the letter out of Billy's hand and read it for myself, starting with the sentence: "You've been highly recommended as a student we might want." "It says right here, 'Financial aid is still available, and arrangements can be made to help defray the costs. Brandenbrook is committed to supporting worthy students with a wide array of scholarships.' 'A wide array,'" I said to Billy. "And I can see you sitting on this lawn, I really can. Next year in their catalog they'll show you playing your guitar."

"You're always dreaming big, Pup." Billy said it with a sigh, like college was a kid-dream he'd outgrown.

"Too big if you ask me," Gram said. She patted Billy on the knee, and struggled from the couch. "I hate to see you disappointed, Billy," she said sadly. "I wish I was a millionaire. I do."

"Does this mean you won't get drafted?" Dare said, excited. "So you don't have to put that letter in the paper after all? You can just go off to Pennsylvania and read books?"

"In someone's stubborn dream," Billy said. He looked at me, then he slid it all back into the envelope: the catalog, the letter, the papers to apply. "Who recommended me to them, Reen?" he asked me in a whisper once Gram had left the room, and I guessed that Carl Grace hadn't talked to Billy yet. "Why would a private school in Pennsylvania write to me at Gram's?"

"How would I know," I lied, but my cheeks were burning pink. I can lie better than Billy, but I hate to lie to him. "But time is of the essence. You want a scholarship to Brandenbrook, you better write them now. It's September in three weeks."

"I was right about the name on that red pennant." Dare returned my shin kick, but his was twice as hard. "And now Billy can skip that stupid letter to the paper! He'll go to school in Pennsylvania, and he'll get to see the Bucs!"

Did you recommend him, Mr. Marsworth? Did your assistant, Carl

Grace? Or did I recommend him with that letter that I wrote??????
Maybe Dr. Price didn't throw my letter in the trash!!!!!!

If you need good news to help your rest, I have it here!!!! After
our summer full of worry, Brandenbrook asked Billy to apply!!!

A THOUSAND BILLION TRILLION GAZILLION THANK-YOUS,
MR. MARSWORTH!
thank you thank you thank you thank you thank you thank you thank you
thank you thank you thank you thank you thank you thank you thank you
thank you thank you thank you thank you thank you thank you thank you
thank you thank you thank you thank you thank you thank you thank you
thank you thank you thank you thank you thank you thank you thank you
thank you thank you thank you thank you thank you thank you thank you
thank you thank you thank you thank you thank you thank you thank you
thank you thank you thank you thank you thank you thank you thank you
thank you thank you thank you thank you thank you thank you thank you
thank you thank you thank you thank you thank you thank you thank you
thank you thank you thank you thank you thank you thank you thank you
thank you thank you thank you thank you thank you thank you thank you
thank you thank you thank you thank you thank you thank you thank you
thank you thank you thank you thank you thank you

I'd keep going, but my arm is falling off. And I have to run
this letter to your house!

Saturday, August 10, 1968

Dear Miss Kelly,

Please don't be alarmed by the strange
script; I've asked Carl Grace to take
dictation while I rest.

What truly joyous news to receive at
this late hour. It feels as though the light
of hope is filling this whole room. Light
of possibility; light of peace for Billy. I
shall imagine him as you have—a thriving
student on that campus, exactly where he
should be. Billy playing his guitar out on
the lawn. Someday you shall see that sight
in person; I am confident you will.

No need to thank me, dear Miss Kelly.
It is you who made this possible in more
ways than you know.

And now, dear child, Billy must apply.

Sincerely,

H. W. Marsworth

Sunday, August 11, 1968

Dear Mr. Marsworth,

Billy's in the Sunday paper!!!! He's right there on 12A!!!!! The second letter under "Readers Write About the War."

It's 5:00 a.m., Gram and Dare and Billy are asleep. I'm writing you by flashlight huddled on Gram's steps. I had to swipe the Bensons' paper, so I could put a copy with this letter because I know you'd want to see it from me first. (Don't worry, Mr. Marsworth, I'll run down to the stand and replace the stolen paper as soon as I'm done writing you this news!)

Billy Kelly published!!!

I just had to brag to you before our family falls apart, and Gram's good name is ruined, and whatever other bad things will happen to us now. (Should I expect a bloody chicken at Gram's door?)

I'm so proud to be his sister!

I've never been so proud. I wish Mom were here to see it!!!!

Billy Kelly famous!!!! Billy Kelly in a paper as big as the Tribune!!!!

P.S. I'm going to knock on Snow Cone's window so she can see it, too!

If we fight and die in the pursuit for South Vietnam's freedom, but deny the young men of America the freedom of good conscience, what kind of country are we? Are we a country of liberty and justice? Freedom for all men? What is it we believe, if we think our young should follow blindly, should be forced to serve their country in a war they think is wrong? Is that what we call democracy? If we imprison our own young for saying they won't kill, are we better than the Communists we're killing to defeat? I can't answer for another, but I'll answer for myself. The fight for freedom starts at home with the right to burn our draft cards, to protest war, to refuse to take a life if our conscience says we can't. It starts with conscience before country, without imprisonment or shame. If my own country won't allow me the freedom to choose peace, what is it that we hope to win in Vietnam?

—WILLIAM KELLY, Lake Liberty

Dear Mr. Marsworth,

So far nothing SUPER horrible has happened from that letter,
unless you count Gram saying she wouldn't read it, then going
back to bed too sick for Sunday Mass, and telling all of us to
skip church, which she never, ever does. (The skipping-church
part doesn't count as horrible.) Or unless you count Dare asking
Billy, "Why'd you send that crap into the paper if you're going
off to school?"

He's out sulking in his tent now, I guess the stink of dog
poop must be gone.

Snow Cone stopped by this morning with a neon peace
medallion she'd made from yarn and wood. No boy would ever
want to wear it, but Billy pretended like he might. At least he
put it on while she was here. She asked Billy for his autograph,
but Billy only blushed.

We're still driving to the cottage in Gram's old Plymouth
like we planned. At least Billy, me, and Snow Cone. (She just
ran home to change into her suit.) Dare says he's staying home
to guard Gram's house from vandals, but Dare's just being
stupid. Nothing bad will happen on a Sunday afternoon.

I feel so proud of Billy's "public record" in the paper I
could burst!

I know pride's a deadly sin, but I don't think the sin is
deadly if you're proud for someone else.

Please, please write me, Mr. Marsworth. I can tell this all to Snow Cone, but you're the one who matters to me most. Is your resting nearly done?

Still Lonely,
Reenie Kelly

Sunday, August 11, 1968

Dear Miss Kelly,

I shall cherish Billy's letter, just as I treasure yours.

What a thoughtful, brilliant boy, although I suppose "young man" would be more apt. At my late age, I can't help but think of Billy as a boy.

It truly meant the world to hear him on the page, to hear the voice of Billy Kelly, that brother you so love.

I hope the Bensons' _Tribune_ was replaced as you had promised; I would hate to think I have a stolen piece of someone's paper.

Sincerely,

H. W. Marsworth

P.S. As told to Carl Grace.

Monday, August 12, 1968

Dear Mr. Marsworth,

I wish you'd been home this morning to see me open up your milk box and howl under the moon. A happy happy howl. I might have woken your whole block, but I don't care. It's worth a wild happy howl when I hear from my good friend.

Are you STILL resting, Mr. Marsworth? Gram's been "resting" here with me. She's been resting in her bedroom since she saw Billy's words in print. For the first time in twenty-two years (that's how long that Gram's been widowed), Gram called in sick today to Brindle Drug. She also called Dad in North Dakota, but he hasn't called back yet. (I don't know how Dad CAN call, Gram's had the phone unplugged.)

Maybe NO ONE read that letter in the paper after all, maybe Billy isn't famous, because nothing bad has happened to us yet. Gram's good name isn't ruined, she ought to go to work. Instead I have to bring her toast and tea.

If you come home, I'll bring you toast and tea. I won't talk your ear off, I promise that I won't.

Florence Nightingale in Training,
Reenie Kelly, Nurse

P.S. While I'm taking care of Gram, I'm going to read through that pack of papers Brandenbrook sent Billy. Don't worry, I won't fill out his application, but he better get it done while there's still time. Are you ABSOLUTELY SURE about the scholarship? Billy still says we can't afford it, and Gram says, "There's no such thing as free lunch." I understand that adage, Mr. Marsworth, but is Brandenbrook free lunch?

P.P.S. Speaking of lunch, it's already past eleven and Gram's still sleeping in the darkness with her bedroom curtain closed. (She's closed every curtain in the house.) I went out to Dare's tent to tell him nothing bad had happened, not one teeny-weeny thing, and he and Float ought to come inside for tuna sandwiches and cards. I won't tell you what Dare said, you're just too good.

P.P.P.S. Tick tock tick tock tick. It's nearly 2:15 now. Gram's gone to the bathroom twice, drank a glass of water, and put an ice bag on her head. I read through Billy's papers, and he needs to write an essay to apply, plus get two letters from his teachers. At least I could write his teachers; I've got time for that.

P.P.P.P.S. I just finished writing Mrs. Lamb and Skip, and I sent them each a copy of the letter Billy wrote. (I found four copies on Gram's street just by checking neighbors' burn bins.)

I did ask Mrs. Lamb to write a letter to Brandenbrook for Billy, because Billy was a favorite, and she always told me that. I know she'd want to see his name in print!!!! I hope Denton Elementary doesn't just stick my letter in her box and let it sit until summer ends. I hope someone in the office calls to tell her she's got mail. (I wish I would get mail!!)

P.P.P.P.P.S. I sent Skip Dennis the Menace, and I told him I was heartbroken to hear he'd lost his best friend Jackie Moon. I know I should have written sooner, but Jackie Moon, and Skip's last letter, still make my stomach hurt. And I feel a little guilty helping Billy, but not Skip. Do you think President Johnson got my letter? Do you think a brand-new president will end the war in Vietnam before I'm finished with sixth grade? Will the Minnesota senator for peace win the next election? Billy says Senator McCarthy will bring the soldiers home, but Gram won't let us put a sign in her front yard.

P.P.P.P.P.P.S. I'm going to sneak this over to get out of Gram's dark house. Just writing about Skip leaves a funny feeling in my throat.

P.P.P.P.P.P.P.S. I think I'll sneak a stop at Snow Cone's house. No company for us, Gram says, not even Snow Cone.

Monday, August 12, 1968

Dear Mr. Marsworth!!!!!!!!

You're home!!! You're home!!!! Did you look out your window
and see me jumping for PURE JOY!!! You hung my paper
chain across your gate just like I asked. It looked like Christmas
morning lit up in the sun!!! It felt like Christmas morning!!!

Could you please come to the window and give me one
quick wave? Or open up your window and yell one quick hello?

Is your resting nearly finished?

Are you fit as a fiddle???

Can you type again??? Will Carl Grace still take
dictation? Is he in your house with you right now?

I'm going to toll your bell tomorrow, in case you'll come
outside!!!! A little sunshine might be good for you, it'd sure
be good for Gram. In case you come outside to meet me,
please bring Clyde!!!

When Gram goes back to work tomorrow (she better go
to work!), I'm going to bake a "WELCOME HOME" cake and
bring it to your house!!!!

Chocolate or vanilla? I have recipes for both!!!!

Your Ecstatic Betty Crocker,
Reenie Kelly

Tuesday, August 13, 1968

Dear Miss Kelly,

Please forgo the cake; I'd much prefer you play with
Dare and Snow Cone. The final days of summer are
swift to disappear.

Sincerely,

H. W. Marsworth

H. W. Marsworth

P.S. A full scholarship is possible with all expenses
paid. If Billy is accepted, Dr. Roland Price will
keep his word.

Dear Mr. Marsworth,

I wished I had a letter when I dropped off your morning paper, and then I double-wished it when I found yours in the box.

You're typing, Mr. Marsworth, which means you must be well!!! I HOPE it means you're well.

Could you please tell me that you're well? I'll leave a YES or NO for you to circle, and put back in your box.

Are you well enough to hear the Kelly news? (Most of it's not happy, so if you're too busy resting, just toss this whole sad story in the trash.) I've got a lot of time to write because I'm still trapped indoors with Gram. Don't even bother asking about Dare.

I'll start with the mostly bad-but-good news because you need to know that first.

I guess folks DID read Billy's letter (that's the little-bit-of-both news, but now it just seems bad) and I can't say how many, but enough that some folks phoned Mr. Casey, and said they'd take their business to the Texaco, and others pulled up to the pumps but they wouldn't let Billy help. Not every customer, but still Billy had to watch while Mr. Casey worked.

When Billy came home from the Conoco, he looked sadder than I'd seen him this whole summer. Gram didn't get out of bed, and Dare refused to come inside, and as soon as Billy plugged the phone back in the wall it started ringing off the hook with angry calls. Calls from strangers and Gram's friends, and Billy listened to their lectures and their insults while I heated up a can of mushroom soup to split for supper.

"I want that phone unplugged," Gram ordered from her bedroom, and Billy yanked the phone cord from the wall.

"They won't call forever," Billy said, but I could tell he wasn't sure. "Did Gram get out of bed at all?" He pulled the last dry heel of Wonder Bread out of the bag, then set it lonely on a plate beside our soup. "Is that all we've got to eat?" he asked. "What did you find for lunch?"

"Tuna fish. The last of Gram's canned dills."

"I guess we'll need to go for groceries."

"Us? Go outside in public? After all those calls that just came in?" I wasn't in a hurry to hear what Piggly Wiggly shoppers had to say to us tonight.

He pulled a dusty can of fruit cocktail from the cupboard. "What else can we do? We can't hide out here and starve. Her canned food won't last forever. And we better buy some groceries while I still have a job."

"You really think you could get fired?" I remembered Mr. Casey standing on the sidewalk one Sunday after Mass, and telling Gram he hadn't had a better summer boy in years.

"I guess I'm scared I might. Mr. Casey can't afford to lose the business, and he can't afford to let me sit while he pumps gas. He's got cars to fix." Billy set the soup and bread down on a plate to take to Gram. "What about your route? Any problems with your customers this morning?"

"Not a one," I said, but I wished Billy hadn't asked that, because to tell the truth, I hadn't thought about our route, or how Dare and I could lose it, or how customers might quit, but then I thought about the Canes with their son gone to the Army, and crabby Mrs. Strait who blabbed to Gram about the book, and the Lonergans and Heanys, who'd booed those peace teens last month at the parade, and the Olsons and the Petersons, who let their little kids throw candy at them, too. All families with a flag in their front yard. "You think they'd quit the paper over this?"

"I think a lot of stuff might happen." Billy frowned, then pointed toward the bedroom where Gram was still inside in darkness. "Like that," he said. "And all of it my fault."

"Not yours," I said. "You didn't make this—"

Oops, hold on, Mr. Marsworth, I have to stop this story because there's someone at Gram's door.

BACK, and now I have a BETTER story, but I don't have time to write it to you yet. Stay tuned this afternoon. For now, I'll drop this letter with a clang, so at least you'll know how glad I was to see that short typed note inside your box.

To Be Continued,
Reenie Kelly

P.S. Are you well? Please circle YES or NO.

Dear Mr. Marsworth,

Okay, before Gram calls us down for supper, I'm going to tell you all that happened when the knock came at the door. (That's right, Mr. Marsworth, Gram is OUT OF BED, even if she's only cooking creamed corn and canned hash.) There's so much I have to tell you, and so much I have to ask, please please please just say that we can meet one afternoon.

You said yourself, August will be quick to disappear.

All I want from August is one meeting with my friend!

Here's the long story that I promised earlier today. I have lots of bad news, too, and a mystery to solve, but first I'll start with story #1.

STORY #1. This Unexpected Tale Opens with a Knock on Gram's Front Door . . .

Knock knock knock.

Enter fancy Mrs. Brindle.

Do you know Mrs. Brindle? Mr. Brindle's pretty wife, but she's rarely in the store. Mrs. Brindle with her gleaming golden Cadillac, her patent-leather purse, and her pink high-heeled shoes. Pink cotton gloves in August. Frosty beehive hairdo stacked up on her head.

Anyway, when I answered Gram's front door, Mrs. Brindle waltzed right in, stinking up the room with sweet perfume.

When I said Gram was fast asleep, that she'd been sick in bed since Sunday, Mrs. Brindle said she'd be glad to wait until Gram woke. Then she sat on Gram's old couch, crossed her ankles, and inched her gloves off slowly like she planned to wait all day.

"You may go about your business," she said kindly, but I couldn't. I couldn't finish off your letter with fancy Mrs. Brindle in Gram's house.

"She won't see anyone," I said. "Not even you."

"Is it that letter Billy wrote to the Tribune?" Mrs. Brindle raised her perfect eyebrows, and I gave a silent nod.

"Please tell her I'm not leaving," Mrs. Brindle ordered. "Not until we've had a word."

"I don't know," I stalled. The last time I'd gone into Gram's dark bedroom, she'd been curled up like a caterpillar staring at the wall.

"I do," Mrs. Brindle said. "Please go tell her now."

I walked into Gram's room and closed the door on Mrs. Brindle, because I knew without Gram saying, she wouldn't want Mrs. Brindle to see her messy bed or Gram curled up in the darkness staring at the wall.

"I heard." Gram sighed. "It's Gwendolyn."

"She won't leave," I said. I handed Gram her flowered housecoat and set her slippers on the floor beside her bed.

"I look frightful." Gram fluffed her gray hair with her fingers. She pinched both cheeks for color and gave another sigh.

"Billy's really sorry," I said to Gram again. I'd already said it four or five times, but Gram just shrugged it off. "He didn't want this trouble for you, Gram."

"Of course he's sorry," Gram said. "And he'll be sorrier than this, you mark my words." Then she opened up her door and hobbled from her room.

"Gwendolyn." Gram sounded like her throat was thick with dust. "I'm not up to guests, as you can see."

"Are you truly sick, Blanche Kelly?" Mrs. Brindle asked matter-of-factly. "Or is this about that letter your grandson wrote to the Tribune?"

"There isn't any difference." Gram eased her way into the rocker like it hurt her bones to sit.

"Don't be silly," Mrs. Brindle said. "You can't stay home sick because of something that boy wrote."

"I'm sick enough," Gram said. "And you don't need the Kellys' trouble at the store. Your business will go bad, and your family has been good to me—"

"Nonsense." Mrs. Brindle waved her gloves, disgusted. "We can't run the store without you, you know that good and well. How dare you leave us in the lurch so you can mope. You didn't write that letter, Billy did. The young folks are all foolish now, you're not the first good family to have trouble with a child."

"All my boys were good—" Gram started, but Mrs. Brindle cut her off.

"Blanche, it's only his opinion. And Billy has every right to say this war is wrong. Dr. Spock believes it's wrong, and we still sell his mother-and-child guidebook in the store."

"You see," I said to Gram, but she said, "Hush."

Mrs. Brindle glanced out Gram's screen door, then lowered her strong voice. "I shouldn't be saying this in public, but I don't want my own boys in that draft. Warren's fifteen now, Rusty thirteen, Len and Les eleven. I don't want a single one sent to Vietnam. (The Brindle kids are rich enough for college, but I didn't tell her that.) It might have to be the women who take the side of our young men against this draft. The mothers and the grandmothers. I don't imagine that their fathers—"

"Sisters, too," I added. "I'm on Billy's side."

"Well, good for you," Mrs. Brindle answered, but she kept her eyes on Gram. "We need you at the store, Blanche. You're strong enough to take whatever flack some folks might give. You're not the kind of woman to go to bed and quit. And every day you're gone is a day that Gordy makes me work the counter by myself. You know I hate that job. Or any job. Gordy's a fine husband, but I don't want him for my boss." She stood up from the couch and inched the gloves back on her hands. "So we'll see you bright and early?"

"But what about your business?" Gram said. "Wasn't Monday slow? Today? Folks will stay away."

"We'll bounce back," she said. "And you know you need the money. I'm not sure that Casey's—"

"No," Gram said. "I wouldn't be a bit surprised if he lets Billy go."

"But he said Billy was the best," I said. "He told you that himself when summer started. Standing on the sidewalk when we were new to town."

"He can't run a charity," Mrs. Brindle said like I was stupid. "If the men refuse to buy their gas at Casey's, or bring their cars in for repair—"

"Well, anyway," I bragged, "Billy's going off to college in Pennsylvania soon. He won't need that job at Casey's—"

"My goodness, Pennsylvania." Mrs. Brindle said it like Pennsylvania was a joke. "Really, Blanche?"

"Oh this girl and her notions," Gram said, embarrassed. "I swear she'll be the death of me."

"Not before tomorrow morning." Mrs. Brindle gave a little laugh. "I have tennis at 10:30." She opened up her patent-leather purse, and handed me a stick of Dentyne gum. "So bright and early," she told Gram. "I'll tell Gordy to expect you. He'll be thrilled."

"What do you say, Reen?" Gram was pushing for a thank-you for that gum.

"I say I'm right about that college. Billy's going to go."

You know I like to have the last word, Mr. Marsworth. And it was good to get it this time, with Gram and Mrs. Brindle acting like my plan for Billy's college was a scheme that couldn't come true. Just so you know that I'm not awful, I ended with a fakey: "Thank you for the Dentyne, ma'am. I'll share half with Float!"

Aren't you glad to get some good news, Mr. Marsworth? Fancy Mrs. Brindle saying Billy might be right about the draft! Gram going back to work!!! Me set free to play with Snow Cone at your cottage all day long!!!!!! (Dare can sulk out in Gram's woods until he rots.)

Aren't you glad to get a happy story from this house?

Well-Mannered Mostly,
Reenie Kelly

P.S. Can you stand a little bit of bad news?
1. So far the Gustafsons and Olsons have canceled their subscription to the paper. Dare already lost four houses, but he says he doesn't care. He says he's going to quit the paper as soon as Dad comes home.
2. Yesterday, Billy got a pile of mail, but none of it was good. He has another stack today, but I put them in the trash. I don't think I like getting mail anymore. You can't believe the horrible, hateful, hurtful things strangers wrote to Billy, and you can't believe how low he looked reading their mean words.

Tuesday, August 13, 1968

Dear Miss Kelly,

Unfortunately, I know well what those envelopes contain.
I'm sorry for whatever vile insults Billy bears. Unless
I am familiar with an address, or it's a bill that should
be paid, I dispose of all suspicious mail now unopened.
Perhaps Billy might consider doing so as well.

Were you able to buy food? Perhaps it would be
helpful if Carl Grace bought some groceries at Piggly
Wiggly for you all.

Sincerely,

H. W. Marsworth

H. W. Marsworth

P.S. I do hope your "last words" were correct. Would you
please confirm when Billy has applied to Brandenbrook? Of
all the good news you might offer, I shall consider that
the best.

Dear Mr. Marsworth,

Someone hurled a brick through Gram's front window, and it crashed into the couch, where Billy was asleep!!! It could've hit his head! That's how close it was. Shards of glass were everywhere, including Billy's skin. Dare came running from his tent the second that he heard it, but he only saw a pickup truck tearing down Gram's hill.

Gram wouldn't call the sheriff—you know why.

That's all I can tell you at 4:30 in the morning.

Gram and Billy are exhausted. I'm exhausted and shaking in my skin.

Billy's going to drive us on our routes.

Shattered,
Reenie Kelly

Wednesday, August 14, 1968

Dear Mr. Marsworth,

Billy never drove us, because someone slashed three tires on Gram's Plymouth, plus they shaving-creamed the front seat so we're stranded. (When Gram walked outside to see it, her tired eyes filled up with tears.)

I KNOW you KNOW who did it, and Dare and I know for sure who did it! Rat and Cutler might be slow to get revenge, but somehow they always do.

Gram and Billy had to walk to work this morning. A mile down to Main Street is a long way for Gram to walk. A long, long way.

Dare and I already carried the broken window to the hardware store, and Mr. Rash didn't seem a bit surprised to hear someone threw a brick into Gram's house. "Probably for that letter," Mr. Rash said, his voice suddenly sour with disgust. "You folks got what you deserved."

He was nothing like the man who had joked with us all summer, or given us Tootsie Pops for shopping in his store. That man was another Mr. Rash. "Could be months before I get to it," he said about Gram's window. Then he walked off to the back room without another word.

Do you think he'll ever fix it? Because he acted like he wouldn't.

Billy taped a filmy piece of plastic over Gram's gone

window, but one hard rain and Gram's living room will flood.

I did my best to clean Gram's car, but it still reeks of Aero Shave, and there's a soapy, slimy feeling I can't scrub from the cloth. Right now, Dare has the Plymouth jacked up in Gram's driveway, and when he finally gets that tire loose we'll haul it down to Casey's to get patched. Dare says only one tire at a time because we only have one jack. When it comes to car repair and tires, Dare gets to be the expert. I didn't spend my days in Denton helping Dad work on our car.

Dare says if Gram's tires can't be patched we'll have to pay for new ones, which means all the college money that we've saved will go to Gram. We know we have to pay, because those slashed tires and that shaving cream aren't really Billy's fault. Gram and Billy blame his letter, but the blame belongs to us. (I'll explain it to you someday, Mr. Marsworth. I'm really too ashamed to tell you now.)

The only good news at the Kellys'? For the first time since that letter, we're back on the same side. Gram made Dare and me walk our routes together, and to tell the truth, I was glad to have Dare with me in the darkness, plotting how he'd fix Gram's car and get revenge once and for all. Dare revved up for action was better than his silence, or me walking on those empty streets alone.

Still Rattled,
Reenie Kelly

P.S. Just in case you left a letter, I ditched Dare at Snow Cone's window while I finished delivering on Hillcrest. (Did you ever think Dare Kelly would have a summer crush? I never did.) Thank you for those few words you left inside your box. Maybe after reading this you'll leave a few more words.

Wednesday, August 14, 1968

Dear Mr. Marsworth,

Did you send Carl Grace to drive Gram home from work????

Gram said he pulled up to Brindle Drug just as she stepped outside at 5:15, and he offered her a ride, and she said yes. (Coincidence or Mr. Marsworth's kindness? I'm going to vote for #2.)

Apparently Gram knows Carl from the drugstore, and she knows he's your assistant, and she still took the ride. Maybe things are changing, Mr. Marsworth. If Gram likes Carl Grace enough to take a ride, she might just like you, too. ☺

Which leads me to a question I've been waiting WEEKS to ask. Have you gotten enough rest for one big question? I'm hoping that you have. I'd forget it if I could, but I just can't.

You know that Kelly-Marsworth tie the sheriff mentioned in Gram's kitchen? The one Gram wouldn't explain?

Well, Snow Cone found a clue carved into a stump out in your woods.

Does D.W.M. + E.E.B.= FOREVER sound familiar, Mr. Marsworth?

Snow Cone didn't tell Dare she found it, and I didn't tell him either, because if E.E.B. is actually Elizabeth (Betsy) Ellen Brighton (later Betsy Kelly) it should be F.J.K. + E.E.B.= FOREVER in that heart. To tell the truth it made me sad to see it, and I hope Dad never sees it, because he always said that Mom was his one and only girl.

251

Am I right that E.E.B. is Betsy?

Did our Elizabeth Ellen Brighton love your David, Donald, Dennis? Were they like Beth and Billy? Is that how you knew Mom? Did she spend time at your cottage just like us?

And is that D.W.M.'s bear on the twin bed in your cottage? Are those his tennis shoes left on your front rug? His scooter in rafters of the shed? His baseball mitt hanging on the hook? Was it D.'s collection of old baseball cards Dare found in a box? (We're not snooping through your shed, but I confess we like to look.)

And if all those things are D.'s, where is he now? Is he living in Lake Liberty? Did he marry someone else the way Mom did? (Did Dad know that D. and E. were once FOREVER?)

Do you have grandkids, Mr. Marsworth? Do they ever come to see you? Am I the only kid that writes you letters? (I hope I'm the only kid ☺.)

Please don't be mad about my questions, and don't say that I'm a snoop. Some things I need to know and this is one. If Mom REALLY IS E.E.B., then D.W.M. + E.E.B = FOREVER is a lot to keep inside. If your D. is kind like you, I guess I'm not surprised Mom loved him once. Was your D. disappointed when Mom married someone else? Did our families turn to enemies when Mom quit D. for Dad?

You can go ahead and tell me, because I won't tell Dare or Billy, or any other living soul, cross my heart and hope to die. I'll keep our secret story to myself.

You can tell me EVERYTHING. In fact, I think you should. Don't you think E.E.B.'s devoted daughter has a right to know???

Impatiently Awaiting All Your Answers,
Reenie Kelly

P.S. I forgot to say it was extra-kind of Carl Grace to offer to drive Gram every day until we get the tires fixed. Billy stayed late tonight at Casey's to see if that first tire can be patched. I guess that means he hasn't lost his job.

P.P.S. I just realized it's been a WHILE since a letter came from Beth. Do you think maybe Beth and Billy aren't FOREVER anymore????

P.P.P.S. Don't you worry, Mr. Marsworth, I'll make sure Billy gets that Brandenbrook application in the mail, even if he works late on Gram's tires, and even if he doesn't have a minute to apply.

P.P.P.P.S. After last night's brick, we've decided to stand guard tonight so no one hurts Gram's house. Dare's taking 12—4, and he's sleeping with his baseball bat in case any trouble comes. I'm taking the first shift, which means I've got the lonely hours until midnight to think of Mom and D., and why they were forever once, and Skip without his best friend Jackie Moon, and Billy getting drafted if Brandenbrook says no, or if he doesn't get a scholarship, or if he has to go to prison just to stay out of the war. And now I'm thinking of those letters calling him a weakling and a weasel, a coward and a traitor, and the one where someone wrote, "You deserve to die a terrible death." I guess I'd rather think of Mom and D. Could you send an honest answer, because the Marsworth-Kelly story is the one I really want?

Thursday, August 15, 1968

Dear Mr. Marsworth,

Nothing in your milk box when I dropped off last night's letter,
but I thought you'd want to know we made it to the morning
safe and sound.

  I was still up on my guard shift when Billy came home
close to midnight, and I eavesdropped through the screen door
while he and Dare talked on Gram's steps. Billy said again that
he was sorry for Gram's Plymouth, and the brick through the
front window, and all the hate that Dare would face now in his
life. He said he'd tried his best to be a brother Dare admired,
someone to look up to, and he hoped someday he'd get to be
that brother once again. "I didn't mean to let you down, Dare,"
he said sadly. "But there are different kinds of courage—"

  "I understand your kind," Dare said, "I do. Even if I can't
agree—" Suddenly he stopped to give Billy a big hug. You
might not know this, Mr. Marsworth, but Dare Kelly doesn't
hug a soul except for Float!!! "Right or wrong about this
conscience stuff, you're still my brother, Billy. Folks come
after one Kelly, they come after us all."

  "But I don't want them after you, Dare," Billy said. "Or
any of my family."

  "We're tough enough to take it," Dare said, and Float
barked to agree, and I crept up to the attic so they wouldn't
know I spied.

Can you believe it, Mr. Marsworth? Dare Kelly's almost on our side!

When Carl Grace drove up for Gram this morning, I ran out to his car to thank him for his help. All his help, including Brandenbrook. Then I asked if you were rested, and if rested meant you're well, and did he think a couple questions in a letter could have worn you out again. (I don't want to wear you out with all my questions.)

"I can't speak for Mr. Marsworth," Carl Grace said quickly before Gram got to the car. "But he was typing in his study when I left."

Does that mean an answer's coming? Does that mean you'll tell me ALL?

I'm heading to the cottage, so you don't have to rush. If you need to nap between the sentences, go ahead and doze.

Still Dwelling on Those Six Initials,
Reenie Kelly

P.S. The first tire can't be patched, but Billy plans to stay tonight to try to fix the second. Don't worry, Mr. Marsworth, I'll find a way to help him get that application done. I can't write the essay (well I "could," but "shouldn't"), but I can help him fill out the papers: name and address, parents—all that stuff.

P.P.S. Mrs. Lamb still hasn't answered, but I wrote to Billy's high school English teacher, Mrs. Lafayette, the only Denton teacher to bring a baked ham to our house when Mom was sick. I remember how young and shy she seemed standing in our doorway, telling Billy she was sorry to hear Mom wasn't well, and how embarrassed we all were to have a real-life teacher see our messy house. A kind, young teacher with a baked ham will write Brandenbrook, I'm sure.

Thursday, August 15, 1968

Dear Mr. Marsworth,

It's nearly eight o'clock at night and still no answer from you yet.

Didn't you see me out there checking? I was at your box three times. If you started it this morning, your letter must be LONG. Or is there someone else you type to, Mr. Marsworth???

D.?

Do you have other children? Grandkids? (I really want to know about those grandkids.)

How can I have you as a best friend, and still have so many mysteries? Don't best friends tell each other ALL? I've told you ALL and MORE and then MORE STILL.

Here's the MORE STILL from today, in case you want a little Kelly news tonight. (Does Clyde still listen to my letters?)

This morning, when Snow Cone, Dare, and I were walking to your cottage, the sheriff pulled up in his squad car to ask what we were doing on that road. "Just walking," Dare said, and I knew he didn't mention your cottage, because somehow that horrible sheriff would destroy the place we love. "No law against that, right?"

"You got a license for that mutt?" The sheriff nodded down toward Float.

"Sure," Dare lied. "But he don't like a collar, so he mostly goes without."

"Not in this town. In this town that dog wears a license or he's going to the pound." Sheriff Cutler pulled a Camel from his pocket and lit the cigarette. "You out here looking for some tires you can tack?"

"No sir," I said. "But someone took a knife to the tires on Gram's Plymouth. Slashed three of them. That ought to be a crime."

"Ought to be." He blew a cloud of smoke into my face. "But I didn't think the Kellys cared much for the law."

We all knew he meant Billy's letter to the paper, but no one said a word. I didn't want him smacking us, the way he'd smacked Steven in Gram's kitchen while we watched.

"We don't take to cowards in Lake Liberty," he said. "A man fights for his country, or else he's not a man. He's not even an American."

"Well, technically, if he's a U.S. citizen—" Snow Cone started in that lawyer voice she likes to use on Dare, and I squeezed her hand to tell her to shut her up.

"Who the h— are you?" the sheriff asked, disgusted. He took a good long look at Snow Cone's face, and then he moved on to her outfit: the homemade tie-dyed T-shirt, a fluorescent peace medallion just like the one she'd made for Billy, those always dusty shoeless feet. "You live here in Lake Liberty?"

"Moira Parks from Hillcrest." Snow Cone answered strong. (Do you think she'd act so strong if she'd been there when he hit Steven?) "And my mother is a lawyer."

"Well, good for you," the sheriff said, "because that Kelly kid will need one when the draft board's done with him. And he's going to need a doctor before that."

"He ain't sick," Dare said, even though we knew that wasn't what the sheriff meant.

"You can bet your a— he will be when we're done." (I'm leaving out the words that you won't like. Or maybe I should skip it all, because I didn't like A THING the sheriff said.)

Then he drove off down Tuxedo, leaving us in dust.

It spoiled our whole day at the cottage. We kept waiting for the sheriff, or else his terrible kid, and we kept thinking of the sheriff hurting Billy because we know that's what he meant.

In case we get attacked, Dare built two sturdy slingshots out of rubber bands and sticks (Snow Cone doesn't want a weapon) and he's collecting ammunition, including mud bombs made of rocks. He's stashed it all up in his tree stand so we're ready if they come. (I know you don't like weapons, but we need to be prepared if someone comes to hurt us, or your cottage, Mr. Marsworth. Don't you think we need to be prepared?)

While Dare worked on his arsenal, I sat with Snow Cone on your front porch and planned a Main Street March for Peace to show that we're on Billy's side against the war in Vietnam. The signs we'd paint. The chants she'd learned in San Francisco. "1, 2, 3, 4, we don't want your stupid war." Dare swears that he's not marching, but he didn't say we shouldn't. Doesn't that surprise you, Mr. Marsworth? I guess his crush on California Snow Cone is changing Dare's rough heart.

Are you still working on that letter? The longer that you take, the more I think that E.E.B. is DEFINITELY Mom. Wouldn't it only take one sentence to tell me I was wrong?

Still Impatient,
Reenie Kelly

Friday, August 16, 1968

Dear Mr. Marsworth,

Billy got fired from the Conoco. ☹☹ The best summer boy Mr. Casey said he'd ever had, and still he let him go!

I knew it when I saw him after sunset trudging up Gram's hill. (I was waiting on Gram's steps to make sure he got home safe.) Even in the darkness, I saw the slow way he was walking, staring at his feet, his hands stuck in his pockets, his shoulders drooping forward like he'd taken a bad punch.

I raced halfway down Gardner with worry weighing on my heart. "Did someone hurt you, Billy?"

"Just my pride," he said. "I lost my job at Casey's, Pup." He wiped his greasy hand under his nose to catch a sniff. (Billy always sniffs when he feels sad.) "Mr. Casey's customers don't want a coward—"

"You're not a coward, Billy." I looped my arm through his so we could walk to Gram's together. "It was brave to write the paper. And all the things you've had to face since then—"

"You might think so, Reen, but you're just one. That brick through Gram's front window. Her car. Those hateful letters folks are sending. The phone calls. The customers at Casey's. If you heard the names they called me, you'd know 'brave' isn't one. And now I can't even help Dad pay—"

Billy stopped, and I knew he dreaded telling Gram and Dare he'd lost his job.

"At least it's better than the draft," I said. "All of this. At least you'll be alive. And if that letter helps you stand against the draft, or keeps you out of prison—"

"All this hatred just for peace?" He sighed the same way Mom used to, when she wished the world were better than it was. "All this for one letter?"

"It's this terrible town," I said. "Everybody's mean." I didn't have the heart to tell him what Sheriff Cutler threatened this morning on the road.

"No," Billy said. "It'd be the same in Denton, only worse. You'd be making enemies of friends. And Dad would be ashamed of me, just like Gram is now. The things they've done to Gram because of me—" Billy hung his head. "Gram's car needs three new tires, and who else is going to hire me?"

"We'll be okay," I said, even though I'm not so sure that's true. I laid my cheek against his arm and smelled his Casey's summer smell of gasoline and sweat. "And pretty soon you'll leave for Brandenbrook." (I admit I choked a little on that last part, because Billy gone to Pennsylvania is a thought that I can't bear. I really can't.)

"Oh, Pup," he said with a sad laugh. "How exactly would that happen? I don't even have a job."

"Tomorrow morning," I told Billy, "we're sitting at Gram's table until those papers are filled out. You get started on that essay. Remember how you sat Dare down after school to make him do his homework, and quizzed me on my spelling, and always checked my math?"

"It's not the same," he said. "First thing tomorrow morning, I'll be looking for a job."

And I guess that must be true, because it's now tomorrow morning, Mr. Marsworth, and Billy's on Gram's front steps circling HELP WANTED ads, and Gram's gone off to Brindle Drug with her face stuck in a frown, and Dare's filling up a bucket with big rocks out in Gram's woods.

I'm dropping off this letter, hoping for your answer, and coming back ASAP to fill out those college papers. If Billy isn't going to do it, then I AM.

If you don't want to tell me about D., or why D.W.M. + E.E.B. didn't last forever, then don't. I'd rather drop the question than lose you as a friend. Please please please, oh please just write me back.

Lonely for My Pen Pal,
Reenie Kelly

Friday, August 16, 1968

Dear Miss Kelly,

I do not wish to exacerbate your sorrows, and somehow I fear
our friendship does just that. Please know there are days
when I can't answer, and things I cannot say, but that does
not mean I do not wish you well. I will always wish you well.
FOREVER.

You have asked me about D., and that unexpected
carving discovered in my woods. To that end, I have
written, and rewritten, and perhaps I'll write again if
I fail yet tonight. There are occasions when the truth is
hard to tell, and this is one.

D.W.M. is my beloved Danny Marsworth, our only child,
a beautiful kind boy we loved more than life itself. Love.
Even after all this time, it pains me to speak of Danny
in past tense. As you know, young Miss Kelly, beyond loss
love does endure.

And I'm afraid that Danny has been lost. Perhaps
you've heard the term "missing in action"? MIA? It's a
military term for lost soldiers who may be dead or living,
no one knows. In August 1950, our beautiful young Danny
went missing in Korea in another senseless war. In truth,
he is considered missing still, along with many thousands
of our soldiers missing in Korea, and many more missing

265

now in Vietnam, and like so many of the families, I
have found it slow and painful to accept the possibility
that Danny must be dead. Even as I type these words,
I feel like I've betrayed my missing son. Surely it's a
father's job to never give up hope his child lives.

And yet every day that Danny's missing is another
day I grieve my son is gone.

His mother, my dear departed Ruth, left this world
sick with fear and grief. On my better days, I tell
myself Danny's true home is in heaven, and his mother
is there with him, just as she would want. God willing,
I will see them both when my time comes.

So I have told you now of D., and may I ask a
question in return?

Don't you think the answer to that carving is
already in your heart? You're a girl like Betsy
Brighton, someday you might carve M.E.K. into a tree
with someone else. Or maybe Dare and Snow Cone will
carve another heart inside my woods. In fact, I hope
they do. Does that mean that it's FOREVER? Forever is
a long time, dear Miss Kelly, when you're young.

And your father? Does it help to know he was a
loyal friend to Danny? The best a boy could have.
True blue like Reenie Kelly. Betsy, Frank, and Danny
spent so many happy summer days down at that cottage;

sometimes I see them still silhouetted in the sunset sitting on the dock wishing on the stars. How I hoped their carefree days as youth could last forever. FOREVER.

The heart can't help but wish.

Perhaps I could have told you sooner, but the story of that friendship was your father's first to tell. I hope someday he does. He loved Danny like a brother; I know he loves him still. When people taunted Danny for being the son of the town "trator," you can bet Frank Kelly was always at his side.

Frank and Betsy Kelly.

Sincerely,

H. W. Marsworth

H. W. Marsworth

P.S. As I wrote once, the apple didn't fall far.

Friday, August 16, 1968

Dear Mr. Marsworth,

I've crumpled up so many bad starts to this letter they're all over my floor.

I'm so sorry you lost Danny, even though I know my sorry doesn't help. And I'm sorry if I made your heart hurt worse by asking nosy questions, and bugging you for answers when the story is so sad.

I know that Mom and Dad loved Danny, and I know they love him still, and I know they will love him FOREVER, just like you do. And I'll love him forever because he was your boy. And he's still at the cottage, he really truly is, and every part of him that lives there— his bear, his mitt, his scooter, his baseball cards, the jacket on the hook, the little fishing rod against the wall—I'll keep them safe from harm. No one can hurt Danny while Reenie Kelly's here. I won't let them hurt you, either.

Never ever ever ever ever, Mr. Marsworth.

I just want Danny to come home. And I want Mom to come home, too. And I want to see the three of them wishing on the stars just like you said.

I wish we all could live forever.

I wish we never had to lose the people that we love.

I wish this letter could be better, I really truly do. I hope you know it means that I love you, Mr. Marsworth, and you'll always have a family as long as I'm alive. I don't want you all alone with so much missing in your heart. I know Mom wouldn't want it either. Mom would want the Kellys and the Marsworths to be one.

Forever,
Reenie Kelly

Friday, August 16, 1968

Thank you, dear Miss Kelly.

Your friend,
Howard Marsworth

Dear Mr. Marsworth,

Here's a little jar of wildflowers I picked out in Gram's woods. I'm sorry it's not fancy, but I remember something beautiful and blooming can be solace for the soul. (I've saved every letter, every single one.)

   You can set this on your table to remember that you're loved.

   And you're not alone in missing Danny. I miss him with you, too.

            Your Faithful Friend Forever,
            Reenie Kelly

Saturday, August 17, 1968

Dear Mr. Marsworth,

How are you this morning? Did those wildflowers
help? Would you like some happy news while we're so sad?
(Sometimes one good thing can help your heart, and I know this
is a good thing that you want.)

Yesterday, when I was crying in the attic over Danny
going missing, and what if Skip went missing now in Vietnam,
Skip MIA like Danny, and what if the draft board forces
Billy to go to Vietnam, and what if just like Danny, he was
lost for eighteen years or more, Billy came up to my bedroom
to ask how he could help.

"Just apply to Brandenbrook," I sobbed. "Don't wait
another day."

And Billy swore he would just to make my crying stop.

Isn't that the best news, Mr. Marsworth?

My eyes were pink and puffy, but I went downstairs to
Gram's table to make sure he kept his word. And there was
Dare, sitting next to Billy, staring at the pictures of that
leafy-tree green campus, and the baseball team, and boys in
sporty sweaters with books tucked under their arms.

"I might play first base for the Quakers," Dare joked when I
sat down. "You going to get me into college, Reen?"

"You'll have to get your grades up," Billy said, like college
might be possible for Dare.

Dare Kelly off at college???

"I can't work a miracle," I said. "You want to go to college, Dare, you better read a book."

"It's not just Dare that needs a miracle," Billy said, like he was telling me a hard truth I didn't much want to hear. "I'm not sure God himself could get me into Brandenbrook two weeks before September, or get us all the cash I'd need to go. You make that happen, Reen, you've got someone on your side."

"Maybe Mom," I said. "She could be a saint by now."

I wish I could've added Mr. Marsworth, and I wish I could have told him all the ways you've tried to help me save him from this war. (I sure wish that we'd saved Danny.) Maybe someday all the Kellys will know the good you've done.

Your Friend and Second Family If You Want Me,
Reenie Kelly

P.S. You didn't leave a note this morning, so I'll check back in a bit. Write back ASAP if you like this happy news!

P.P.S. If Billy went missing in a war, I'd never give up hope. Skip either. I'd feel just like you do, Mr. Marsworth.

Saturday, August 17, 1968

Dear Miss Kelly,

Indeed, that happy news is most welcome at my house.

While you're busy working miracles, could you see to it that application makes it to the box?

Even in a miracle, Billy must apply ASAP, as you would say.

Sincerely,

H. W. Marsworth

H.W. Marsworth

Dear Mr. Marsworth,

It's done!! It's done!!!

I walked with Billy to the post office, and I watched with my own eyes while he licked the extra stamps, then slipped it in the box. He didn't have the recommendations from his teachers, and he says his essay's weak, and Denton High has to send his transcript, but he mailed what he could.

(Billy swears Brandenbrook won't accept him in mid-August, but he put the application in the mailbox anyway because, "Saying no to you, Pup, is like talking to a wall." I don't care if I'm a wall. At least he sent it, Mr. Marsworth! If there wasn't ANY hope for Brandenbrook, I know you would've said. You would've said so, right???)

Here's a little bit more news I hope will make you happy: I'm on my way to Snow Cone's to paint PEACE signs for our protest. We're going to march on Monday at 2:30 outside Piggly Wiggly, because Snow Cone says mothers buying groceries might be on our side. Do you think you can come? Can Carl Grace march with us?

So far we're keeping it TOP SECRET, because I don't want Gram to tell me I can't march. Gram's tired of the trouble, and I don't want more trouble, but I'm marching now for Billy, and for Danny, and for Skip and Jackie

Moon, and all our pen pals in the Fourth Platoon, and all the people dying on both sides, including all those children Snow Cone says we're killing. "No man is an island," Mr. Marsworth, and every death diminishes me just like John Donne said, and I want the people in this town to know it isn't just my brother who believes this war is wrong.

The hateful calls and letters just won't quit, and sometimes people yell, "Get out of Lake Liberty," or "The Kellys are all commies," when they drive by in their cars. What's a little bit more hate in this dumb town? They can hate me right with Billy, at least he's not alone.

This morning we woke up to a dead squirrel on Gram's front steps.

And a mess of broken eggs smashed on her car.

(Shouldn't I skip that bad news? I think I probably should. I've tried to keep things cheery because I know now you don't need another ounce of sadness in your heart.)

Anyway, the good news is I'm going to march for PEACE, and you should come and join us if you have the strength to stand. I'd be so proud to march beside you, Mr. Marsworth.

Standing Up for Peace Now,
Reenie Kelly

P.S. On our way home from the post office, we stopped at Rash's Hardware to ask about Gram's window, and Billy had to listen while Mr. Rash called him a deserter, and a traitor to his country, and he asked us how Frank Kelly could raise a coward son. "Good men died so you'd be free," he said to Billy, and he said he'd fix Gram's window when Billy did what's right. I guess that means we'll have sheet of plastic for a window at least until Dad's home.

Sunday, August 18, 1968

Dear Mr. Marsworth,

I know now all the news of war must make your heart hurt worse, and I don't want to make you suffer, but this is news I think you'll want to know. I can't bear to write it, so please read it for yourself.

Every letter that Skip sends me just gets worse. Is that the truth of war? I guess it is.

At least he's still alive. At least he isn't missing. At least he has a chance to heal. At least he wasn't killed like Jackie Moon, and all the other good guys that he lost.

Still, I don't want him to be wounded. I don't want him to go home a one-armed boy.

Of course I'll be his pen pal for the rest of our long lives. Always and forever, I'll never quit on Skip.

Praying for My Pen Pal,
Reenie Kelly

P.S. We're all at work on get-well cards, including Dare. Snow Cone, too. If you want to add your own, I'll mail it with the rest.

278

Hey there, Reenie Kelly,

I got to keep this short and sweet, or not so sweet. You ought to know that I've been wounded. Got my back and arm shot up pretty good. I took a bullet to the lung, but I'm alive. Other guys were KIA, and that part hurts the worst. I can't think of anything, but those good guys that we lost. I got a Purple Heart here at the hospital, but what good is a medal when the guys you loved are dead? I'd rather have them living than earn a Purple Heart.

I don't feel much like a hero, that's for sure. Maybe that's ungrateful, but it's true. Folks should hear the truth about this war.

My left arm looks like a mangled hunk of beef a dog gnawed to the bone. If they can save some of the nerves it might still work. Either way, I hope I'm going home. Good riddance, to this war. I hope my friends and family like me still. I'm not the kid they last saw, that's for sure.

I could use some Reenie Kelly letters to lift my spirits. I'm in the hospital in DaNang, but I'll get you your letters here. Next stop, Louisiana, if Uncle Sam decides I'm sufficiently destroyed to be discharged.

Is Billy squared away for college? I sure hope so.

Do you mind a one-armed pen pal, if they have to take my arm? I hope and pray it doesn't come to that.

> Your Friend,
> Skip

Sunday, August 18, 1968

Dear Mr. Nichols,

I would like to join your devoted friend, Miss Kelly,
in praying for your health. In every way that you
can heal, body, heart, and spirit, I pray with time
you will. I shall pray as well that you are discharged
to your family. With great sacrifice and courage, you
have served your country honorably, but home would
be the best place for you now.

                              Sincerely,

                         H. W. Marsworth

                         H. W. Marsworth

Monday, August 19, 1968

Dear Mr. Marsworth,

I snuck your letter into my care box with our get-well cards and a batch of Gram's good fudge and a rainbow-colored bracelet Snow Cone braided out of yarn. This afternoon our package will leave for Vietnam. I hope all the love we sent will help Skip heal.

Do you think his arm will heal? Will he end up with a hook? Don't worry, I didn't write that, I kept it to myself. I just know if it were Billy, he'd hate to lose an arm. Anybody would, including Dare.

I'm going to walk for Skip on Main Street at 2:30 this afternoon and for all the other people in that country who don't deserve to die.

In case there's any chance you'll join us, we've made lots of extra signs. Snow Cone is sure some mothers at the grocery store might march. Yesterday I made a sign that said ARMY PFC SKIP NICHOLS, PURPLE HEART, COME HOME. On the other side I painted: PATRIOT FOR PEACE. (That means I love peace AND my country. Snow Cone taught me that.)

Could I make a small confession? I'm a little scared to march this afternoon. I'm scared of what might happen when folks see us with our signs, and hear us singing peace songs, and saying war should stop. I can't forget those teens that marched for PEACE in the parade, or that soldier in the wheelchair with the sign against the war, and how angry people acted, or how mean Sheriff Cutler might be to us all.

But then I think of Skip, and how scared he was of war, and how his left arm has been mangled, and that bullet in his lung, and I think of Billy hated for one letter to the paper, and I know they need me standing with them, so I will.

You'd think the right thing would be easy, but it's not. I'd feel so much better if I had you at my side.

Piggly Wiggly, 2:30.

War Protestor,
Reenie Kelly

P.S. I just found out that Dare and Billy are both coming!!!! Dare marching for peace??? You better come to Main Street to see that for yourself!!!!

Dear Mr. Marsworth,

I wish you could have seen it, the first part and the last part
(the middle was a mess), but the very very best news is that
we didn't march alone!!!!!!!!!!!!!!!!!

At first it was just the four of us standing down on
Main Street with our signs, and singing "Where Have All the
Flowers Gone" while Billy played guitar, but then a mother
with a baby in a stroller and a young boy clinging to her leg
crossed the street to say how proud she was to see us all.
She picked up a sign, and gave one to her son, and then three
bikinied girls jumped out of a Mustang to stand there with us,
too. "Keep playing," one told Billy, and the three girls started
singing, and then two more women came from Piggly Wiggly,
and one shaggy, pimpled boy dropped his bike against the curb
and grabbed a sign. Folks were gathering on Main Street, but
no one said we had to stop.

When fancy Mrs. Brindle got out of her Cadillac to march
with us, I couldn't believe my eyes! She didn't pick up a sign, but she
spread her two gloved fingers in a peace sign.

That's the first good part that I promised.

Once we started down the sidewalk, angry men from
Parker's Barber came out to curse us all, and the Legion men did,
too, and Mr. Rash yelled that we belonged in Russia. Kids rode
up on bikes and started booing with the crowd. In the middle

of that mess, Rat and Cutler grabbed hold of my Skip sign, and ripped it right in half while people cheered. Dare tackled Cutler to the ground, and I had Rat by the neck, and mothers started scolding, and Billy handed his guitar off to a stranger and stepped in to stop the fight. Gram ran down from Brindle Drug, because someone must have told her, and Sheriff Cutler pulled up in his squad car and said we were all under arrest. Except he only handcuffed Billy, before he shoved him in the car.

"You better take me, too," I said, climbing in the backseat of the squad car next to Billy. "This was my idea."

"You arresting all the Kellys?" Dare said, and he squeezed in next to me, and then Gram got in the car.

"For heaven's sake, you kids!" she said. "What's going on?"

"Get out," Sheriff Cutler ordered, but nobody would move. I was glad we'd left Float safe inside Gram's house.

"You may as well arrest me, too, Stu," Mrs. Brindle said. "I'm not going to send my sons to Vietnam."

"We have a right to peaceful protest," Snow Cone added. "My mother is a lawyer." But before she'd hardly said it, Steven Cutler plowed her facefirst to the ground.

"Snow Cone!" I yelled, trying to shove my way past Dare and Gram, but then we were all out of that backseat except Billy, and Dare was pounding Steven Cutler's ugly face with his big fist.

"Darrel Kelly!" Gram yanked Dare by the T-shirt, and Sheriff Cutler grabbed his arm.

"Everybody calm down." It was Mr. Brindle's low voice rising in the crowd. He'd come down from the drugstore wearing his white smock. "Can we have some calm here, please?"

"You're all under arrest," Sheriff Cutler growled again.

"Really, Stu," Mr. Brindle said, taking hold of Mrs. Brindle's elbow. "You can't arrest women and children. You've got mothers in this crowd."

I looked over at the squad car, where Billy still sat handcuffed, and hoped somehow he counted as a kid.

"Don't tell me how to do my job," Sheriff Cutler said.

I helped Snow Cone to her feet and wiped her bloody palms clean with my shirt.

"These good folks just want peace," Mr. Brindle said. "Including Gwendolyn. We might not agree—"

"You can bet your life we don't." Sheriff Cutler spit down at the sidewalk.

"You can't take one without them all," Mr. Brindle said. "And you don't want them all. That little blonde in the bikini is Mayor Hanson's youngest, Suz. You think he wants to pick his daughter up in jail? Let the Kelly boy go free, send these good folks home."

"Good folks, my a—." Sheriff Cutler snorted, but he yanked Billy from the squad car, unlocked those horrible handcuffs, and told him to get lost. "All of you," he said to our whole crowd. "And next time you want to protest, don't do it in my town.

Get into the squad car," he snapped at Rat and Cutler, and they ducked into the backseat still sneering at us all.

I guess that's the middle and the end, but the end was so much better. Gram was mad as a wet hen, but she went back to the drugstore, and Billy made friends with those bikini girls, and Snow Cone's hands were scraped bad, but she said they hardly hurt, and a few of the young mothers told us we were brave, and all of us agreed we'd march again to stop this war.

I guess not everybody hates us, Mr. Marsworth!!!

"1, 2, 3, 4, we have friends against this war!!!!"

Peace Marcher,
Reenie Kelly

P.S. I'm going to write this all to Skip now, because I know he'll be glad to get a second letter while he's sick!!!!

P.P.S. I hope you're proud we stood for peace. Please tell me if you are.

P.P.P.S. Did people march for peace when Danny went to war?

Tuesday, August 20, 1968

Dear Miss Kelly,

I am quite proud you marched for peace, and as far as I'm
aware, you would be the first to organize a peace march
in Lake Liberty. I shall dare to hope it's not the last.

At the same time, a march for peace that devolves
into a scuffle has clearly missed its mark. I am
troubled by the violent image of your hands around
Rat's neck.

If you continue with this squabble, someone could
be seriously hurt.

Peace begins with peace.

Have you learned that lesson yet?

Sincerely,

H. W. Marsworth

H. W. Marsworth

P.S. Carl Grace carried word home of the melee. He'd arrived
late to your protest, just in time to see Dare tackle
Steven Cutler to the ground. You can imagine my dismay
when I'd heard your march had taken that bad turn.

Tuesday, August 20, 1968

Dear Mr. Marsworth,

I'm glad our peace march made you proud, even if you think
we wrecked it with a fight. (We're not the ones that wrecked
it.) And I understand the lesson: PEACE BEGINS WITH
PEACE. Billy said the same thing, and Snow Cone said it, too.

Next time I'll let Rat and Cutler rip my sign. (Or at least
I'll do my best.)

Gram's crabby with us too, not because we fought, but
because of all the other ways that we've gone wrong.

Here's our WRONG LIST from the lecture Gram gave to
us last night:

We are . . .

Wrong about the war

Wrong about our country

Wrong to protest down on Main Street

Wrong to use Skip's Purple Heart on any kind of sign

Wrong to drag in mothers and their children

And Mayor Hanson's daughter

And for heaven's sake—even Mrs. Brindle

Wrong to write that letter

Wrong to "compromise" Gram's reputation

Wrong to bring this kind of chaos to her town

Wrong enough to get her tires slashed

And a dead squirrel on her doorstep

And a brick through her front window that isn't even
   fixed
Shaving cream and eggs
Wrong enough that Father Gleason came by after
   supper to say this nonsense had to stop
Neighbor against neighbor
Wrong enough that Ardis Lindstrom called Gram to
   say the bridge club doesn't want her anymore
Thirty-seven years of bridge, and Gram's best friends
   kicked her out
Wrong enough that Gram just can't go on
She didn't make this war in Vietnam and she can't
   stop it
And neither can three kids
And what will Billy do in prison?
And how will Dare and I make a single decent friend
   when school starts?
She doesn't mean that ragged, shoeless girl from
   California
But good kids from Lake Liberty
Who will want to know the Kellys now???
Nobody, that's who!!!!

Gram's list was probably longer, because she ranted through
our supper, and she kept up with the ranting after Father

Gleason left, and in between her rant, she kept saying that she loved us, but when it came to the war in Vietnam she'd finally had ENOUGH. ENOUGH. E-N-O-U-G-H.

When she'd finished with her ranting, she went into her bedroom and closed the door again, and we could hear the muffled sounds of sobbing, but when we asked if we could help her, she just said it was too late.

"We're sorry about your bridge club," Billy said through the closed door, then he opened Gram's directory and dialed Ardis Lindstrom on the phone. He said Blanche Kelly loved her country, and she loved folks in Lake Liberty, every lifelong friend, and she wasn't on his side against the war. Not even one small bit. He begged her not to blame Gram for something he had done. "Gram agrees with you," he said, in his gentle Billy way folks love so much. "And your bridge club means the world to her."

And you know what, Mr. Marsworth? I think Billy got Gram back in her bridge club, that's how sweet he was.

This morning he's driving to Excelsior to try to find a job. Gram says after yesterday no one in Lake Liberty will hire him again.

Dare says he's sick of all the trouble, so we're heading to your cottage for a TUESDAY SUN-AND-FUN-AND-FISH DAY Dare says he's earned in spades, and he's made me triple swear I won't waste the day on peace, or war, or Skip, or Billy and the draft. (Deep down, I know Dare agrees with Gram, but if he has to choose between this hateful town and Billy, it's Billy's side he wants. Also, he's on the side of Snow Cone now—his great big summer CRUSH!)

D.F.K. + M.J.P.

Don't be surprised to find that in your woods.

Your Future Peaceful Marcher,
Reenie Kelly

Wednesday, August 21, 1968

I had to tell you quick that Dare's been hurt, and the doctor won't say yet how bad it is. Once I drop your paper, we're on our way back to the hospital to sit with Dare again. Gram wouldn't sleep at home last night in case Dare went into a coma. Please pray for Dare this morning, and all day if you can.

Wednesday, August 21, 1968

Dear Mr. Marsworth,

I'm writing from the lobby of the hospital while Gram's upstairs keeping watch over Dare, and Billy's sitting there beside her worried for them both. Billy sent me out for fresh air, because he knows this place reminds me of the last days we had Mom. I don't even have to say it, Billy knows.

And what if we'd lost Dare? That's all I can think now.

I don't know where to start so this makes sense.

Maybe with the ambush. I guess I should start there.

Yesterday, when we got down to your cottage, Rat and Cutler were waiting in Dare's tree stand with the weapons that Dare made. The slingshots and the mud bombs, but they also brought a BB gun, so we were beat out from the start.

We'd barely walked into your woods when I was hit hard by a mud bomb, and I can't explain how much that mud bomb hurt. (Dare had packed his bombs with rocks.) When the second one hit Snow Cone, she ran out of the woods. I wanted to run with her, but Dare headed toward the tree stand to fight them face-to-face, and I knew he'd need my help.

We started climbing up those wood rungs Dare had hammered to the tree, and the whole time we were climbing, they bombarded us with BB shots and mud bombs. There was nothing we could do but duck our heads and dodge. It was worse than I can tell you, Mr. Marsworth. Boom boom boom boom boom.

And then somehow Dare lost his footing, and he tumbled from the tree, and I watched him fly right past me and crash onto the ground.

"He ain't hurt," Cutler said, but blood was gushing from Dare's head, and I could see the bones and guts inside the gash. I shook Dare hard and called his name, but he wouldn't budge.

I begged him to wake up, but I couldn't even get a blink.

Float was licking at Dare's face, and whining something terrible, but Dare didn't move an inch.

Snow Cone watched it from the road, and ran for help.

I was sure that they had killed him, and every time I close my eyes, I still smell Dare's blood mucked in his hair, and see him lying openmouthed, unconscious, and all the terror that I felt, shaking him awake, it's still here in my body, even now.

I hope you've never had to see that, Mr. Marsworth.

I hope you'll never have to worry your brother might be dead.

The cowards Rat and Cutler didn't come down from the tree stand, they just called Dare a faker and told him to get up.

Dare still hadn't moved when I heard the wail of the sirens, and Dare was still unconscious when Sherriff Cutler got out of the car.

I don't want to write about that man, I really don't.

Or those near-killers, Rat and Cutler.

I bet he beat them both, he was steaming mad about the BB gun and mud bombs.

I hope they go to jail where they belong.

If one good thing comes from Dare being hurt, it's those two bullies locked in juvie until the day THEY die.

Billy says we should be grateful Dare's out of danger now. (That's the GREAT news, Mr. Marsworth!!!) He's wide awake with a jagged line of thick black stitches, and blood still crusted in his hair, and a brand-new scar to go with all the others that he's earned. His right arm's in a cast, and he's too dizzy yet to read, or keep his balance walking or do division in his head. The doctor says a couple weeks of bed rest ought to help Dare heal. Billy's right about the grateful, but I still want Rat and Cutler to pay for what they've done. Someone has to stop the terrible things they could do next.

Ooops—Billy just got off the elevator. I'll write more when I can.

Hater of All Hospitals,
Reenie Kelly

P.S. It's bedtime, Mr. Marsworth, and tomorrow morning Dare is coming home! Already!!!! Dad says it's too expensive to pay a hospital to feed Dare root beer Popsicles and all the ice cream he can eat. OH!!!! THAT'S THE BIGGEST NEWS TODAY! Dad called from North Dakota, and we all passed the phone around Dare's room, and we each got one quick minute, except Dare got five or ten. The rest of us just listened while Dare joked with Dad about having Dad's hard head, and how he'd look twice as tough with one more scar, and the cast on his right arm itched, but he'd scratch it with a stick as soon as he got home. "They got me saying ABCs." Dare laughed his tough guy laugh. "That's how dumb they think I am."

Dare was quiet for a minute, then he said, "No, don't come home just for me, I'll be all right." His voice choked up a little, and we all watched Dare listen to whatever Dad said next. "Sure I'm sure," Dare finally said, and we knew what Dad was asking: He was asking twice if he needed to come home.

If it were me, I'd tell Dad to come home. I want Dad to come home.

I'll never leave my kids for one whole summer. Never ever, Mr. Marsworth.

P.P.S. Can I tell you something secret, Mr. Marsworth? It was strange and sad and lonely to hear Dad's growly voice after all these months. He sounded beat and worried, and a little grumpy, too. "What in God's name happened, Reen?" he asked, but he didn't wait for my answer, and I'm not sure I could have told him, because too much has happened here this summer with him gone. "Gram says you're scrapping with the Cutler kid, and mouthing off on Vietnam, and marching like a hippie, and somehow Billy wrote to the paper to say that he won't serve."

"We're both against the war," I said, and I wondered if he'd read a single letter that I'd wrote. "I wrote that to you, Dad. You didn't write back."

"I don't have the hours, Reen," Dad said. "And I've got three of you to write. Gram can't take the trouble you kids are dishing out."

I looked across the bed where Gram had her wrinkled hand over Dare's good arm. Her gray curls were flat and frizzed. Her eyes exhausted.

"We're sorry," I told Dad. "But Billy got her back into the bridge club."

"What is that about Gram's bridge club?" Dad said, confused. "Look, you can't turn against your country, no matter what you think about this war. You or Billy. You're old enough to know that."

"We're not," I said. "And he might still go to college."

"On that scholarship?" Dad said, and I was glad he'd read THAT letter. "To Brandenbrook? Who's behind that, Reen?"

"I guess that college just found him," I lied, and I wished I could have said, "It was your best friend's father, Mr. Marsworth," but I kept that to myself, because it isn't what you want. Maybe someday, Mr. Marsworth.

"That so?" Dad said like he'd caught me in that lie. "I'm almost out of time, Reen, and I want a word with Billy. Be good for Gram, love you to the moon."

"Love you, too," I said, and I tried to picture Dad's wide face, the freckled skin, the red hair shaved close to his head, or to remember his big arms, the strong way Dad would hug me, sometimes Dare and me together, squished against his chest. "I'm saving Billy, Dad," I said. "You remember what Mom wanted?"

"Of course." Dad sighed again. "All of us love Billy. Now put him on the phone."

I don't know why I wrote that, Mr. Marsworth, one long boring conversation word for word. Maybe you don't care what a dad says to his kid. But I know you liked Frank Kelly, and maybe after all these years you'd want to hear his voice. It's good to hear a voice. Does he sound much like he sounded as a kid? How long has it been since you and Dad have talked?

I hope when he comes home we can be the Marsworths and the Kellys once again.

P.P.P.S. I'm doing Dare's WHOLE route now. Me, all by myself. Billy begged to help, but I said no. The sack is twice as heavy, but I'm not the weakling that I was when I got my route in June. If I'm late dropping your paper, I hope you won't be mad. Dare says he'll be down for just a week. I bet he's right!

Wednesday, August 2I, 1968

Dear Miss Kelly,

Thank you for your letter.

I cannot tell you how concerned I've been since
learning of Dare's fall.

The news came to us from Mavis Barnes, the
dispatcher for the sheriff, and when she said
there'd been trouble at my cottage, I feared first
for you and Dare.

There was little she would offer, except to say
Dare tumbled from a tree, and he'd been taken by
ambulance to a city hospital for help.

Please say how I might help you, dear Miss Kelly?
Is there something I can do for Dare? Or any of
your family?

After Mavis phoned, I asked Carl Grace to drive
me to the cottage, so I could see the tree stand
where Dare fell. I so wished your summer refuge had
remained a place of joy.

May I tell you one good thing? Sometimes one
good thing can help the heart. (I remember what you
write me.)

Despite the harm that's come to Dare, you have
made a place of peace out of that cottage, and I hope
you will return. The fresh white paint, the angry
words all gone, the weeds cleared from the yard,
those shutters cobalt blue. That little garden of

bright marigolds you planted near the porch. It all
looks nearly as lovely as those years when Danny
spent his summers running through those woods with
Frank and Betsy at his side. I should have come to see
it sooner; I'm sorry that I didn't.

Thank you, dear Miss Kelly, for giving it your
love.

I'm aware in many ways you've had a summer filled
with strife, but I hope you will remember all the good
you have accomplished. Ingenuity. So much good for
one young girl to bring into the world.

I have no doubt your great love for your brother
will help Dare Kelly heal.

Your Friend,

H. W. Marsworth

H. W. Marsworth

P.S. I went into the shed to find that box of Danny's
baseball cards you once told me Dare admired. Please
pass them on to Dare with my best wishes for good
health. Danny's cards are his to keep. They aren't
much good to anyone sitting in that shed.

P.P.S. I shall eagerly await your updates on Dare's
health.

Thursday, August 22, 1968

Dear Mr. Marsworth,

Baseball cards, and a gallon of fudge ripple, and Carl Grace
with Gram's new window, and a stack of brand-new comic
books for Dare!!!!!!!!!

You sent all that to the Kellys because Dare fell from your
tree???

We don't blame you for Dare's accident, no one thinks that
it's your fault. It could have happened anywhere those rotten
boys had been. Still, Dare's delighted with the baseball cards and
ice cream, and the Spider-Man and Batman comic books. Right
now, he's upstairs in Gram's attic (Dare and Float get my twin
bed, I get the floor) with Danny's precious baseball cards spread
out on the sheet. He's quizzing Snow Cone on the players while
she decorates his cast.

What else? The new window made Gram teary. (She
would never say that, please don't tell her that I told!) Did you
know Carl Grace had to take it to another town just to get it
fixed? Mr. Rash won't do business with the Kellys anymore.

Carl Grace and Billy hung the window in the frame, and
now the sun is gleaming through that bright glass, and Carl
Grace and Billy are talking in Gram's driveway, their heads
bent close together like the two of them are friends. Do you
think they're talking about Brandenbrook??? I hope so.

Gram's gone to the drugstore, and I'm trying to write this

letter, but in between, I'm opening the door to the women of Lake Liberty, with their get-well hot dishes, and brownies, and coffee cakes, and worried questions about Dare. Even Ardis Lindstrom delivered warm blueberry cobbler. She asked kindly after Dare, so I guess not everybody holds a grudge over our protest. Or at least they don't hate Gram.

Earlier today, Mrs. Brindle brought Dare a basket filled with candy, which she said he had to share: Tootsie Rolls, Turkish Taffy, Snickers bars, Bazooka gum, Twizzler sticks, Starbursts, Milky Ways, and more, and she told Billy he could scrape and paint her boathouse if he still needed summer work. She can't pay what Mr. Casey did, but at least Billy could earn some.

That's a lot of kindness. Don't you think so, Mr. Marsworth?

Wait! Breaking news out in Gram's driveway . . .

Carl Grace just reached into his car for an envelope for Billy. Now they both looked back toward Gram's house to make sure that no one saw. (I saw, but I'm a spy.)

Did Carl Grace have news from Brandenbrook??? Is it something about Vietnam? The draft? Why would he have an envelope for Billy? Tell me if you know!

I'll try to worm it out of Billy, but just in case I can't, will you get it out of Carl Grace and write back ASAP?

Not Too Nosy for My Own Good,
Reenie Kelly

P.S. Guess what, Mr. Marsworth!! Billy just climbed into Carl Grace's car and left without a word. Carl Grace and Billy going where???? And to do what?????

P.P.S. Okay, Billy finally came back to Gram's on foot, and he won't tell me where he went with Carl Grace or why. He just said, "Go play now, Reen," but he said it in a sad way that made me worry more.

"Did you get bad news about the draft?" I asked, but he said no. "Brandenbrook?" I said, because I could see the cloud of worry in his eyes. "You're not getting sent to Vietnam?"

"I'm right here with you, Pup," he said, but then he said to go upstairs with Dare and Snow Cone, while he sat alone on Gram's old sofa, staring at his hands the way he does in church.

I didn't go play with Dare and Snow Cone. Right now, I'm holed up in Gram's bathroom finishing this last P.S. to you. Could you talk to Carl Grace ASAP???? Will you find out where they went? Or why Billy wants to mope down on Gram's sofa by himself???

And where did Billy put that envelope? It wasn't in his hand when he came into Gram's house. Do you know what was inside it, Mr. Marsworth???

I'm only going to worry, Mr. Marsworth.

I'm going to run this to your house now. PLEASE answer me tonight!!!!

Thursday, August 22, 1968

Dear Mr. Marsworth,

I went back for an answer, but my letter was still there. When you pick it up tomorrow morning with your paper, you'll find this second batch of weird news waiting in your box. And I hope you'll answer both my letters, because:

1. I'm worried about Billy.

2. I know you won't believe what happened here tonight.

In a strange day that just got stranger, Rat (Tony RATacheck to be precise, Gram won't let me call him Rat) showed up at Gram's front door with his Rat mom. Gram had the nerve to let OUR MORTAL ENEMY come into our house. Him, and his crappy homemade card, and his Jiffy jar of money, and a stupid blue balloon.

Tony Rat Baloney. Tony Phony. That's all that I could think of when he mumbled he was sorry, and he hoped that Dare was better, and he hoped we could be friends.

FRIENDS????????????????????

He said it all to his ripped sneakers and Gram's floor, without a single look at me, until his mother yanked his chin up, and made him say a second sorry.

"Get lost," I said, and I headed toward the attic stairs so I could be the first to tell Dare that Rat was in OUR HOUSE.

"You get back here, Reen," Gram ordered. "I mean it. Right now, Miss."

"But Dare," I said. "He wouldn't want him here."

"You let Dare get his sleep," Gram said. "You can listen to this now."

I sat down on the attic steps, so I could hate him from a distance without seeing his rat face. After everything he'd done—nearly killing Dare, Misery, the worms shoved down my shirt, papers stolen from my customers, the Milk Duds at the movies, the dog poop in Dare's tent, that day they fought me on the street, kicked me in the stomach, and started this whole war, that chicken on your gate, Gram's tires slashed—I wasn't going to listen to that kid.

"Your brother gonna be okay?" Rat finally asked.

"You mean King Kong?" I said, sarcastic. "He has a name."

"It's Darrel," Gram said.

"Okay," Rat said. "Will Darrel be all right?"

"In time," Gram said. "But his injury was serious, and it could have been much worse. He may have some trouble reading, at least for a short while. And dizziness. Plus the doctor bills. The hospital."

"Oh Blanche," Mrs. Rat said, "I'm so sorry, I just am." Her white waitress shoes were filthy, and her Country Café uniform was stained with food and grease. "We'll help out all we can, I swear we will. Tony has his paper route, and he'll give you what he's saved, plus all he earns. And I'll—"

"You didn't throw those rocks," Gram said. "We shouldn't

305

have to pay for the mistakes these kids all make." Gram said "all" like we were just as bad as Rat.

"I suppose that's true," Mrs. Rat said, and she gave a glance toward Billy. "Don't you think the war this summer is bringing out the worst?"

"The worst," Gram said, like she was blaming Billy instead of blaming slimy Rat for nearly killing Dare.

Mrs. Rat must have agreed, because she suddenly asked Billy, "Are you the one that wrote the paper?"

"I am," Billy answered firmly. "But that's not Dare and Reen—"

"Of course not," Mrs. Rat said. "But when you write against our country, and our soldiers, even children will get angry, and they should. Tony's father was a Green Beret."

"Billy didn't write against our country, or our soldiers," I corrected Mrs. Rat. "He wrote against the draft, and the war in Vietnam."

"Same thing," Rat said. "All of it is traitor talk."

"I'm not a traitor, Tony," Billy said. "I just disagree. You shouldn't hurt Reen or Dare for what I've done."

"No one's hurting anyone," Gram ordered. "This fighting can't continue, I'm sure we all agree to that. Letter or no letter."

"Absolutely," Mrs. Rat said.

"It's not from Billy's letter." I crossed my arms to keep from shaking, and I kept my butt glued to that step so I wouldn't

306

bolt across the room to smash that scrawny kid. "They've been mean to us all summer, before Billy ever wrote against the draft. Ask him what he did! Just ask! To us and Mr. Marsworth."

"Let's leave Marsworth out of this now, Reen," Gram said, and Mrs. Rat didn't argue. "I was under the impression Tony's here to make amends for what he's done. Not start another fight."

"That's right," Mrs. Rat agreed, and she nudged Tony with a shove. "Tony?"

"I made a card for Darrel," Rat said. He passed it off to Gram, then he handed her the money jar, and the sagging blue balloon. "And I guess I'm going to visit every afternoon until he's well. My mom got a book on baseball from the library, I guess I'm coming here to read so he can rest."

"You're not coming HERE," I said. "And, Dare hates books."

"Me too." Rat shrugged. "My mom had that idea."

"Then you can read the sports page to him, Tony," Mrs. Rat said. "Or find something else to do to be his friend. Bring Battleship or checkers."

Rat sitting in my bedroom playing Battleship with Dare?????

"No way," I said.

"Good thing Reen's been all for peace this summer," Gram said to Mrs. Rat. "Peace, peace, peace. What better place for Reen to start than her own house. She can put her money where her mouth is."

"I'm not for peace with him," I said. "Not ever."

    "Peace is peace," Gram said. "Make an enemy a friend, that's how it starts."

    That's REALLY what she told me!!!!!

    AAAGGGGGGHHHHHHHH. Make an enemy a friend????

    The only good news in this letter is Rat gave Gram all of his money: $137.62. It's his savings since first grade and I got to see his pale chin shake when he left it in Gram's hand. I hope he cried the whole way home.

    Please please please write back ASAP.

                              Disgusted,
                              Reenie Kelly

Friday, August 23, 1968

Dear Mr. Marsworth,

It's ten o'clock this morning, and I've been back to your house twice, but you haven't written me a word. Do you think Rat will really come to Gram's this afternoon? Do I have to let him in? Dare says we're going to lock the doors and windows, and hide until he leaves.

Snow Cone says it's like the Paris peace talks, and this is how war ends.

Right now she's in the attic trying to talk Dare into peace, and Billy's at the Brindles' asking about work, and I'm impatient in Gram's living room waiting for your word.

If you don't know about that envelope Carl Grace gave Billy, where it went or what it was, I might just do a search of Gram's garage. (I've already searched through Billy's papers, and underneath the cushion of Gram's couch. You'll be proud to know I kept my nose out of Beth's letters.)

Did you talk to Carl Grace yet? Where did he take Billy in his car?

I don't like it when you're quiet for too long!

On the Hunt Now,
Reenie Kelly

Dear Mr. Marsworth,

I found that yellowed envelope hidden behind a can of paint in Gram's garage.

I wish I'd never solved this mystery. Never ever. Ever. Ever. Ever. But I did, and now I can't take it back.

How could you, and Mom, and Dad, and Gram, keep such a GIANT secret, Mr. Marsworth???

Did Billy know the truth before Carl Grace gave him Mom's letter in that card???? Did you want Billy to have it???? Why would Carl Grace make Billy see that now???

You knew the truth from the beginning and you never said a word.

I'm going to sit outside your house until you see me face-to-face. I'm going to ring your bell ten thousand trillion times, and I won't stop.

If you want to keep my friendship, you have to come outside!!!

You can't be a brave man and hide inside your house.

Reenie Mixed-Up Kelly

December 24, 1962

Dear Mr. Marsworth,

I think of you alone this Christmas season, and I wish there was a way, despite our misunderstandings, and our grief, and all the unintended pain I may have caused, to somehow be a friend to you again. It isn't right for you to spend a holiday alone. Why not join us at the Kellys' for tomorrow's Christmas roast? We'll be in town for such a short time, and it's difficult to say how many years will pass before we're in Lake Liberty again.

I hope someday you'll trust I still love Danny, as you do; I have loved him all along. And Frank's love for his best friend has never faltered. We did not give up hope Danny would be found, but Billy needed family, and a father. As painful as it was to build a life with Danny missing, Frank and I believed it's what Danny would have wanted for his son. To you it was betrayal; I'm sorry for the suffering we've caused.

I won't say that it's been easy, but what marriage ever is? The children keep us busy: Reen and Dare with all the energy you'd expect from

Kelly kids, and gentle Billy as intelligent and thoughtful as your beautiful lost son. The children are all Kellys, as they should be, but when Billy's old enough to know the truth, Frank and I intend to tell him he had another father first.

I'll tell him all about the boy so kind he couldn't kill insects. A boy I loved from age seven until forever with my great big young-girl heart. A boy who enlisted in the Army to prove he loved his country.

A boy we lost too early.

This is a hard truth for a child as young as Billy, but one I promise you we'll tell. Right now Billy is thriving as a Kelly, without the terrible weight of all that we can't answer: "How did my father disappear? When will he be found? What if he's still living? Or held captive in Korea?" Those questions are the weight we all must carry, but they're too much for a child.

For now, we just want Billy loved and happy. Wouldn't Danny want the same thing for his son? I think he would. And Billy is the apple of Frank's eye. He's a musician and a scholar with Danny's wide, bright mind. He's my confidant and rock as Danny was. A devoted older brother to adoring Dare and Reen.

A boy much loved by all, including Blanche. A boy who calls himself a Kelly with great pride.

Someday you'll love him, too. I'm sure you love him now.

In case you won't come to us for Christmas, I've enclosed a recent picture of the kids for you to see. Billy is too old to visit Santa, but he went with Dare and Reen. That's how sweet he is.

He looks so much like Danny; I'm sure you'll see that for yourself.

Perhaps in time, with healing, our two families will be one. I hope you will forgive me.

Blessed Christmas, Mr. Marsworth, and may peace prevail at last. Peace between our families, and peace on earth for all.

Much Love,
Betsy Brighton Kelly

Dear Mr. Marsworth,

I can't quit thinking of Mom's letter.

I know you hear me ringing. You must see me at your gate, but you won't even come outside.

Did you give Carl Grace that letter? Did you want Billy to know who his true father really was? Did Mom or Dad tell Billy??? Did you meet Billy and not me??? Did he visit you this summer at your house??? Does he already know Clyde?

Mom should have told the truth to me before she died. She should have told us all from the beginning.

Do you know what it's like to have a GIANT family secret?

Or to find out your family's not the family you always thought it was????

Don't you think someone should have told me, Mr. Marsworth?

Please come out to see me. I'm going to sit here at your gate until I get an answer, so you better answer soon. If you aren't strong enough to see me, send out Carl Grace instead.

Not Leaving,
Reenie Kelly

P.S. Billy isn't a REAL Kelly??? How can that be true?

P.P.S. Did you stay mad at Mom and Dad for getting married? Were you against our family all these years?

P.P.P.S. At least come out and get my letters, Mr. Marsworth!

Dear Mr. Marsworth,

I'm not really gone. I'm spying from the oak tree, and I'm staying in these branches until someone comes outside. You or Carl Grace, I'll take either one.

Do you know how strange it is to read a Christmas letter that Mom wrote? To see her handwriting I love. To hear her voice, just the way she sounded when she spoke. And what happened to that Santa picture? I'd like to see it now.

Is Billy why you wrote me, Mr. Marsworth? If I hadn't been his sister, would the two of us be friends? Was it only knowing Billy that you wanted all along? Why does he get to be your grandson, when I know you best of all? I never had a grandpa, Mr. Marsworth. And now Billy gets to have you, and keep you for himself.

I said I'd be your family, do you remember that I did?

Why didn't Mom ever tell me? Why'd everybody make believe that Billy was Dad's son? Isn't eighteen years a long time for a lie? Wasn't it a big lie for us all???

Come outside to see me, Mr. Marsworth.

Dad's in North Dakota, and I want answers now.

Double-Crossed by Friends and Family,
Reenie Kelly

Dear Mr. Marsworth,

I'm home now in Gram's cramped bathroom, pretending to run water for a bath while I write to you instead. There's a lot I need to tell you, and I need to tell you now. (I can't write in Gram's attic with Dare and Float hogging my room.)

First, did you see Billy come to find me in the tree across the street? Did you or Carl Grace tell him I was there? Billy said he'd been searching through Lake Liberty since he'd found Mom's letter gone from Gram's garage. Gone like me.

"Come on down so we can talk," he begged, but I wouldn't move an inch. He couldn't climb up to get me, and I wasn't coming down. "Pup." He sighed. "You weren't supposed to snoop in Gram's garage. That letter wasn't meant for you right now."

"You're telling me." I was so mad I could have screamed or cried, but instead I curled into a rock. "Did you know the truth before Carl Grace gave you Mom's letter?"

Billy sighed again. "I did," he finally said. "Dad told me just before I turned eighteen. Before I had to register. He knew I'd see it on my birth certificate."

"Before you turned eighteen? And you didn't tell me or Dare? And Dad didn't tell us either?" I tried to see his face, but he was shadowed by the leaves. "I'm not going back to Gram's. Not ever. I don't even know my family. Or anybody now."

"Reen," he said. "You know that isn't true." He reached

up for my foot and gave it a soft tug. "Come on down. Nothing's changed."

"It has," I said. "The Kellys aren't the Kellys. Mom and Dad just made that up. You're not even Dad's—"

"Please don't say that I'm not Dad's, please don't. Because that's why Mom and Dad didn't want anyone to know. Because they knew folks would say I'm not a Kelly. Maybe even you and Dare would think it. Or other people would. And I'd start to feel it, too. I want to be Dad's son."

As soon as Billy's voice broke, my heart was sick with sorrow for the mean things I'd just said. I dropped down from the tree and put my arm around his waist.

"I didn't mean it, Billy. Of course you're still Dad's son. It's the secret that I hate. I think they should have told us sooner. Maybe from the start. Told the truth about our family."

"You know Mom did her best, Reen. She always always did. I don't want to say now she was wrong."

"Okay," I said, ashamed. "But did you get to meet him, Billy?" (As sorry as I felt, I hoped his answer would be no. Shouldn't I be the first to meet you, Mr. Marsworth? I've been asking this whole summer.)

"Danny?" he said sadly. "He died before—"

"No," I said. "Mr. Marsworth. Danny's dad. Your grandpa." I pointed toward your big brick house across the street. "He lives right inside there, Billy."

"I know where he lives," he said. "But he's not my grandpa, Reen. I mean, not really. I don't even know him."

"But he could be your second family. Our second family."

Billy gave a little laugh. "I don't need a second family."

"I might," I said. "Because I think that's what Mom wanted. Didn't she say that in the Christmas letter? That the Marsworths and the Kellys should be one?"

"And what about _that_ Christmas letter?" Billy said, confused. "Did you ask him for it, Reen? Did you meet Mr. Marsworth on your route? Because strangely Carl Grace told me Mr. Marsworth wanted _you_ to have it. Someday. When I thought the time was right. And I should let you know that Christmas visit to his milk box wasn't just a dream."

I knew it, Mr. Marsworth! I knew that snowy memory was real!

"That letter was for me?" I asked. "Mr. Marsworth wanted _me_ to have it?"

"He did." Billy crinkled up his face the way he does when he's confused. "Is there something you're not telling me? What Christmas visit, Reen? When did you go to his house? Did Mom take you without me? And isn't he a recluse?"

"Kind of, sort of," I said, smiling. Don't I deserve a secret, Mr. Marsworth? "But if you want to be his family, I can be his family, too. You won't be the only Kelly."

"That's sweet, Reen." Billy laughed. "But I don't think we'll all be one family. That's not the way it works."

That might be what he thinks now, Mr. Marsworth. But, you know I have my ways of changing Billy's mind ☺.

The story doesn't end there, but it's all that I can tell you, or all I want to write because Dare's pounding on the bathroom door to use the toilet.

Oh, wait—

Okay, here I am again. Now I'm writing to you by flashlight while I listen to Dare snore.

What else?

When I told Gram I knew Billy's truth, and, the long lie about our family had been wrong, she said, "Some things are best unsaid while kids are young. But I'm truly sorry, Reenie, if you feel you've been deceived. That wasn't our intention."

Gram HARDLY EVER says she's sorry, Mr. Marsworth, and I'm glad this once she did. Still, we left Gram at the table and took our dinner to the attic to tell Dare.

And do you know what Dare Kelly did? He broke down in a sob. Great big messy tears streamed down his freckled cheeks, and Float was whining with him, and licking at Dare's face to make the sobbing stop.

"First Rat inside my house," Dare said, blowing his snot into my sheet. "And then you two come upstairs to tell me this. Dad wouldn't live a lie like that, I know he wouldn't. Pretending to be Billy's—"

"Dad didn't pretend," I said, because I'd already hurt Billy saying Dad wasn't his dad. "He's Billy's dad. He is. They didn't want Billy to be different from us, Dare. Mom or Dad. They didn't want us to say he wasn't Dad's true son."

"They kept the secret for our family," Billy said to Dare. "Or me. I guess it was mostly me they wanted to protect. But you know I'm still your brother. Nothing changes that."

I still have a hundred questions, Mr. Marsworth. No matter what Gram says, I'm old enough to understand it all, and they should have told us earlier, because a lie this big is wrong. Even so, Billy IS my brother, and I'm glad you're in our family, I really, really am.

You're my family now, through Billy.

I hope you want another Kelly as your family, Mr. Marsworth. And please say it WASN'T ONLY BILLY that made you be my friend.

Ready for a Second Family,
Reenie Kelly

P.S. Okay, not a hundred questions, but a couple: Did you come to Gram's that Christmas? Did you and Mom make up before she died? Are you still sad that Mom and Dad got married, when Danny didn't come home? I know why that hurt your feelings, Mr. Marsworth. We wouldn't want Dad to marry someone else with Mom still in our hearts.

P.P.S. But if Mom didn't marry Dad I wouldn't be here, and Dare wouldn't be here either, and we wouldn't be Billy's family, and you wouldn't have me for your friend.

P.P.P.S. Tomorrow afternoon I'm taking Billy to the cottage, to show him every little piece of Danny still left inside that shed, and the D.W.M. + E.E.B. = FOREVER on that stump. Then we're tearing down Dare's tree stand, and destroying every weapon before someone else gets hurt. Dare wouldn't agree to that, but he'll find out after it's done.

P.P.P.P.S. Why don't you come down to the cottage for a chance to meet us both???? (If you came to Gram's in '62 that meeting doesn't count. Billy says he can't remember, and I DEFINITELY don't.) I'll keep my eye out, Mr. Marsworth. I'll listen for your car.

Friday, August 23, 1968

Dear Miss Kelly,

It is too late for me to type, but Carl Grace
shall take dictation as I rest.

I'm sorry I was out during your desperate
search for answers. That letter was truly meant
for later, perhaps in many years. At my age, I
can't be certain of tomorrow, or my aging heart,
so I chose to give it to Billy for safekeeping. I
hope your family will forgive me for whatever
harm it caused.

And I hope you will forgive me, too, Miss
Kelly. A secret of such consequence was difficult to
keep, yet it was not mine to tell, and so I couldn't.

Your parents have raised Billy, and Billy is
their son. He was never mine to claim, except in
love. Child of my child, and yet I understand he
wants to be a Kelly first and foremost. Perhaps
in some bright future I will know Billy at last.

As for that Christmas invitation I received
so long ago...

Have you any memory of a man outside
your door?

I could not bear to join your family, but I'd brought a Christmas gift for Billy, a boxed set of Beethoven albums I thought he might enjoy.

"You can't just bring a gift for Billy," your father said, embarrassed, while I stood there at the door with one wrapped package in my hands. "Not with Dare and Reen—"

"Of course," I said, ashamed, and I understood immediately just how wrong I'd been to bring one gift, to single Billy out from you and Dare. (All for one, as you would say.)

"Oh, Frank," your lovely mother intervened, but he was right.

"My apologies," I offered. Then I hurried away quickly from a place I didn't belong.

Even after all these years, I can still recall the cold light of that Christmas, and the great humiliation I'd brought upon myself.

Do you understand, Miss Kelly? I'm certain that you do.

All is as it should be. Billy has a family rich with love. You and Dare have Billy. I would be selfish to wish otherwise.

Sincerely,

H. W. Marsworth

P.S. May I make a small confession? Perhaps it was true in the beginning, that I welcomed news of Billy in your letters, and I welcomed our shared worry about Billy and the war. And of course every word you wrote of Billy was an unexpected gift. But the great gift of sharing Billy wasn't the only reason I continued our correspondence. I wrote because I knew in you I'd found a true-blue friend. And you were right again, Miss Kelly. What shut-in doesn't need a true-blue friend?

P.P.S. Would you grant me one small favor? Please accept Rat's attempts at friendship, and offer some small kindness to encourage him in return. The path to peace is rarely easy, but peace is always possible. If anyone can forge a path out of the wilderness, it's you.

Saturday, August 24, 1968

Dear Mr. Marsworth,

Maybe that Beethoven gift was wrong OR maybe Dad was wrong, because I didn't need a present, and I doubt that Dare did either. If you'll come to Gram's again, with a present just for Billy—especially a boxed set of Beethoven—Dare and I won't care. (Believe me, we won't care a lick about Beethoven.) No one here will scold you like Dad did.

I don't blame you for the secret, I just wish we'd had the truth from the beginning. I wish Mom and Dad had trusted we wouldn't love Billy less. When I talk to Dad, I'm going to tell him that.

Have a happy Saturday. You'll get an update on the cottage tonight when I get home, UNLESS you decide to join us. (Hint, hint, hint.)

Always True Blue,
Reenie Kelly

Saturday, August 24, 1968

Dear Mr. Marsworth,

Your cottage is a place of peace again!! We demolished all our weapons, the mud bombs and the slingshots, then we tore apart Dare's tree stand, and covered up his bloodstain with fresh dirt. I don't ever want to look at that again.

When our demolition work was finished, I pulled Billy through the thick brush toward that tree stump Snow Cone found.

"Wow," Billy said, and then we stood in holy silence like we were staring at Mom's grave.

"D.M.W. + E.E.B.," Billy read aloud. "FOREVER."

"Just don't tell Dad you saw it," I said. "Or Dare. He won't want to see another boy's initials carved with Mom's."

"I don't much like it either, Pup." Billy traced Mom's letters with his finger, before he moved on to the D. "FOREVER," he repeated. "But you know that I'm an orphan, right?"

"An orphan? You're not an orphan, Billy."

"Well, my real parents are both dead." He brushed his shaggy bangs back from his face. "You know, Mom and Danny were my parents. So that makes me an—"

"You said yourself that you're Dad's son," I said. "You are, and always will be."

"That's what I'd like to think," he said. "But the truth is that I came from Mom and Danny, which means I'm Danny's

326

son, regardless. I'm half Danny's, that's a fact. And I've never been like Dad, Reen. You know, not the way Dare is. Or tough like all the Kellys. Even you. I've always been a little different. A mystery, I guess."

"You're not a mystery to me," I said. "You stand for peace like Mr. Marsworth. And both of you like music. And poetry. And he loves great big words, and books, and smart ideas like you do. Maybe Danny was the same."

"Poetry and music?" Billy stared at me, suspicious. "How do you know what he likes? I've lived here this whole summer and I haven't seen him once. Not even at the Conoco. And yet he let <u>you</u> play down at his cottage. Then he gave me that strange Christmas letter he wanted <u>you</u> to have." Billy waited for an answer, but I didn't say a word. "You <u>must</u> have met him, Reen. Do you see him on your route? Does he come out to the gate?"

"No," I said, "not really."

"Spill the beans," he said, then he looked long into my face like he could see into my soul.

"I just know him," I said finally, because I can't lie to Billy when his kind brown eyes are begging for the truth. "We're pen pals, more or less."

"Pen pals?" Billy blinked, confused. "You mean like you and Skip?"

"A little bit," I said. It felt strange to lose that secret, like

I'd opened up a jar to let a butterfly go free. "Except Skip is in the Army, so he doesn't answer much."

"You're pen pals?" he repeated. "You write letters? You and Mr. Marsworth? You write letters and he answers?"

"That's the way a pen pal works," I said.

"But Dad said he hasn't heard a word from him in years. And he never wrote to me in Denton. Never once. Yet he's your pen pal in Lake Liberty?"

"Because you couldn't be singled out," I said. "And he knew you were a Kelly first and foremost. But he needs to meet you, Billy, and you should meet him, too. Family should know family. And if you want him to write a letter to you first, I can—"

"Please don't ask him, Reen," he said. "Promise me you won't."

(I DID make that promise, Mr. Marsworth, so I won't ask you to write to Billy, but if you decide that for yourself, it'd sure be smart. Billy needs you for his family, and I think you need us, too. "No man is an island," didn't you teach me that?)

"We all can be a family," I told Billy. "The Marsworths and the Kellys, like it was when Mom was young."

"You think that's what Dad wants, Reen?" Billy asked. "Or Dare? Or Gram? She's upset enough that I've gone against the draft. You think she wants a Marsworth—?"

Please don't let that hurt your feelings, Mr. Marsworth. I

just thought you'd want to know why Billy Kelly hasn't begged to meet you A HUNDRED TRILLION TIMES!

"I think it's up to you, just like the draft. You have to follow your own conscience," I told Billy. "Meet him if you want."

"He hasn't asked to meet me either," Billy said. "He sent us Carl Grace with comic books, and ice cream, and Gram's window, and that Christmas letter for you. And—" Billy waved the flies back from his face, and looked out toward the clearing.

"That's his way of being friends," I said. "Because I know he loves you, Billy. Even living all alone, with only Clyde to call his family. Or locked behind that spiked fence that nobody can cross. I honestly believe he loves us all."

"Clyde?" Billy asked.

"His cat."

"So I guess you know it all," Billy said, half-laughing. "Leave it up to you, Reen."

"Not everything," I said. "But one thing I know for certain is our families should be one."

And I really do believe that, Mr. Marsworth.

It's what Mom would have wanted for us all.

Ready to Be Family,
Reenie Kelly

P.S. Time is of the essence. A wise man taught me that.

P.P.S. Billy helped me get that rocker from your rafters in your shed. In case you come down soon to see us, I wanted you to have a place to rest on your front porch. You don't have to meet us at Gram's house.

P.P.P.S. I should have stayed down at the cottage, because Rat and Dare and Snow Cone are playing poker in my room, which means I have to write you from Dare's tent. Imagine the stink of sweaty feet and wet dog, musty towels and boy BO. I have to keep my head outside the flap to breathe fresh air. Still, I'd rather leave Gram's house than play a game with Rat. Dare must have lost his marbles when he fell out of that tree because he let Rat in Gram's attic! And Snow Cone just wants peace at any price. I'd rather write my best friend than play poker with them all.

P.P.P.P.S. Will you think about a meeting, Mr. Marsworth??????

Sunday, August 25, 1968

Dear Miss Kelly,

Although I'm not an advocate of gambling, perhaps
you could try a hand or two of poker with young
friends. An old recluse won't run with you at
recess, or stop at Brindle Drug for a soda after
school. September will come soon; I'd like to picture
you at school in the company of friends.

Sincerely,

H. W. Marsworth

H. W. Marsworth

P.S. You have a lovely view of family, dear Miss
Kelly. Of course in every way that truly matters,
all of us are one.

P.P.S. I remember what you ask me: Please inquire
of Billy where he went with Carl Grace, and let him
know he has my blessing to tell you that truth now.
I do not wish to keep more secrets from my friend.

Sunday, August 25, 1968

Dear Mr. Marsworth,

You want us to have your cottage???????????????

That's what Carl Grace told Billy!!!!!!!!!!

You're GIVING it to me, and Dare and Billy for all
time????????????

Three kids with their own cottage!!!!!!!!!!!!!!!!!!!

How can we ever ever ever ever ever thank you, Mr.
Marsworth???????????????

Billy says we have to ask Dad for his permission, but
the truth is that we don't. Billy's eighteen now, he can say
yes for himself. And I've said yes already, and Dare said
HECK YES, ARE YOU KIDDING!!!! OF COURSE I WANT
THAT HOUSE!!!!!! Even Gram said it's high time we had
a house to call our own. (I think Gram might just be glad
to have us gone. ☺)

"Lord knows all four of you can't squeeze into that
attic. At least Reen will need her own room. And Dare can't
spend a Minnesota winter in those woods. And I guess if
Mr. Marsworth thinks that Billy—" Gram started, and then
stopped. "I mean, that isn't really charity."

"It isn't only Billy," I told Gram. "Mr. Marsworth gave it
to us all."

And I know it isn't charity, it's love. Love love love love
love. Love for Billy, and us all!!!!

You're a true friend to the Kellys, Mr. Marsworth. Mom knew that all along! I knew it all along!!!

It's the best news of the summer!!!!! The best news of my whole life!!! The Kellys living at your cottage!!!! That entire slice of shore all to ourselves. We can wake up summer mornings and eat breakfast on the dock. Swim any time we want. Dare says we'll learn to ice-skate with a frozen shore all to ourselves.

Don't you worry, Mr. Marsworth, the Kelly kids will fill your house with love.

I have to rush to Snow Cone's house to tell her our great news!!

Do you think she will believe it???? A cottage of our own?????

I'll drop this letter to you first, and I'll ring your rusted bell. It's a happy day for ringing!!!! I'd ring a hundred bells outside your house now if I could!!!! I'd put on a parade!!!!

Every bone inside my body is blowing up with joy!!!!

Thank you thank you thank you thank you thank you thank you thank you thank you thank you thank you thank you thank you thank you thank you thank you thank you thank you

A MILLION TRILLION ZILLION THANK-YOUS WILL NEVER BE ENOUGH!

                                        Overjoyed-Ecstatic
                                        Reenie Kelly

P.S. I won't take no for an answer if that's all Dad has to say about your cottage being ours. I'm absolutely positively never taking NO!!!!

P.P.S. I'm going to spend the whole darn day playing games with Rat, including poker, and feeding him Rice Krispies bars, and making him my friend. That's a small price for your cottage. I hope that makes you proud.

Dear Mr. Marsworth,

I can hardly sleep a wink tonight, can you?

Could you meet me at the cottage before the summer's done? Shouldn't we go inside so I can see where we will live?

Could you come to us for Christmas? Christmas at the cottage?

Would you like to come some morning to fish with Dare down at the dock?

Wouldn't you like to sit with Billy on the front porch talking about peace? Or poetry? Or college? You could listen to him sing. Shouldn't we do it before Brandenbrook? (I haven't given up on Brandenbrook, have you?)

You can rest in your old rocker while you tell me about Danny, and every happy cottage memory you have. And all your memories of Mom. And I can tell you about Denton, and the years of Mom you missed.

Would it make you sad or happy if I slept in Danny's room with that old bear?

Do you want everything inside to stay the same forever?

Just the way you left it? Including that 1950 calendar?

We'll love every bit of that old cottage just like Danny did.

I hope you won't mind if we clean it up at least? We'll want to make that cottage spick-and-span.

> Your Best Friend in the Whole World,
> Reenie Kelly

P.S. Tomorrow, when Billy's finished at the Brindles', he's going to drive us to the cottage so we can picture it our own. Dare's still a little dizzy, but he wouldn't miss it for the world. He's already making plans for all the fix-up work he'll do when Dad comes home.

P.P.S. We know you offered money for repairs, but what work the Kellys can do, I promise you we will.

P.P.P.S. Could we go inside to see it? Dare and I want to do that.

P.P.P.P.S. Billy's writing you a thank-you!!! And of course you know a letter is the first step toward a friend!!!

Monday, August 26, 1968

Dear Mr. Marsworth,

Reenie asked me to deliver this, because she said you'd want to read it, and she's too brokenhearted now to come out of her room. She won't even talk to me or Dare. Snow Cone came by this afternoon, but Reen wouldn't see her.

I'm not sure how well you know Reenie, but if you know her just a little, you've probably heard how much she loved Skip. She was so proud to have him for a pen pal, even though we all thought a stranger in the service was an odd friend for a kid. And Dad worried, because his letters seemed to make the war too real. Too real for Reen at least. I wish I'd had the chance to thank him for telling Reen she had to find a way to keep me from this war, or for saying I shouldn't serve.

He might have saved my life, but he lost his.

Perhaps that's the truth of every fallen soldier, I don't know.

I honestly don't know.

It seems wrong that I'm still living, when another boy is dead.

Sincerely,
Billy Kelly

P.S. Mrs. Lamb was Reenie's fifth-grade teacher. In fact, she taught us all.

Dear Reenie,

I'm sorry I've been slow to respond to all your letters. Even teachers can be busy; I hope you'll understand. It's been a summer spent with family, especially my son.

You might recall my youngest, John? He used to stop by after school to help me wash the blackboards. He's the baby of the family, our only boy, and unfortunately he got his letter from the draft board. I can't tell you how difficult it is to send your own son to this war. When John is done with basic training, he expects that he'll be sent to Vietnam. Of course we're praying for a safe assignment, as every parent does.

I'm pleased that Billy's choosing college; I hope the scholarship you're counting on is still possible this year. I recommended him quite highly, and the letter you requested has been sent. In all my years of teaching, I don't think I've taught another boy as kind as Billy Kelly, or quite as pensive either. I suppose I'm not surprised to hear he's objecting to this war.

I only hope he doesn't take a stand against our John, or march against the brave men who are fighting for us all. Every soldier in this battle deserves our country's gratitude. I hope you learned that from our pen pals; I definitely did.

And on the subject of our pen pals—I'm terribly sorry, Reenie, but I'm afraid I have been charged to deliver some hard news. Tragically, your pen pal, Skip Nichols, has died in Vietnam. Apparently an infection from his war wound spread into his blood. I understand he was hoping to go home.

I know how sad this news must be, especially for you with your mother gone so young. Please know you were a bright light in a dark time for our troops. You brought joy to another and for that you should be proud.

When I think of you today, I see you standing in my classroom, reading with such relish a funny letter you'd just finished, or reading us the news Skip had written of the war. Of course we all adored our pen pals, but I think it's safe to say you loved yours more than most.

Please take comfort in these words from Lieutenant Kohl: "Could you please tell Reenie Kelly, Skip looked forward to her letters, we all did. She kept us laughing through some dark days, that's for darn sure. Sometimes when Skip was really down, we'd say, "Hold on for Reenie Kelly. You got another letter coming, and she'll be waiting for an answer, you know she always is." I think Skip got more letters from one student than all of us combined. If she needs another pen pal, we've got plenty waiting here."

I hope you'll write to him, dear Reenie. There are thousands of our soldiers who long to hear from home. My son, John, will be among them now.

My deepest sympathy.

Love and blessing to the Kellys.

In Friendship,
Mrs. Lamb

Tuesday, August 27, 1968

Dear Miss Kelly,

May I offer you my friendship face-to-face in
this hard time?
     Shall we meet down at the cottage? Today at
I2:I5?
     To paraphrase you, dear Miss Kelly: "When
you're sad a friend can help."
     Would that help or harm you, because I only
wish to help.
     Please answer yes or no.

                         No Child Is an Island,

                         Howard Marsworth

                         Howard Marsworth

P.S. If your brothers would be willing, I hope
they'll sit with us as well. "All for one," as you
would say. I think it would be best to meet you all.

P.P.S. I should forewarn you, dear Miss Kelly:
My pallor is quite ghostly. I'm afraid you'll
be alarmed to meet a man so frail. Letters can
disguise an aging heart.

Yesyesyesyesyesyesyesyesyesyesyesyes
yesyesyeyesyesyesyesyesyesyesyesyes
YESSSSSSSSSSSSSSSSSSSSSSSSSSSSSS

Tuesday, August 27, 1968

Dear Mr. Marsworth,

Do you know my biggest worry before I met you face-to-face this afternoon?

I was afraid you might not like me, or I might not like you either, but the thing I worried most about was that our letters might just stop. After a summer of my begging you to meet me at your gate, to be my friend in person, I was suddenly afraid you wouldn't want me to write you anymore.

I have to write to you, Mr. Marsworth.

I do.

And you have to write to me, because even while we talked today on your front porch (our front porch now, too!) I couldn't tell you ALL my feelings, I just couldn't. A letter helps me say what's in my heart.

And I bet it helps you, too. Both of us were shy this afternoon for two good friends! ☺ I still feel a little shy alone here at the cottage writing to you now.

I guess that I'll just say what's in my heart.

First, it wasn't true EXACTLY when I said Billy had to work at Mrs. Brindle's, and that Dare didn't want to come. The truth is, I didn't invite them, because deep down in my selfish heart I wanted us to talk all by ourselves. You and me, just like our letters. And I was

343

happy when I saw you had left Carl Grace at home. When it was just you on that front porch it almost made me cry. (I'm still as weepy as I was when you were here.)

And you're right, you looked pretty small and frail, but your warm handshake was still firm.

"Give a man a handshake," you said with a quick laugh, and I'd forgotten that I wrote that, until you reminded me I did. I can't believe you've saved all my letters, Mr. Marsworth. Of course I've saved every word you wrote me, but I didn't think you'd do the same. Someday we have to read them all together, word for word. Let's do it at the cottage, sitting on our porch.

What was the second thing you said? I wish I could remember.

Maybe—"You've done a fine job on that paper route, your mother would be proud."

I think I might have blushed. I know I wished I had invited Dare and Billy after all, because once I was with you, I could hardly say a word. Loquayshous (not sure about that spelling!) Reenie Kelly, who can usually blab and blab.

Instead I just stood there tongue-tied, hoping you could be like a friend who hardly said a word. Finally, I sat down on the porch step like I always do with Dare, while you sat there on the rocker, and I truly couldn't believe that you were real! Or that meeting you was real! Or that you wore a starched shirt and a bow tie even in the August heat, or that you looked older than I'd pictured in my mind.

You talked about the weather, and I talked about the lake, and we were nothing like our letters until you mentioned Skip.

"I'm concerned for your young spirit, dear Miss Kelly," you said, serious and slow, and suddenly you sounded like my pen pal, but in person. (Not your wobbly voice, but the way you use your words.) And when you said love was all that matters, and that my missing Mom and Skip would last forever, because you still missed Ruth and Danny, you were exactly like your letters, and I hope whatever I said back to you (I don't remember what I said) sounded like the Reenie Kelly you wanted for a friend.

I didn't tell you, Mr. Marsworth, but I could feel my own throat closing while I listened to you talk. I was thinking about Danny as a boy down at the cottage, and going missing in Korea, and never coming home, and Skip's family at his funeral, and how they'd never get to see their boy again, and Billy leaving me for college, or getting sent to prison, but either way at least he'd be alive. And I was thinking you were right again: Love endures all.

"I like that," I said, smiling, but I couldn't keep back the tears. (Thank you for that handkerchief, it's in my hand right now!)

The second thing I want to tell you:

I'm sorry that I gave you that quick hug. I hope that I didn't scare you, Mr. Marsworth, or hurt your tender bones, or make you need to leave abruptly, because suddenly Carl Grace was in your driveway, and your pale cheeks were flushed, and you rose up from your rocker to "bid a quick farewell." Farewell, and we'd hardly talked at all!

I'm not sure what you meant when you said, "Perhaps for this first meeting brevity is best."

Could you please explain that to me now?

That wasn't a long meeting, even for a first.

Are you ready for a second? Please say yes!

Here's the third thing I need to say about this afternoon:

As soon as you were gone with Carl Grace, I used that key you left me, and went into the cottage to see it for myself.

It smells a little like Gram's crawl space, summer hot and dusty, but I like all the pictures of Danny on the wall. Danny as a baby, and Danny as a boy, and his high school graduation, and Mom and Dad and Danny on the edge of your old dock. All Danny pictures, but I see Billy, too. Your boy is living still in Billy, and before the summer's finished, you'll see that for yourself.

Don't forget you promised me you would.

Time is of the essence.

When I'd finished with the living room and kitchen, I went into Danny's bedroom to hug that old-time bear. It smelled like grass and cherries, and a little like your woods, and I sat on that twin bed and hoped it'd be my own.

And you know what I saw next, Mr. Marsworth?????

That sweet gift with the letter you'd left for me in Danny's room!!!

I can't believe you had that picture of us framed, or that you've kept it at your bedside table all these years the way a grandpa would.

Billy, Dare, and me all seeing Santa.

Every night for all these years you got to see us, Mr. Marsworth.

You better take it back now, so we'll be with you again. You shouldn't be alone in that big house.

> Until Tomorrow and Tomorrow and Tomorrow,
> Reenie Kelly

P.S. I came home from the cottage to the most amazing news!!! This afternoon while we were talking, Dr. Roland Price called Billy to say he'd been awarded the Daniel Marsworth Scholarship for Peace!!! Every penny of his college paid just like you promised!!! Not charity, but earned by Billy's good grades and his peaceful Marsworth heart!!! We did it, Mr. Marsworth, we made Mom's dream come true. Our dream!!! Or I should say you did it??? Yes, I should! We want you to come for supper! Everybody does! Get ready, because I'm going to clang your bell until you finally answer YES! You know how much I hate to hear a no!

Tuesday, August 27, 1968

Dear Miss Kelly,

I remember what you ask me.

This would be the photograph your mother gave me long ago.

I have kept it framed and faded at my bedside through the years, and in that way you've kept me company much longer than you know.

Now it shall be your keepsake, a gift from your good mother.

The Kellys at the cottage, right where they belong.

Until Tomorrow,

Mr. Marsworth

Author's Note

Dear Reader,

Don't you love a letter? A letter is the perfect way to share your thoughts and hopes and fears with someone else. It's why I'm here this morning, writing my own letter to you now.

I have some things I need a friend to hear.

When I began this book five years ago, I didn't set out to write about the war in Vietnam or the damage that endured beyond that war. Nor would it be possible for me to write a book that would give voice to the millions of civilians and soldiers of all nationalities killed and wounded in Vietnam, Laos, and Cambodia, or the suffering experienced by survivors and the families of survivors, including refugees from war-torn countries forced to make new homes in unfamiliar lands, and those who have been wounded recently by weapons the U.S. and other armies left behind. While their stories must be told and told again if we ever hope to learn the lessons of this war, they belong to voices other than my own. My greatest wish for this book is that it will inspire you to read and listen beyond it to the stories told by those voices.

In truth, I began this book drawn by the spunk of Reenie Kelly, an eleven-year-old girl uprooted to a small town and hoping for a friend. In early drafts, it was the Kelly family story that I followed, and up until Mr. Marsworth suddenly appeared in one short letter, I didn't know who he was or that his own life had been scarred by war—his refusal to serve in World War I and the loss of his beloved son in the Korean War. I didn't know this book would become the story of a friendship between an aging conscientious objector and a scrappy letter-loving girl.

Yet, there I was in 1968 with Mr. Marsworth and Reenie Kelly in Lake Liberty, Minnesota, watching as they bonded over the shared fear that Billy could be drafted for the war in Vietnam. What did that threat mean to Reenie and her family? To reclusive Mr. Marsworth? The community of Lake Liberty? What did people in a small Midwestern town know and understand about the war in 1968? What did they believe? How did they treat people who disagreed with their beliefs? Were peace activists welcomed or despised?

Luckily, like Reenie Kelly, I'm always eager to learn more. I've spent the last five years considering those questions, and a hundred more that came up as I wrote. I've read letters, books, and oral histories, talked to friends and strangers, watched documentaries on wars and 1968, and after all that research, I have so much more to learn. About all wars. About humanity. About how to make peace possible. My work is just beginning; I hope you'll learn more with me, too.

So while this was never meant to be a book about a war, I hope in some small way it has become a book of peace. Inspired by the peacemakers, the conscientious objectors, the brave activists who are punished or imprisoned, the marchers, the letter writers, the justice seekers, the poets and the dreamers. I hope we find a way to make a better world our work. Maybe then we can begin to end the wars around us. Or stop a war before it starts. Or realize that the damage done during a war never really ends.

That's the second wish that's in my heart this morning as I finish up the final pages of Reenie Kelly's book: A wish for peace far into your future, and the future of all children on this earth.

I'm leaving now to drop this letter in your box. I hope you'll write me back ASAP. I hope you'll tell me what you're doing to make a better world.

Your Story Dreamer,

Sheila

Acknowledgments

Thank you to all who have been with me through the years I wrote this book—family, friends, and students—those who cared about my progress, and those who kept the faith. As always, endless gratitude to my amazing family—Tim, Mikaela, and Dylan—who have shared this book since its beginning. Thank you for reading and rereading and rereading every draft, and believing it would end. I could not write without you. Honestly. This book only exists because of you. Thank you to the men who lived through the draft years of the Vietnam War and shared their stories: Gary Gorman, Allen Learst, Gordon Salisbury, Jim Perlman, Rod Nelsestuen, and others. I am especially grateful to the book Dear America: Letters Home from Vietnam, edited by Bernard Edelman. I carried that collection of letters close to my heart. So, too, Dear Dr. Spock: Letters about the Vietnam War to America's Favorite Baby Doctor, edited by Michael Stewart Foley. Thank you to Ann Melrose and Patricia Jones for answering my questions about Quakers, Susan Wolter Nettell for reading with careful attention and kindness, Callie Cardamon for loving the early pages of this book, Loren Taylor for proofreading on short notice, Tricia Hummel and Dick Mammen for Rollo's second home, Maeve and Meghan Maloney-Vinz for your expert advice that early morning, Josie Sigler for so many important conversations, Jamie Titus for keeping me centered and well, and Marty Case for sharing this writing journey with me, always. Thank you to the wonderful people and places that gave me quiet rooms to dream this book into being: The Studios of Key West, Tyrone Guthrie Center, Anderson Center for Interdisciplinary Studies, Clare's Well, Malmo Art Colony, and Lynn and Frank James. Thank you to the Minnesota History Center for your invaluable archives and for the work you do keeping history alive. A huge thank-you to my treasured agent, Rosemary Stimola, and my visionary editor, Stacey Barney, who saw a book within a book within a book and kept me moving toward that light; I would only work this hard for Stacey Barney. Thank you to my incredibly generous assistant editor, Kate Meltzer, and all the folks at G. P. Putnam's Sons whose work and contributions made this story real. I know the wait was long; thank you for believing. And finally, thank you to the staff at HCMC TBI Clinic—especially Helen Mathison and Courtney Mitchell—for helping me find my way back to my work. In more ways than any of you know, you made this possible.

Other Voices on 1968, the Experience of War, and Work for Peace

For Kids and Adults

Thanhha Lai, *Inside Out & Back Again,* 2011 (novel)

Thanhha Lai, *Listen, Slowly,* 2015 (novel)

Bao Phi and Thi Bui, *A Different Pond,* 2017 (picture book)

Rita Williams-Garcia, *One Crazy Summer,* 2010 (novel)

Rita Williams-Garcia, *P.S. Be Eleven,* 2013 (novel)

For Adults

Thi Bui, *The Best We Could Do,* 2017

Clayborne Carson and Kris Shepard, editors, *A Call to Conscience: The Landmark Speeches of Dr. Martin Luther King, Jr.,* 2001

Bernard Edelman, editor, *Dear America: Letters Home from Vietnam,* 2002

Michael S. Foley, editor, *Dear Dr. Spock: Letters about the Vietnam War to America's Favorite Baby Doctor,* 2005

Larry Gara and Lenna Mae Gara, editors, *A Few Small Candles: War Resisters of World War II Share their Stories,* 1999

Le Ly Hayslip with Jay Wurts, *When Earth and Heaven Changed Places: A Vietnamese Woman's Journey from War to Peace,* 1989

Rufus M. Jones, *A Service of Love in War Time: American Friends Relief Work in Europe,* 1917–1919, 1920

Dr. Martin Luther King, Jr., *The Trumpet of Conscience,* 2010

Maxine Hong Kingston, editor, *Veterans of War, Veterans of Peace,* 2006

Viet Thanh Nguyen, *Nothing Ever Dies: Vietnam and the Memory of War,* 2016

Bao Phi, *Thousand Star Hotel,* 2017

James W. Tollefson, *The Strength Not to Fight: An Oral History of Conscientious Objectors of the Vietnam War,* 1993

Kao Kalia Yang, *The Song Poet: A Memoir of My Father,* 2016

DVD

The Good War and Those Who Refused to Fight It: The Story of Conscientious Objectors in World War II, 2002

The Trials of Muhammad Ali, 2013

The Draft, 2015

The Vietnam War: A Film by Ken Burns & Lynn Novick, 2017

Nobel Peace Prize

In 1947, the Nobel Peace Prize was awarded to the Quakers. To read more about their work and why they were selected for the prize, you can visit the Nobel Prize website: nobelprize.org.

Gunnar Jahn, chairman of the Nobel Committee, said the following in his presentation of the award: "The Quakers have shown us that it is possible to translate into action what lies deep in the hearts of many: compassion for others and the desire to help them—that rich expression of the sympathy between all men, regardless of nationality or race, which, transformed into deeds, must form the basis for lasting peace."

TURN THE PAGE FOR A SAMPLE OF
SHEILA O'CONNOR'S
Sparrow Road

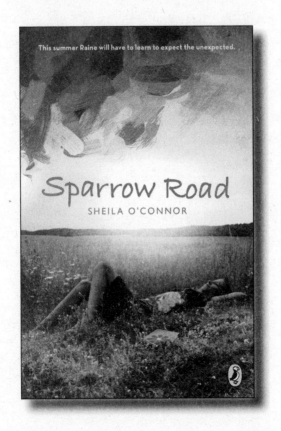

This summer Raine will have to learn to expect the unexpected.

Sparrow Road

SHEILA O'CONNOR

In the shadowed glow of headlights the old pink house looked huge, rambling like the mansions on Lake Michigan. A fairy-tale tower rose high above the roof. The pillared front porch sagged.

"However humble," Viktor said. He steered his truck to a slow stop. "I give you Sparrow Road."

"*You* own this place?" I gasped. Viktor's rusted truck reeked of mud and grease; his sunken face was covered in white whiskers. He looked too poor to own a country mansion, even one as worn as this was.

"Raine!" Mama jabbed her elbow in my ribs. "Viktor owns the whole estate."

"The main house," Viktor said as if he hadn't heard me, "is where the artists sleep. Your cottage is a short walk through the meadow." It was the most I'd heard him say since he met us at our train.

"Well, it's nothing like Milwaukee, that's for sure." Mama gave me a weak smile.

1

Just hearing Mama say *Milwaukee* made me miss it more. Already our apartment seemed another world away, a place where Grandpa Mac waited, lonesome with us gone. I thought of Grandpa Mac standing sad-eyed at the station, the secret fifty-dollar bill he stashed in my back pocket. *In case of an emergency,* he warned, like he knew one was ahead.

"I would assume"—Viktor cleared his throat as if those few words wore him out—"the four artists are asleep at this late hour." Only one small curtained window was lit up in the house. He opened up his truck door. "I shall get your bags."

"I don't want to stay," I said the second Viktor left us in the truck. Sparrow Road looked haunted-mansion creepy, the same way Viktor Berglund looked when I saw him at the train. A man so thin he looked more skeleton than human; a man with ice blue eyes and a face as cold as stone.

Mama touched my cheek. "Sweetheart, we can't leave."

"Grandpa Mac said he'd come to get me. Day or night. All I have to do is call. We can go back to the station, wait there for a train." I still had the good-bye apple muffins Grandpa baked us in my backpack. A bag of wilted grapes. Grandpa's fifty-dollar bill.

"We can't," Mama said. "And Grandpa Mac is far away. For the first time in a long time, it's only you and me." She wove her sweaty fingers between mine.

2

Your mother's done some crazy things, but this? Suddenly Grandpa Mac's worries were moving into mine.

"But you don't even like to clean," I said. Grandpa Mac always joked that Mama's middle name was Mess. Now I'd lose what was left of my good summer so Mama could cook and keep house for some artists in the country.

"Raine," Mama said. "We've been over this already. A hundred times at least."

We had. Still, none of Mama's reasons for this job made an ounce of sense to me. "But Sparrow Road?" I said. "You had a job back in Milwaukee."

"Sweetheart," Mama said. She opened up the truck door. "This is going to take some brave from both of us."

It took more than brave for me to follow brooding Viktor across the dew-soaked meadow. It took Mama's hand clenched around my elbow and a night so black I was too afraid to stay in Viktor's truck all by myself.

"The bats," Viktor warned. "Don't be startled by the swoops."

I pressed in close to Mama. A symphony of insects rattled in the grass. "Are there snakes?" I asked.

"Raine's used to the city," Mama said to Viktor.

Even the country air smelled strange. A mix of fresh-cut grass and lilacs, rotten apples, raspberries, and pine. Maybe fish, like a lake might be nearby.

3

"And to think," Mama said like she hoped to get some happy conversation started. "Just three days ago, I was serving lunch to crabby customers at Christos."

"Three days ago," I added, "I was stacking shelves at Grandpa's store." All the Popsicles and candy I could eat. Our portable TV tucked behind the counter. Brewers' games on Grandpa Mac's transistor. Chess with Grandpa's best friend, Mr. Sheehan, when the afternoons got long. The summer job I loved, and Mama made me leave it.

"Oh, Raine." Mama faked a cheery laugh. "You spend every summer in that store. Besides, we'll only be here a few weeks."

"Eight," I moaned. "If you make us stay until September."

Mama gave my arm a sharp, be-quiet squeeze. "Raine's tired," Mama said, like I was six instead of twelve. "Ten hours on a train. That long ride from the station. She needs to get some sleep."

Sleep. I wasn't going to sleep a wink at Sparrow Road. Grandpa Mac always said he couldn't get to sleep without the song of sirens, the noise of neighbors humming through our walls, the roar of city traffic on the street. It would be the same for me.

"Tomorrow," Viktor said, "I shall take you on a tour. Tomorrow is a Sunday. On Sundays we may speak."

"Speak?" I said.

"As I explained," he said to Mama, "every day is silent until supper. Every day but Sunday."

"What?" I said. "Silent until supper?"

"I assumed she knew the rules," Viktor said like his mouth was dry with dust.

"She does," Mama lied. She tried to nudge me forward, but I wouldn't take another step. A thick swarm of mosquitoes feasted on my skin. Tomorrow I'd be covered in red welts.

"I don't." I slapped down at my leg. "Mama never mentioned any rules."

"Just a few," Mama said. No one hated rules more than Mama. "Like there won't be any newspapers."

"Is that it?" I asked. No newspapers was nothing like silence until supper.

"Or television," Viktor said to Mama. "Or radio. Or music. Not at any time."

"What?" I said. "No TV until September? No radio? And we can't even talk?"

"Molly," Viktor said. "If it's a problem for the child?"

"It is," I answered.

"Raine's not a child," Mama said. "She'll make it through just fine."

"The artists," Viktor said, "they require quiet. They only have the summer for their work. As it is, it's already July."

I wasn't going to talk to any artists. The second I saw daylight I was calling Grandpa Mac. Collect. Just the way he taught me.

"Of course," Mama agreed. "We won't disturb the artists. We'll have enough to keep us busy, as you know."

"Let us hope," Viktor said.

"As for the rules," Mama added quickly, "we completely understand."

"I don't," I said again. "I don't understand at all."

Our cottage was a tiny Snow White house where a gardener used to sleep. Inside it smelled like dust balls and old clothes;—abandoned, like no one had lived in it for years. There was a sunken couch, a painted wooden rocker, and a little purple table just for two.

"Well, it's cute," Mama said when Viktor left.

"Cute?" The walls were butter yellow, the white lace curtains grayed. "Maybe in a rundown dollhouse kind of way." I rolled my eyes at Mama. I didn't care about the cottage. "No TV? Silence until supper? All those stupid rules you didn't tell me?"

"I was going to," Mama said. "Just not on our first day." She wiped her palm across the dusty table. "Don't worry, Raine, we'll make it our own place."

The only place I wanted was Milwaukee. I lugged my suitcase up the narrow staircase to the tiny slanted bedroom where Viktor told us we would sleep. Heat pressed down from the ceiling; a hint of breeze blew through the open window.

"How is it?" Mama asked, but I didn't answer.

It was daisy wallpaper peeled away in patches, two sagging beds, a broken mirror nailed to the wall. I flopped down on the musty mattress, hugged a flimsy pillow to my chest. At home, Beauty would be purring on my bed. Grandpa Mac would be watching some old western on TV.

"Love you to the moon and back," I whispered to Grandpa Mac. It's what I always said before I went to bed. A single tear trickled down my cheek. *Love you to the stars,* he said to me. *Good night, sweet girl. I'll see you in my dreams.*

The strange thing is, I slept. Long and deep, the way I sometimes did with fevers. When I woke up the next morning the spicy smell of coffee filled the cottage and Mama's bed was made.

"Mama?" I called. She never made her bed.

"Down here, sleepyhead," Mama almost sang. "Come see, Raine. I've been cleaning up our cottage. And everything looks better with the sun."

Downstairs, Mama sat at the little purple table—her long red curls still wet from washing, her denim overalls rolled up to her knees. The smell of dust had already disappeared. Warm white light poured through the open windows. "Getting ready for our week." Mama patted a stack of yellowed cookbooks. "I found these in the cupboard. The birds wouldn't let me sleep."

I slumped down in the chair and wiped the sleep out of my eyes. "I need a phone," I said. "This morning."

"There's no phone, Raine. I'm sorry." But sorry wasn't in her voice.

"No phone?" I looked around the cottage. "No phones at Sparrow Road?"

Mama shook her head. "The artists come to Sparrow Road to get away."

"Right. No talking. No TV." I dropped my head into my hands. Six days a week of silence, now I couldn't even find a phone. "But what about emergencies? A fire? Someone could get hurt." I was two when Grandpa Mac taught me how to phone for help.

"In an emergency," Mama said, "I'm sure a call can be arranged."

"Okay," I said. "It's an emergency today."

Mama stared into my eyes. "This isn't an emergency. It's change. I know that you're unhappy, but we'll get used to it. We will."

"But why?"

Mama turned the pages of her cookbook like an answer would be there. "I told you, Raine, I came to do a job."

"You had a job at Christos."

"Another job," Mama said. "A job that wasn't in Milwaukee. And I'll have my Christos job when we go home." She slapped the cookbook shut. "Raine," she sighed, "not everything's a mystery." It's what she always said when she

9

was tired of my questions or when she held a secret she wasn't going to tell.

"I know," I said. "Not everything. But this?" Our move to Sparrow Road was a mystery to me.

"But hey!" Suddenly she jumped up and an unexpected smile lit up her worried face. "If you're looking for a mystery, I've got a real one you can solve." She grabbed my wrist and pulled me toward the counter. "Look!" she cried. "Like Easter!"

Underneath a drape of emerald velvet was a lilac wicker basket filled with water-colored eggs, a jelly jar of flowers, warm banana bread, and two small tangerines. On a torn scrap of paper WELCOME had been glued in golden glitter. "I found it here this morning, at our door."

"Weird," I said. "Viktor didn't make this."

"No," Mama said. "I don't think so either." I heard a hint of wonder in her voice. Like maybe something was a mystery to her. "And this?" Mama handed me a linen napkin, white, with the towered house embroidered in the center and my initials *R.O.* stitched into the corner. "There's a second one for me," Mama said.

"So someone knows our names," I said. "Someone besides Viktor."

"Yes," Mama said. "Someone who must be happy that we're here."

Mama was right. Sparrow Road looked different in the sunlight. Outside, miles of rolling hills formed a patchwork quilt of green, wildflowers swayed graceful in the meadow, and the sky seemed to stretch forever in a perfect, deep blue sea. It was a pretty place I might have loved with Grandpa Mac and Mama. A vacation place without Viktor and his rules, and all the silent days I had ahead.

When Viktor came to take us on the tour, I let Mama walk beside him. I was happiest a few steps back, away from Viktor's stony quiet, his icy eyes, his sunken face covered in white whiskers. Plus there was something I was watching—the friendly way they talked, the way Mama seemed too sweet, too comfortable with a man as cold as Viktor. Too at home, like she and Viktor knew each other before he met us at the train.

He led us down a steep path to a lake. "Sorrow Lake," he wheezed when we'd made it to the shore. "But here, I need a rest." He sat down in the shade while Mama and I left him for the dock.

"Sorrow Lake?" I said to Mama, when I was sure Viktor was too far away to eavesdrop. "Isn't that a strange name? And how can Viktor own a lake? No one owns Lake Michigan."

Mama shook her head. "So many questions, Raine."

"Did you know Viktor before he got us at the train?"

"Know him?" Mama closed her eyes, tilted her face up toward the sun. "Viktor hired me. It's how I got the job."

"But did you know him in Milwaukee? Or some time before now?"

Mama opened up one eye and gave me a mean squint.

"You just seem to know him, like he might be your friend."

"Viktor is my boss." Too many questions got on Mama's nerves. "I'm here to work for him."

I slipped off my flip-flops and dipped my toes into the lake. A school of minnows skittered near the surface. "So can we swim after the tour?" I wanted something happy up ahead, something besides Viktor's boring tour and Mama planning out her menu for the week.

"We'll see." A flush of red washed over Mama's face. Already, her pale Irish skin burned a little pink. I didn't have Mama's coloring or beauty. I was dark-eyed, dark-skinned, with straight black hair, and skinny, where Mama was all curves. "This afternoon," Mama said, "I need to go with Viktor into Comfort."

"Comfort?"

"It's a town not far away. It's where I'll buy the groceries."

"You? You mean you're going without me?"

Mama kept her eyes closed. "Viktor's truck," she said. "There isn't really room for three."

"There were three of us last night." We were crowded knee to knee, but we still fit.

"Another time. Today you'll have to stay here by yourself."

"Alone? At Sparrow Road? Mama, there's nothing here for miles except for hills!"

"The artists," Mama said, although we hadn't seen them. "Surely one of them would be near if some emergency occurred." Sparrow Road had cast some kind of crazy spell on Mama. At home Mama worried when I walked six blocks to the library. Mama always acted like I'd be snatched off of some street. Grandpa Mac did, too. Now she was going to leave me in the country by myself?

"I want to go with you. There's room for me in Viktor's truck."

"No." Mama stood, then offered me a hand. "I'm afraid today I'll need to go with Viktor."

By the time we finally made it to the main house, I was too mad at Mama to listen to Viktor's dull descriptions. Instead I kept my eyes out for an artist, someone who'd be nearby at least while Mama was in town.

"Well, it certainly is spotless," Mama said the minute we stepped inside the house. I could tell she was relieved.

It was almost spooky clean, like a house where no one lived. The dark woodwork was all polished, floors and ceiling beams and benches. Crystal chandeliers sparkled in the sun. It smelled like Holy Trinity, our church back in Milwaukee—hot candle wax and lemon polish, a trace of sweet perfume. A wide, grand wooden staircase curved up from the front room.

Viktor cleared his throat. "The artists keep it tidy." He raised his lanky arm and pointed down a hallway. "Our poet, Lillian Hobbs, has the room off of the library."

"A poet?" Mama said, surprised. "How nice. Raine writes."

"I wrote," I said. "In fourth grade." Back when my teacher, Sister Cyril, told me to put my imagination to good use. But I didn't want Mama to tell my past to Viktor. Not a word.

"Our other summer artists—Josie, Eleanor, Diego— all reside upstairs. And each one has a shed where they create. Although Lillian and Eleanor often work here in their rooms." He'd already pointed out the little sheds as we'd walked across the meadow. Two in the tall grass. Two tucked back in the woods. "Of course the artists' sheds, their rooms, all those spaces are totally off-limits. Always. Like the silence until supper; that rule must be honored. The artists came for quiet. They must be left alone."

Viktor made it sound like every rule was for me, like there was no place for a kid at Sparrow Road.

"We understand," Mama said. I could tell she wanted to get Viktor off the rules.

"And here"—Viktor led us to a gleaming tiled kitchen where copper pots hung from silver hooks—"is where you shall prepare the evening meals. As you wished."

"You *wished* to make the meals?" I asked Mama, but Mama just ignored me.

"Every day but Sunday," Viktor said. "On Sundays you are free."

The smell of peanut butter and warm toast lingered in the kitchen. Maple syrup that reminded me of home. Earlier, an artist must have eaten breakfast. I wondered where they were this morning, what they looked like, if one of them would be here when Mama went to town. Close enough to help if something happened?

And which one left that basket at our door?

© Devon Cox

Sheila O'Connor is the critically acclaimed author of *Sparrow Road*, winner of the International Reading Award, and *Keeping Safe the Stars*, as well as novels for adult readers that include *Where No Gods Came*, winner of the Michigan Prize for Literary Fiction and the Minnesota Book Award. A graduate of the Iowa Writers' Workshop, Sheila also writes poetry, short fiction, and creative nonfiction for audiences of all ages. She is a professor in the Creative Writing Programs at Hamline University, where she also serves as fiction editor for *Water~Stone Review*.

You can visit her website at sheilaoconnor.com.